his secret daughter

BOOKS BY MELISSA WIESNER

his secret daughter

Melissa Wiesner

bookouture

Published by Bookouture in 2023

An imprint of Storyfire Ltd.
Carmelite House
50 Victoria Embankment
London EC4Y 0DZ

www.bookouture.com

ISBN: 978-1-80314-851-9
eBook ISBN: 978-1-80314-692-8

For my sister, Pam, who loves both show tunes and mysteries

Emma Havern's hands were coated in slick amber clay when the phone rang. She leaned across her pottery wheel to peek at the name lit up on the screen. Alicia, her best friend. Emma's gaze shifted to the half-formed flower vase still spinning on the stand in front of her and then back to the phone.

Maybe she'd let it go to voicemail.

About thirty seconds after the phone stopped ringing, it lit up again.

Emma sighed and switched off the wheel, reaching for a rag to wipe her hands. Except for her daughter, Maya, or the high school, she wouldn't stop in the middle of work to answer the phone for anyone other than her best friend of over ten years. Still, their decade of shared history didn't keep the exasperation from creeping into her tone. "Alicia, I'm working."

"I know you are, honey," came a clipped voice through the phone's speaker. "Which is why I'm calling. Have you showered today? Have you stopped to have a bite to eat?"

"Well..." Emma didn't want to lie. Besides, Alicia would see right through her. "Not exactly..."

Alicia sighed. "Most of us drown our sorrows in a nice glass of Cabernet. You drown yours in clay and ceramic glaze."

"I'm not drowning my sorrows," Emma protested. "I have a show coming up."

"You still have to eat."

Emma sighed and swiped her hands on the terracotta-streaked rag in her lap. "Okay. I'll go make a sandwich. Will that make you feel better?"

"Temporarily."

"What would make you feel better permanently, so I can get back to work?"

"Talk to me, honey," Alicia urged in a softer tone. "I know you're hurting."

Emma pushed her stool away from her pottery wheel and crossed the room to the utility sink against the opposite wall. Tapping the phone to speaker, she left it on an overhead shelf while she plunged her hands under the warm water. "There's nothing to talk about. I told Noah if he left for that work trip last month, he shouldn't bother coming back." She stared at the rainbow of splattered paint on the wall behind the sink, as if it might contain the answers to how she and her husband had ended up here. "He left anyway."

Emma could still picture the strain on Noah's face, his brow furrowed, the lines deepening around his eyes. Still hear the apprehension in his voice when he told her he had to go, he didn't have a choice.

You always have a choice.

"He loves you. I know he does."

"I think he's having an affair."

Alicia went silent for a moment. "Did you find proof of that? Why didn't you tell me?"

"No, there's no proof. Only..." Emma's shoulders slumped. "I'm not naïve. What else could it be? If it were any man besides Noah who'd suddenly started acting distant and traveling constantly... what would you think he was up to?"

"I'd think..." Alicia sighed. "Okay, you're right. But it isn't any man. It's *Noah*."

Alicia had been Emma's best friend since she'd moved to Grand Rapids over a decade ago. Neither of them had family in the area, and it had been so long now that they thought of each other like sisters. Alicia had known Noah for ten years, too.

"What about counseling?" Alicia asked.

"With his travel schedule? I don't think so."

"Do you think you'll divorce?" Only Alicia could ask a question like that so directly.

Emma's heart constricted. She hadn't let her mind wander in the direction of divorce. It hurt too much, so she'd been burying her head in the sand—or the clay, in this instance.

She dried her hands and then slipped out the door of her pottery studio into the backyard. "I don't know," Emma finally said, sinking into a chair under the shade of her favorite maple tree. Across the lawn, a burst of spring perennials bloomed in an improvised display of shapes and colors. Emma had planted them years ago when they'd first bought the house. She and Maya had wandered the garden center to pick out the brightest, boldest hues they could find, without any thought to a formal layout or design. It had turned out better than it would have if they'd carefully planned it all out. It was easy, unfussy, so unlike the house where she'd grown up with its manicured lawns, boxwood topiaries, and rose gardens that required a full-time gardener to maintain.

Emma loved this garden, loved the yard that Maya had spent hours in when she was young, making up games with the neighborhood kids instead of shuttling off to tennis lessons like Emma had in her own childhood. And then there was her favorite part of the yard: the art studio tucked under an oak tree on the back edge of the property.

She'd been surprised when Noah had found a job in Grand Rapids, Michigan and proposed moving their family away from Boston to a place where they didn't know a single soul. But it had been a good job, with plenty of room for advancement and a lot less travel than his previous job. At least until the last few years.

Noah had found them this house in a neighborhood full of kids, with great schools for Maya, where Emma could go back to work as an art teacher when she was ready. The art studio had finally convinced her. It had even come with the pottery wheel and kiln.

Looking back, Emma wondered if that move had been the beginning of her and Noah's slow slide toward this separation. As promised, Noah's job had certainly had plenty of room for advancement. But as he rose in the company, the traveling had picked up again. At first it was just a minor inconvenience for Emma to juggle work and solo-parenting Maya when Noah was out of town. But then, about two years ago, Noah began to schedule trips almost weekly. And not only was he gone so much of the time, but he was distracted and distant for the few and far-between moments he was actually around. Emma had tried arguing with him, begging him to send one of his associates, and finally she'd resorted to ultimatums.

The last straw had come about a month ago when Noah's boss had asked him to attend yet another out-of-town work meeting. Emma couldn't believe he'd even considered going. Maya had been rehearsing her part in the school production of *Mamma Mia!* for months, and the performance was the day of his trip. Noah had looked genuinely devastated as he'd packed his bag and headed out to the car. But not so devastated that Emma's pleas for him to stay, or the knowledge that it would break their daughter's heart, had changed his mind.

"Emma, come on." Noah had sighed, lifting his suitcase

down the porch steps and carrying it to the car. "You know if there was any way I could say no, I would."

Emma had trailed after him. "There is a way you can say no. Just say it. Tell them you can't go."

He'd tossed the suitcase in the trunk of the car and pressed his palms to his face like he was utterly exhausted. Something about that gesture had irritated Emma even more. What did he have to be so tired about? All Noah had to do was go to work, while she'd be the one to stay home and break the news to their daughter.

"I just need a little more time to get this client's project wrapped up," Noah had pleaded.

"You've been saying that for years." She'd crossed her arms over her chest. "You promised that when we moved here, there wouldn't be any more traveling."

Noah had sighed again, dropping his hand to his sides. "Things change. Life happens."

"If you go on this trip and miss Maya's show, I want you to move out."

Noah had paused with the door to the car trunk halfway shut, and for a moment, Emma thought she saw fear cross his features. Then he shook his head and closed the door firmly, leaving his suitcase inside.

Now, Alicia's voice cut into her thoughts. "How is Maya handling the separation?"

Emma sighed. "Oh, you know. She blames me, of course, for asking him to leave." Despite the number of times Noah had let Maya down, he could do no wrong in their daughter's eyes. "She's holding out hope that I'll let him come back." Emma reflexively reached for the wedding ring she'd always worn on a chain around her neck so it wouldn't get in the way of her pottery. Was it time to take it off? Maybe she was holding out hope that Noah would come back, too. She and Noah had been so happy for a long time; that's what made his distance so confusing these past few years. But Emma didn't only want him to be there physically. She wanted that kind of connection they used to have. But he just kept making promises that he never seemed to be able to keep.

Maybe Noah really *was* having an affair. Or maybe he just loved making money more than he loved his family. He wouldn't have been the first man in her life who felt that way. But she'd chosen him because she thought he was different than her father.

"Maya is nothing if not dramatic." Emma could hear her best friend's amusement through the phone. Alicia had two boys whose life revolved around their soccer team. The only drama she usually had to deal with was the endless piles of dirty sweat socks; while Emma's daughter carried her love for theatrics into all areas of life, especially her interactions with her mother.

"Someday, she'll understand that marriage is long and complicated and not always just a matter of *letting him come back*," Emma said. "But now doesn't seem to be the time."

"Well, you know I love Noah like a brother, but I'm on Team Emma all the way."

"Thanks," Emma said, grateful for Alicia's support. "I don't know if Noah and I are going to divorce. He wants to move back, and he says he'll stop traveling so much as soon as he gets this latest project sorted out. But he's been saying that for the past few years, and nothing seems to change."

Emma had been sure if she stood her ground and asked Noah to move out, it would finally wake him up to the fact that she wasn't just making empty threats. She held her breath every time she dropped Maya off for her Saturday visits at his new apartment, hoping that would be the day Noah would tell her he'd talked to his boss, or started looking for a new job, or *anything* to show he was prioritizing their family over work. But he just kept begging her for a little more time and making empty promises that things would be different soon.

"Well, if there's anything you need," Alicia said. "You know I'll be there in a second."

"I might take you up on that..." Emma trailed off as she spotted movement near the house, in the direction of the street. "Alicia, hold on a second." Emma slowly rose to her feet as two police officers appeared on the stone path that led from the sidewalk to the yard in back.

"Hello?" The female officer called.

"Alicia," Emma murmured into the phone. "I've got to go. I think Maya's been skipping school again."

"Oh, dear," her friend replied with another hint of amusement at Emma's struggles with her daughter. "Don't ground her for too long. You're lucky she's not smoking pot behind the school like I did."

Emma didn't feel so lucky. She hung up the phone as the police officers approached.

"Hello," the officer called again. "Are you Mrs. Emma Havern?"

Emma sighed. This wasn't the first time the police had shown up at her house. She supposed she was fortunate that Maya's theater friends were generally a nice group of kids, and that they spent so much time in the school's auditorium that she didn't have to worry much about them drinking or using drugs like Alicia had suggested. But they'd been caught skipping school last month to take the train into the city to catch a matinee performance of *Wicked*. They probably would have gotten away with it if they hadn't decided to break into an impromptu performance of 'Dancing Queen' on the train platform, drawing the attention of the metro police.

"What song was Maya singing this time?" Emma asked, wryly.

"I'm sorry. We're not sure what you mean." The male officer

looked at her sideways. He had a nametag on the front of his uniform that said MONROE.

"Aren't you here for my sixteen-year-old daughter, Maya? She's been skipping school again?"

"No, ma'am, we're not here about a teenager." Officer Monroe shook his head.

A frisson of alarm zipped through Emma, and she slowly rose from her chair. If they weren't here about Maya skipping school, why *were* they here?

"We came to talk to you about your husband, Noah Havern, ma'am." The female officer glanced down at her notepad. O'BRIAN, her nametag said. "I'm afraid we have some bad news."

Emma grabbed her wedding ring again, as her body went hot and then cold. Something had happened to Noah? *Oh, God. Please let him be okay.*

"Your husband was in a car accident out on Route 37. A tractor trailer veered from the opposite lane and hit his vehicle," Officer O'Brian said. "I'm sorry to have to tell you that he's in a coma."

Emma took an audible breath, trying to process the officer's words. An accident... *A coma?* She slowly blew out the breath. A coma was terrifying, but at least Noah wasn't...

She shook her head. It was unthinkable.

Instead, she forced herself to focus on the police officer's words. The accident had occurred on 37, a road that passed right by Noah's new apartment. Thank God he'd been in town, and he wasn't traveling for work in some far-off state. They had excellent hospitals in Grand Rapids, and she could get there right away.

She opened her mouth to ask where the ambulance had taken Noah, but Officer Monroe began speaking again. "We want to reassure you that the child is okay."

Emma's heart clutched. *The child?* What was Maya doing

in the car with Noah, in the middle of the day? Why would he take her out of school?

"They've taken her to the hospital along with your husband for observation," O'Brian continued. "But aside from a small bump on her head, the doctors don't think she has any injuries."

Emma grabbed the back of the chair to steady herself. "I thought you said you weren't here about Maya. But now you're telling me she was in the car, too?"

Monroe checked his notepad, flipping through the pages, his eyebrows knitting together. "You'd asked about a teenager. There was no teenager in the car. The child who was in the accident with your husband is a little girl about two years old."

Emma's head snapped up. "*Two years old?* I..." She trailed off, shaking her head. "Who is the child?"

"To be honest, ma'am," Officer Monroe said, jotting something down in his notepad, "we assumed you'd know."

There had to be an explanation. Maybe it was a friend's child, and they'd called Noah to pick up the girl because of an emergency? Except nobody they were close with had young children anymore. The local families they socialized with all had kids who were Maya's age. And why would any of the families in their acquaintance call Noah, and not Emma, anyway? He traveled so much they barely saw him, while everyone knew Emma from school events and activities.

"I don't know anything about a two-year-old." Emma pressed a hand to her temple as the blood began to pound in her ears. She'd suspected that Noah was hiding something, but... *a child?* It made absolutely no sense that Noah would be with a child she'd never met, never even heard of, unless—

Officer O'Brian's voice cut into her thoughts. "Were you acquainted with Coral Butler, ma'am?"

"Who?" Emma's gaze swung to the other officer.

"I guess we'll take that as a no." Officer Monroe jotted something else in his notepad.

"Yes." Emma's brain was flying in a thousand different directions. "I mean, correct. I've never heard of Coral Butler."

"There was also a woman in the car with your husband," Officer O'Brian explained.

"I..." Emma trailed off again, trying to make sense of this new information. A woman in the car? Who was she? This child's mother?

"She had a purse with ID, so we were able to identify her." Officer O'Brian held up a cell phone to show Emma a photo of a driver's license. "Are you sure you're not familiar with this woman?"

Emma took in the picture of a pretty blond woman, maybe a couple of years younger than she was. *Coral Butler*, the name on the driver's license said. Dazed, she shook her head. "No, I've never seen her."

"We have a couple of officers out tracking down more information on her now. Seeing if there's any relation to the child."

Who is Coral Butler? But then Emma processed the rest of what the officer had said. "You identified her from her driver's license? Is she in a coma, too?"

Monroe and O'Brian exchanged a glance. Finally, Monroe gave a little nod, and then turned his gaze back to Emma. "No, ma'am. She's not in a coma." He tucked his notebook into his back pocket. "Coral Butler died in the accident."

"Oh my God." Emma leaned weakly into the back of the chair.

Officer O'Brian stepped up, taking Emma by the arm. "Ma'am, you don't look well. Maybe you should sit down."

"No." Emma breathed heavily, pulling away. "No, I'm fine."

She had to focus. Noah was in a coma, and Maya would be home from school in a few hours. Emma needed to get over to the hospital, talk to the doctors, and figure out what to do next. Now, more than ever, Maya was going to need her to be strong.

But as Emma hurried into the house to grab her purse and

car keys, she couldn't seem to keep her legs from shaking, and by the time she made it to the front door, her heart was pounding so hard she needed to stop and lean against the wall to catch her breath.

What was Noah up to? What secrets was he keeping?

And, more importantly: *Who were the mysterious woman and child in his car?*

2

"I'm here to see my husband." Emma leaned into the counter at the nurses' station. "He—" She choked out the words. "He was just admitted. They said he's in a coma."

Emma had been able to hold it together for the drive to the hospital, concentrating her full attention on making the correct turns and stopping at red lights. But ever since she pulled up in front of the building and an ambulance drove past, siren wailing, she'd been fighting back tears.

The young nurse behind the computer looked up at her with kind eyes. "I'm so sorry. Of course you can see him right away." She moved the mouse and clicked something on the screen. "What's his name?"

"Noah Havern." Her voice broke at the end.

The nurse nodded, typing something on her keyboard. "Yes, I have his file right here." She glanced down at a clipboard. "Let me just get you his room number."

"Has there been any improvement in his condition?" Emma's heart filled with hope. The officers hadn't shared any information other than the fact that Noah was in a coma. Maybe it was just a small bump on the head, and now he was awake. Maybe Emma would walk into his hospital room and find him sitting up in bed, charming the nurses, and ready to give her a completely reasonable explanation about who this Coral Butler person was, and why there was a two-year-old girl in his car.

But the nurse shook her head with regret. "No, I'm so sorry. It looks like he's the same as he was when they brought him in a few hours ago." She pushed her chair back and stood up. "Let me show you to his room. I'm Brittany, by the way."

"Emma Havern." Emma followed the nurse down the hallway, her sneakers tapping on the gray tile floor. They passed a room on the left with the door open, and she couldn't help but glance inside. An older woman sat next to a hospital bed where a man about the same age lay sleeping, or maybe he was in a coma, too. Above the man's head, machines beeped and whirred. The older woman looked up, face pale and drawn, and her eyes met Emma's. *That poor woman.* Emma quickly looked away and kept walking.

A few doors down, Brittany turned into a room, and Emma followed. Brittany reached up to tug aside a curtain, revealing a hospital bed just like the one where the old man down the hall lay hooked up to machines.

Except this man—

Emma braced her hand on the wall to keep herself upright. This was Noah. The man she'd loved for twenty years. The father of her child.

Emma stared at her husband stretched out on the hospital bed, and all hope that she'd find him sitting up and awake flew right out the window. Noah's face was the same color as the white gauze taped to his temple, masking what was probably a gash where he'd hit his head. The lower part of his face had a series of small red slashes that looked like they'd been carved there from shards of glass, maybe from the windshield shattering. An IV ran from a bag on a pole into his arm and a bundle of small wires connected to a heart rate machine disappeared under his hospital gown.

Noah's chest rose and fell rhythmically, and it was a small comfort that at least he seemed to be breathing on his own. Brittany bustled around the room, pulling open the window blinds to reveal a sweeping view of downtown Grand Rapids, smoothing the sheet covering Noah to his chest, and fluffing the pillow beneath his head. Then she turned to Emma, and her eyebrows knit together.

"Are you okay?" She made her way back toward the door. "You don't look well."

Emma allowed the nurse to take her arm and guide her to a vinyl-covered chair next to the bed. "I'm fine—" Limply, Emma sank into the seat, unable to tear her eyes away from her husband stretched out before her. "It's just such a shock." They'd told her Noah was in a coma, but nobody had mentioned all the cuts and bruises. Or the other injuries. Peeking out from beneath the sheet, Emma could see a cast on Noah's leg that extended from his knee over the heel of his foot, and a brace on one arm. What else was that sheet hiding? What other damage had Noah's body sustained in the crash?

"Of course it's a shock." Brittany pressed a comforting hand on her shoulder. "I'm so sorry you have to see your husband like this."

Emma turned to the nurse, gazing up at her with pleading eyes. "What can you tell me about his injuries? Will he be okay?"

Brittany gestured toward the bed. "In addition to the bump on his head, he does have some broken bones. He fractured both his tibia and his wrist, as well as a couple of ribs. It will be a long road, and he may need surgery for the tibia, but the bones should heal with physical therapy and rehab."

"Okay," Emma said, breathlessly. They could handle physical therapy and rehab. But first, Noah would need to wake up. "What about the coma? When do you expect him to come out of it?"

Brittany's hand slowly slid off Emma's shoulder. "Well…" She paused as if weighing what to reveal, and Emma's heart thudded at her hesitation. "I think you should probably talk to the doctor. He's the one who reads all the test results. I'm not really qualified to speculate on someone's prognosis."

Emma eyed the nurse warily. She'd been hospitalized a couple of times—to have her appendix removed in college, and when Maya was born in an emergency C-section. The one thing she knew about nurses was that they were the first line of command and *always* knew what was going on with their patients—usually better than the doctors who popped in and out of hospital rooms, never staying for more than a few minutes. So, if Brittany was dodging her questions, what was she avoiding saying?

Emma couldn't help but think the worst. "When can I see the doctor?"

"I'll page him and let him know you're here. He's doing rounds on the other end of the hall, so he should be able to get away to come and talk to you pretty quickly."

Emma was almost sorry the doctor could come so readily. If he was willing to jump out of his rotation to talk to her, what kind of news was he about to deliver?

Brittany took another walk around the room, pressing a button on one of the machines suspended above Noah's head and adjusting his IV bag. "I'll be back to change this in a bit. Can I bring you anything? Coffee? Juice?"

Emma's insides churned. "No, thank you. I'm fine." She was pretty sure that if she put anything in her stomach right now, it would come right back up. Then poor Brittany would have two patients to deal with.

"Is there someone I can call for you? Someone who can come so you won't be alone?"

Emma shook her head. She should call Alicia back, but first she wanted to talk to the doctor and have some news to share. It was hard to believe it was only an hour ago when she and Alicia had hung up the phone. Emma's biggest worry in that moment had been Maya skipping school, and now here she was, trying to figure out how to tell Maya that her father...

Emma closed her eyes to block out the view of Noah's bruises and bandages. The machines and monitors. Maya was going to be devastated to see him like this. How was Emma going to prepare her?

She took a deep breath and blew it out slowly. There was no sense in getting ahead of herself. The doctor would be in any minute, and maybe he'd tell her it wasn't as bad as it looked. Either way, she needed to hold it together for her daughter. "I'll call my friend after I talk to the doctor. But thank you."

Brittany gave Emma's shoulder one more squeeze. "If you need anything, just push the call button over there." Then she left, pulling the curtain back across the door behind her, and Emma was alone with Noah.

She slid her chair closer to the bed and reached out to take his hand. It felt dry and cold. Emma dug through her purse and pulled out the lotion she always carried because the clay she worked with sucked all the moisture from her hands. She squeezed a dollop and began massaging it into Noah's palm.

It was the first time she'd touched him like this for a long time. He'd only moved out a few weeks ago, but for months before that they'd barely any spent time in the same room together. He was usually darting off to his next meeting or business trip, radiating stress and nervous energy. Looking over her shoulder while she tried to talk to him, or glancing down at his phone, clearly waiting for the moment he could slip off and get back to work.

This was the first time she'd seen him truly still in months. Why did there have to be a terrible car accident in order to make it happen? Emma's gaze roamed over Noah, and her heart slid into her throat. Though she'd asked him to move out, it wasn't because she'd stopped loving him. No, if anything, she'd hoped that a little distance would help them to come back together again. That maybe he would come to his senses and realize that he still loved her, more than his job and—it was humiliating to admit it—more than the woman he was having an affair with.

Emma took a shaky breath. She'd never actually found any evidence he was cheating on her, but so many signs had been pointing in that direction. And now, there was this mysterious woman, Coral Butler, in Noah's car. Could it be that—

Her thoughts were interrupted by the sound of the curtain rings sliding on the metal railing behind her, and Emma turned around to find an attractive middle-aged man in blue scrubs stepping into the room.

The doctor. That was fast.

"Hello. You must be Mrs. Havern."

"Call me Emma," she said weakly, bracing herself on the arms of the chair to pull herself to her feet.

"No, no." The doctor motioned her to stay seated. "Please don't get up." He crossed the room to the opposite wall and grabbed the chair there, dragging it closer so he could face her, his knees inches away. "I'm Ryan Woodward." He held out his palm.

Emma reached out to shake his hand, and it was warm and firm as it closed around hers. *So different than Noah's lifeless hand resting on the bed*, she thought, and then cringed at the word *lifeless*. Her husband had always been full of life. It was one of the reasons she'd fallen for him all those years ago.

"It's nice to meet you, Dr. Woodward." Emma lied, because there was nothing nice about making his acquaintance in this cold, stark hospital room while her husband lay hooked up to machines.

Dr. Woodward leaned back in his chair and propped a sneakered foot on his opposite knee. "I wanted to tell you a little bit about your husband's condition."

Emma held her breath.

"From what the paramedics reported, your husband's car was hit by an oncoming vehicle, bounced off the guardrail, and rolled twice before coming to a stop in the median."

"Oh," Emma whispered, imagining the sound of squealing tires and crunching metal. "Oh my God."

"He sustained a number of broken bones. His tibia is broken, his wrist has a small hairline fracture, and several rib bones are cracked."

Emma nodded. Brittany had already gone over this. "The nurse said that with physical therapy, he should recover from his injuries."

Dr. Woodward cocked his head. "From those injuries, yes. But your husband also sustained a significant head injury in the accident that has led to edema, or swelling, in his brain."

Emma's heart pounded. "His brain is swelling? That can't be good. Can it?"

Dr. Woodward nodded. "When a body part is injured, you'll often see increased blood flow to that area, which causes swelling. In a sprained ankle, for example, you wouldn't be very worried about a little bit of swelling. It means your body is sending white blood cells to the site of the injury to help with repair." Dr. Woodward took in a breath and blew it out slowly. "In a brain injury, however, there is only so much room for the tissue to swell before it starts to bump up against your skull. So, Noah's brain swelling is a concern."

Emma took in that information. "What can you do about it?"

"We have a couple of medications we're administering

through his IV to reduce the swelling. At the moment, we'll monitor it to make sure it doesn't get any worse. Sometimes with head injuries, it's just a matter of waiting it out and letting him heal."

"And he's just—" Emma waved in Noah's direction where, aside from the bandages on his head, he looked peaceful. "He's just sleeping?"

"Well, not exactly." Dr. Woodward leaned back in his chair, the vinyl squeaking as he moved. "When someone is asleep, they can be awakened by stimuli like noise or pain. Noah is alive and he looks like he's sleeping. But he's unresponsive to any sort of stimuli."

Emma's stomach quaked at the word *unresponsive*. Noah had always been a deep sleeper, and sometimes she'd have to shake him and yell his name to wake him up in the morning, even with his alarm clock blaring right next to his ear. But this was different. Noah wasn't simply lost in a heavy dream. Noah was—

She had no idea where Noah was.

Emma smoothed her hands together to rub in the last of the lotion she'd been applying to Noah's skin. "So, how do we know how bad it is? How likely is he to wake up?"

"Good question." Dr. Woodward nodded. "We have a test called the Glasgow Coma Scale. We use it to assess the level of coma by looking at motor response, verbal response, and whether Noah's eyes are opening."

"What did Noah score?"

Dr. Woodward hesitated. And then, "Noah scored a three."

"Out of how many points?"

"He could score up to nine and would still be in a comatose state. Fifteen is fully conscious."

Emma recoiled. "*Noah scored a three out of fifteen?*" She clutched the arms of the chair. Oh God, she was going to faint.

"Please don't be alarmed."

Was he serious? "How can I not be alarmed?"

"There's another test called the Full Outline of UnResponsiveness, or FOUR. Noah scored much higher on that. We're encouraged, for example, that he's breathing on his own, without a respirator."

"But aren't basic bodily functions the lowest form of brain activity? I mean, you don't even have to think about it to breathe." What if the coma scores never improved? What if this was all Noah's body would ever do? "Will my husband be able to wake up and function normally? Will he be the old Noah?" And if he wouldn't be... what would she do?

"Mrs. Havern," Dr Woodward said, leaning in toward her. "This injury is very recent. It may be that it simply needs some time to heal. When the swelling goes down, he might very well wake up and be back to his normal self."

"You said he might. What are the alternatives?"

The doctor hesitated again. Finally, he sighed. "The swelling could cause permanent damage, in which case, he could wake up but experience changes to his cognitive abilities."

Emma wrapped her arms around her midsection, suddenly cold. "What kind of changes?"

"Mood changes, personality changes. Or he may be unable to communicate in the same way or complete the activities he used to be able to." Dr. Woodward looked her in the eyes. "There are a lot of possibilities, and it's important that we don't start to speculate until we know more."

Emma couldn't help speculating. She tried to imagine Noah —her bright, brilliant husband—a different person. Unable to communicate in the same way. Unable to work or to do the things he enjoyed. What would she do?

Emma straightened her shoulders. She'd take care of him and get him the best care that she could. He might not be the same, but he'd still be Noah, the man she loved. The father of her child.

With the thought of Maya, Emma's heart cracked open. Noah may have been absent these past few years, but she'd never doubted for a minute that he loved Maya. She knew he'd been devastated to miss their daughter's last musical performance, which had made it all the more confusing that he hadn't been willing to say no to his work trip so he could be there. Would he ever have another chance to see Maya up there on stage? Would he even recognize his own daughter?

Emma pressed her hands to her temples. She was getting ahead of herself again. The doctor had said that once the swelling went down, he might wake up and be completely fine. "Okay, so we just wait for him to heal and wake up."

"Well." Dr. Woodward cleared his throat.

Emma's gaze swung in his direction, her heart sinking again. "What is it?"

"Well, I want to make sure you're prepared for all possibilities." Dr. Woodward's eyes softened. "There is the possibility that Noah won't wake up at all."

3

TWENTY YEARS AGO

"Watch out!"

The voice registered in Emma's ears only a second before something came flying over her shoulder, whistling only inches from her ear. She jumped sideways, narrowly avoiding a blow to the head, but her easel didn't have the same kind of reflexes. The mystery object smashed into her painting, sending it flying across the lawn and into the grass. In the commotion, she dropped her paint palette, and it landed face-down, the oil paints splattered in the dirt like a rainbow-hued crime scene.

Damn it. Those paints were expensive, and ever since her dad had cut her off from her college fund, Emma been entirely on her own, financially. Loans paid for tuition, and her job at the restaurant covered rent and food—barely. She'd recently taken a second job teaching arts and crafts at a preschool three times a week just to buy paint and clay. Emma eyed the mess on the ground. That was at least three hours of making paper bag puppets and gluing pipe cleaners to popsicle sticks, just for those supplies alone.

Emma rescued her painting from the grass and found the offending object lying a few feet away. Someone had thrown a football, probably one of the students chasing each other across the expansive student union lawn that stretched between maple trees and nineteenth-century stone buildings on her upstate New York college campus. She turned around, looking for the owner, and saw a tall, blond guy, who looked to be an upper-classman, running in her direction, a cocky grin on his tanned face.

"Oops," he said, stopping with his sneakered-feet only inches from her upside-down palette on the ground. One of her paint brushes stuck out from under his heel. "Guess that one got away from us." He held out his hand to take the football, and Emma's spine stiffened. He wasn't going to help her pick up her supplies? Or even bother to apologize?

She clutched the football to her chest with one hand and checked out the damage to her painting with the other. The paint was smudged, and there was a small tear in the canvas on one of the corners. She might be able to fix the paint smudges before they dried, but repairing the hole would take time she didn't have between classes and her jobs, not to mention more money to buy the glue and a canvas patch.

"Damn it," she repeated, this time out loud.

The guy's blue eyes roamed over her painting. "Hey, that's pretty good," he said, seemingly oblivious to the damage he'd wrought. "Are you an artist?"

"No, I'm a window washer," she snapped, shoving the football under her arm so she could set the easel straight and put the painting back on it.

"Ha ha, hilarious." The guy winked. For the first time, Emma noticed the Greek letters on his T-shirt. She didn't know much about fraternities and sororities—pledging wasn't something she had much time for or interest in—but she recognized these.

Theta Chi Delta.

It was the exclusive national fraternity her father had

belonged to when he was a student at Cartwright University, a fact that gave him an enormous amount of pride. "If you're a Theta Chi Delta, you're welcome in any circles," he used to tell her, when he reminisced about his college days. What he really meant was *wealthy, upper-class circles*, which is all her father ever really cared about. "If you put Theta Chi Delta on your resumé, you can land any job you want, gain access to any country club, and hold your head up high, knowing you're the best of the best."

From an early age, Emma had known in no uncertain terms that she was expected to attend Cartwright and pledge Theta Chi Delta's sister sorority—the one her mother had been a member of. Emma had done what she was told and enrolled at Cartwright, but when it came to choosing her major and pledging the sorority at the end of her sophomore year, she'd rebelled for the first time in her life. She just couldn't imagine spending the rest of her life working in her father's financial consulting business and mingling at the country club. Her father made sure she'd paid for it, cutting off all financial support.

It just *had* to be a Theta Chi Delta who'd destroyed her art supplies and damaged her painting, didn't it?

"Nice tree." The blond guy nodded at her canvas, and Emma tensed up. Sure, there was a tree in the painting, but the subject of her work had little to do with foliage. He'd entirely missed the young girl in the foreground, and he certainly hadn't registered the longing on her face as she watched the other kids playing without her.

Or maybe he simply couldn't relate. He was a Theta Chi Delta after all. *Welcome in any circles.*

"Do you ever do nudes?" Theta Chi Delta cocked his head and gave her a grin. "I'd be happy to pose for you." And with that, he turned his body into the over-exaggerated shape of a bodybuilder flexing his muscles.

Emma rolled her eyes. Like she hadn't heard that line a hundred times before.

"Dude," a voice from behind her called. "You look like an idiot."

Emma spun around to find another guy who also looked to be an upperclassman approaching. This one was taller than Theta Chi Delta guy, had darker hair, and wore a faded Cartwright University T-shirt. He stopped next to Emma and cringed when he noticed the mess on the ground. "I'm so sorry about this." With one hand, he picked up her palette, and with the other, he gestured at the football. "May I?"

Emma handed the ball over, and the dark-haired guy passed it to Theta Chi Delta, giving it an extra shove into his midsection.

"Oof," Theta Chi Delta grunted, wrapping his arms around the football.

"Hey," a third male voice called from across the lawn. "We're in the middle of a game here." A group of guys in athletic clothes stood with their hands on their hips, staring in Emma's direction.

Theta Chi Delta gave them a thumbs up, and then turned back to Emma. "Let me know what you decide about me modeling." He hitched his chin at her. "I'm easy to find. Just ask around for Cooper." And then he turned and headed back across the lawn, tossing the football into the group waiting for him.

What a douche.

A loud snort came from the direction of the dark-haired guy; and at that moment, Emma realized that he was still standing there, and she'd said her comment out loud. Her face flushed. "Sorry," she muttered.

He shot her a grin that seemed more genuine and less cocky than his friend's. "Nah, it's okay. Cooper *can* be a bit of a douche. Just don't tell him I said that."

"I don't plan to converse with Cooper again." She surveyed the ground where her paintbrush lay broken, a casualty of Cooper's heel. Her palette knife stuck straight up in the lawn a few feet away. She grabbed it before someone stepped on it, too.

"Again, I'm really sorry about this." The dark-haired guy waved her palette for emphasis, and Emma's gaze drifted to his hand smeared with multicolored paint. It was a strong hand, rough and a little callused. As if he worked in construction or maybe as a carpenter, instead of attending one of the East Coast's most prestigious Ivy League universities. Another contrast to Cooper, aka *Theta Chi Delta*.

"The football was an accident," the guy continued. "But we should have been more careful."

"It's fine." Emma took the palette and handed him a rag. There was no sense in making a big deal out of it. He was right, it was an accident, and not his fault that a little spilled paint had her pulse racing over the replacement cost. He'd have no way of knowing this was stressful for her. Most kids at Cartwright could call home if they needed money, and their parents would have a check in the mail the next day.

Be honest, Emma told herself. *A year ago, you would have called Daddy for money, too. Quit playing poor little rich girl, and get over it.* Despite her financial woes, she was still better off than most. Her first two years of college had been paid for. And she could always pick up an extra shift or two at the restaurant to buy more art supplies.

"I'm Noah, by the way." The guy swiped the rag across his fingers, and again, Emma was drawn to the strength in those hands. She wondered what he could do with a ball of pottery clay.

"I'm Emma." Her eyes drifted upward, past the wide shoulders beneath the sleeves of his T-shirt until they met his gaze. Unexpectedly, her heart fluttered.

"It's nice to meet you, Emma." When he gave her back the

rag, his hand brushed hers. A wave of heat worked its way up her arm. Something about the tiny flicker in his eyes told her he felt it, too.

Emma backed away and focused on cleaning up her supplies. She had no idea why she was having such a strong reaction to this guy, but she didn't have time for it. The restaurant was expecting her for her shift at 4:30 p.m., and she needed to finish her painting by the time it was due in class on Tuesday. Besides, if Noah was Cooper's friend, he was probably a Theta Chi Delta, too. And the last thing she planned to do was to get involved with a Theta Chi Delta. That fraternity represented everything she didn't want. Everything she'd actively avoided in her life.

"Wow."

The admiration in Noah's voice had Emma pausing as she packed up her paint tubes in their travel case. She spun around to look at him. "What is it?"

Noah stared past her at the canvas propped on the easel. "Your work. It's gorgeous."

"Oh." Emma braced herself. Maybe he really liked how she painted *trees*, too.

"Yeah..." He squinted at the painting, and if Emma didn't know better, she would have said that he almost looked a little emotional. "The girl's face. She looks so lost, like she's always on the outside looking in. She reminds me of... someone I know." He blinked, and then seemed to shake it off as his mouth curved into a smile. "Anyway, it's really compelling."

Emma flushed again, this time with pride. Painting wasn't her specialty—her true love was clay, sculpture, and pottery—but the painting class was a requirement of her major. Many of her fellow students spent their summers studying art in places like Florence and Amsterdam, and now they were enrolled in Cartwright's prestigious Bachelor of Fine Arts program. They lived and breathed studio art, while she'd opted for art education to guarantee herself a job after graduation. Emma knew she was talented, but her father's criticisms had ensured that she always doubted whether she was good enough.

But this guy—Noah—seemed genuinely moved. She might not be the most technically talented artist in the program, but she'd compelled him to connect with her work, and it meant everything.

"Thank you so much," she said, breathlessly.

"Do you always work outside on the lawn like this?"

"It's hard to get studio space—I'm not an art major, I'm in art education, so I come second in line for available space." Emma shrugged like it didn't matter where she worked. "Besides, I get more inspiration from being outside, watching people interact."

"Well, whatever you're doing, it's working. Listen—" He took a step toward her, so close she had to tilt her head back to look up at him. "I don't know what your plans are for later tonight, but if you want to—"

At that moment, the clock in the tower of the Cartwright Memorial Chapel chimed, as it did every hour, on the hour, vibrating across the lawn and cutting Noah off mid-sentence. It took Emma a moment to register the sound, but when she did, her heart slammed into her chest. "Oh, no." She glanced at her watch. "It's four o'clock. I have to go. I'll be late for work."

She spun around, frantically throwing her art supplies into her bag and tucking her painting into her portfolio case.

"How can I help?" Noah asked, handing her a tube of paint he'd rescued from the ground.

"The easel. Can you fold it up?"

Noah grabbed the easel, and as soon as he picked it up, one of the legs fell off. "Oh, no." He turned it over, trying to screw the wooden piece back on. "I think I broke it."

Emma's heart sank. First the paints, and now this. He didn't break it, the football did. "It's fine," she lied, grabbing the easel from Noah and shoving the pieces into her carrying case. "It doesn't matter. I just need to get to work." *Now, more than ever.* It wasn't just paint anymore. She'd need to buy a new easel, too. Emma tossed the strap of her bag over her shoulder, picked up her easel and portfolio case, and took off across the lawn in the direction of her dorm room. If she ran, she might be able to grab her uniform and slip in the restaurant's kitchen door undetected.

Behind her, Noah's voice called out, "Emma, wait! Can I get your number before you go?"

For a moment, Emma considered turning around. Noah had been kind to stay and help her clean up her supplies, instead of taking off like Cooper had. And there'd been that moment when she'd felt that connection between them. But she shook off the notion.

I need this job. Much more than I need a date with a Theta Chi Delta.

Emma hefted her bag higher on her shoulder and kept running.

———

The next afternoon, Emma pushed open the doors of the Kingston Arts Building after her class and squinted in the sun slanting through the maples overhead. It was another beautiful day. She'd love to find a spot on the lawn—away from the football-throwing frat boys this time—and finish her painting. But her easel was broken, and she needed to buy more paint.

Emma sighed and turned in the direction of town. At least she'd made decent tips last night. The Cartwright Inn was an upscale restaurant that mainly served patrons like the people her parents were friends with at the country club. Emma had spent countless hours at country club dinners listening to her parents talk about expensive wines, so at least she knew which bottles to suggest when someone asked for a recommendation. Who would have guessed that knowledge would actually be useful someday? And what would her father think if he knew she'd recommended his favorite bottle of Bordeaux three times this week?

He'd probably quit drinking it.

Emma was just heading down the path toward town when a voice called her name. She turned around to find Noah jogging toward her, a white envelope in his hand.

"Hey." He skidded to a stop in front of her, breathing hard. "I'm glad I caught you."

"Noah—?" Emma looked at him sideways. "How did you know I'd be here?"

"Please don't think I'm a stalker or anything. You mentioned you're an art education major, and I looked on the schedule and saw that a bunch of their classes let out around this time. So, I thought I'd take my chances that maybe you'd be here." His lips curved into a rueful smile. "And now that those words just came out of my mouth, I realize how stalkerish they sound, don't they?"

"Maybe a little," Emma said, but she couldn't help mirroring his smile. A small part of her was flattered that he'd gone out of his way to find her. She didn't want to admit it, but that flutter in her chest was back.

"Well, I felt terrible about how we knocked over your paints and broke your easel yesterday." Noah's face turned serious. "So, I took up a collection with the guys, and we bought you a gift certificate for the art store in town."

Emma's eyes widened as he held out the envelope. "Oh, you didn't have to—"

"Of course we did." He straightened his arm, pushing the envelope closer. "Please take it. Everyone felt really bad when I told them what happened. Even Cooper." Noah gave her a sideways smile. "I don't know much about art supplies, but I described what I thought you were using, and the guy at the store said this should probably cover it."

Emma reached out to take the envelope and, once again, she felt the heat of his hand brush her fingers. His gaze shifted to hers, and she could tell he felt it, too. Emma looked away, forcing herself to focus on the envelope in her hand instead of his dark eyes. She peeked inside and found a certificate for her favorite art store, and $500 listed under the amount. "Oh." She looked up, startled. This would more than cover the supplies she'd lost, plus almost everything she'd need for next semester. "It's too much money."

"Take it. Please." Noah shoved his hands in his pockets so she couldn't hand it back. "The guys really want to give it to you."

She glanced at the certificate again. God, she really needed this. "Thank you so much," she finally said, tucking it into her purse. "You said the guys contributed? Who are they? Your fraternity?"

"Yeah." Noah shrugged. "I'm a member of Theta Chi Delta. Have you heard of it?"

Did he really think she hadn't heard of it? Most members of the fraternity called themselves "Thetas" and assumed you knew exactly who they were. And on this Ivy League campus, most people did.

"Yeah, my dad was a *Theta*."

Noah cocked his head. "Really?"

Emma shrugged. "I don't really care about all that old boy's network stuff, to be honest."

Noah leaned in, a smile tugging at his lips. "Can I tell you a secret, but you swear upon pain of death that you won't tell anyone else?"

Emma returned his grin. "Well, when you put it that way, now I'm dying to know."

"I don't really care about stuff like that either."

"Really? Why did you join, then?"

Noah looked past her, and his eyes clouded over. "I don't talk about it much, but my parents passed away right before I came to Cartwright."

Emma reached out and grabbed his arm. "Oh my God. I'm so sorry."

He gave her a sad smile. "I think when I got here, I was looking for a community. A place that would feel a little bit like a family. And a fraternity like Theta seemed to be the best place to find that."

Emma felt terrible for judging him. "That makes perfect sense. I hope you found your community. Your family."

Noah met her eyes, and that same spark she'd felt earlier crackled between them. "I think I'm getting closer."

4

"Mrs. Havern?" Dr. Woodward's voice dragged Emma back to the present. "Are you okay?"

Emma blinked and stared at the doctor. Had he really just told her that there was a good chance that the man she'd fallen in love with all those years ago might never wake up?

She wrapped her arms around herself and, suddenly, she couldn't stop shaking. "Isn't there anything that can be done? A surgery to release the swelling in his brain, or—something...?" She dropped her hands helplessly in her lap.

"Unfortunately, no." Dr. Woodward shook his head. "At this stage, the only thing we can do is wait and see. The best thing you can do for Noah is to be here with him. Talk to him."

Emma glanced up sharply. "Can he hear me?"

Dr. Woodward nodded. "There's quite a bit of evidence that patients in a coma are aware of conversations and people around them, even if they can't respond. So, the more you can be here to talk to him, to hold his hand, and let him know you love him, the better."

Emma wondered fleetingly if Noah would want her to be

there. If he'd even want to hear her voice. She was the one who'd asked him to leave.

"Visitors are encouraged, and there are no set visiting hours, so if you or any of your family wants to come and sit with Noah, you're welcome day or night."

Maya.

Emma's heart dropped to her stomach. She still had no idea what she was she going to tell their daughter about Noah. Maya adored her father, it would break her heart to know that there was a chance he might never wake up. Emma's gaze flew to Noah's face. She wondered how Maya would react to all the scrapes and bruises and other injuries. Could Maya handle seeing her father like this?

But how could she possibly keep Maya away? Emma had no doubt in her mind that if there was one person who could drag Noah out of this state of unconsciousness, it was his daughter.

"Our daughter, Maya, is in high school. Should I bring her here right away?"

Dr. Woodward glanced at his watch. "School won't let out for a couple of hours, right?"

Emma nodded.

"I wouldn't rush over there to take her out early." He gestured in Noah's direction. "The fact is that nothing is likely to change in Noah's condition right now. Not until the swelling in his brain goes down a bit, and that could take days. Maybe weeks. It's important that you understand that there likely won't be a quick fix here."

Emma's gaze skated across the whirring machines and beeping heart rate monitor to the bandage on Noah's face. Her wish that he'd wake up any minute wasn't going to come true. He could be lying there for—*who knows how long?*

Dr. Woodward leaned in. "I know the waiting can be frustrating for families. But just because it doesn't look like anything is happening, doesn't mean it isn't. Noah's doing the hard work of healing in there. In the meantime, I recommend that you and your daughter try to keep some semblance of a normal schedule. Eating, sleeping, schoolwork. I see a lot of families come through here, and these situations are much, much harder on the ones who don't take care of themselves."

Emma released a heavy breath. "I'm going to have a hard time convincing Maya that she can't be here twenty-four, seven."

Dr. Woodward smiled. "I have a teenage daughter, so I understand where you're coming from. Absolutely bring her here after school and have her hang out and talk to Noah. But if you want my advice beyond that..." He trailed off.

Emma glanced at her husband's chest rising and falling in the bed. When it came to Maya, she and Noah used to be a team. It was one of the things she'd missed most during all of Noah's travels these past few years, and especially since he'd moved across town. Parenting a teenager was hard, and Emma was never sure if she was doing the right thing. She turned back to Dr. Woodward. "I'd love your advice."

"Well, if it were my daughter, I'd make sure she kept up with her classes, sports, even seeing her friends once in a while."

"She has a part in the school musical."

"Great, that's great." Dr. Woodward gave her an encouraging nod. "Make sure she's going to her practices and keeping up with schoolwork. It's going to be better for her mental health than sitting here all day long. And as hard as it sounds—" He looked at her. "That goes for you, too."

Emma thought about the vase she'd left on her pottery wheel in her mad dash to get to the hospital. She couldn't imagine how she'd be able to focus on work right now. But the doctor was right about Maya. As a junior in high school, this was an important year for her. Emma couldn't allow her to get behind or it would make this situation even harder. "You're right. Thank you."

Dr. Woodward nodded and stood up. "I'll be checking in regularly, and if you need anything, just ask one of the nurses." He headed toward the door, and then he stopped and turned back around. "There's a police officer outside. I believe she wants to talk to you about the woman in the car who passed away... And about the child. Is it okay to send her in?"

In the shock of seeing Noah like this, and finding out his prognosis, Emma had pushed Coral Butler and the two-year-old in the car from her mind. There was only so much shattering news she could process in one moment. But now, her gaze slid back to Noah. Was it possible he'd been having an affair with Coral? And if so, was he in love with her? How would he react if he knew Coral had died in the accident? If what the doctor said was true and Noah could hear people talking to him, then Emma was tempted to break the news in case that might wake him up.

It was a horrible way to think. But if it would bring Noah back, and spare Maya the pain of seeing her father like this, Emma was willing to try anything. *And,* Emma realized, she was angry as hell that he'd put her in this position of having to reckon with this woman and child; that she might have to be the one to explain the unthinkable to Maya.

"Emma?"

"Yes." Emma shook herself out of her dark thoughts. "Sorry, yes. Send her in."

Dr. Woodward nodded and headed out the door. A few moments later, a middle-aged woman in a white button-up shirt, gray pants, and no-nonsense black shoes entered the room. She was holding a notepad and pen. "Mrs. Havern, I'm Detective Diane Vargas. May I speak to you for a few moments?"

Emma stood up from her chair. "Yes, please come in."

"Would you prefer we meet outside? So, we don't disturb..." Detective Vargas gestured toward Noah.

"No, this is fine. The doctor said it's good for him to hear our voices."

Detective Vargas's gaze paused on Noah, taking in his injuries, and then she stepped into the middle of the room. "First of all, I want to tell you that I'm sorry for what happened to your husband."

Emma nodded politely. "Thank you."

"He was driving," the officer continued. "But he wasn't at fault. A tractor trailer crossed over the center line and hit your husband's car. We're still investigating whether there were substances involved with the other driver."

Emma nodded. At least she could assure Maya that Noah had been driving safely.

"And we're sorry for the loss of Ms. Butler. Were the two of you close?"

Emma shook her head. "I didn't know Ms. Butler."

"Oh." Detective Vargas cocked her head. "I didn't realize..." She made a note in her notepad. "We were hoping you might be able to give us some information about her."

"I'm sorry. I was hoping *you* could give me some information about her."

Detective Vargas's gaze skated across Noah and then back to Emma. Did the detective have the same suspicions as Emma about Noah and Coral's relationship? Cheating husbands were probably commonplace in her line of work. Still, Emma couldn't help flushing with mortification. She never thought she'd be in this situation.

"Well, we ran Ms. Butler through the system, and she doesn't appear to have a record. A squad car is headed over to the address on her driver's license right now. We're hoping we can find some information about family or next of kin."

"And the child?" Emma prompted. Who was the child in Noah's car?

Detective Vargas raised an eyebrow. "You don't know the child, either?"

"I'm afraid I don't."

"There were some toys and a children's book in Ms. Butler's purse, so right now we're working under the assumption that the child was in her care. Likely she was the parent or guardian. But hopefully, our officer can learn more when they arrive at the residence."

Emma remembered the panic she'd felt when she'd thought the child in the car was Maya. "And how is she—the child? The officers who came to my house said she only has minor injuries?"

"That's correct." Detective Vargas nodded. "She's just down the hall. They'll keep her overnight for observation, since she has a small bump on her head. But they expect to release her tomorrow."

"They didn't send her to the children's hospital?"

"The paramedics brought Coral and your husband here. They assumed that the three of them were related, and brought the child here, too."

Of course the paramedics assumed Noah was related to Coral and the girl. They'd probably looked like a family out for a drive.

Was that what they were?

"We hope to find a family member before they're ready to discharge her." Detective Vargas pulled out a card from her pocket and handed it to Emma. "If you think of anything else, please give me a call."

Emma tucked the card into her purse. "Will you let me know when you find out more about Coral Butler and the child? They were with my husband, after all. I'd like to know..." *God, its humiliating to admit this.* "... what they were doing together... where they were going..."

Detective Vargas's eye twitched, confirming Emma's suspicion that the police officer believed Coral and Noah were having an affair. Who wouldn't think that, if a man and a woman his wife had never heard of were spending time together in the middle of the day?

"Of course," the officer said. "I'll reach out if I learn anything new. In the meantime, I'll let you get back to your husband."

A moment later, Emma was alone with Noah. She approached the bed slowly and stopped with her hands on the bedrail. "Who *is* Coral Butler, Noah? Were you having an affair with her?"

Noah's chest rose and fell, but he said nothing.

"And what about the child. How do you know her?"

Emma stared at her husband. Silence stretched across the room, only interrupted by an occasional whoosh of a machine or a voice drifting in from down the hall.

Emma's hands tightened on the rail. *Down the hall.*

Detective Vargas had said the little girl was in a room down the hall. Emma's heart ached at the thought of it. If she was Coral Butler's daughter, the poor baby had just lost her mother. Was she asking for Coral? Was she all alone in that hospital room? Emma pictured Maya at that age, reaching her chubby little arms in the air so Emma or Noah would pick her up. Waking up at night and crying for Emma to come in and soothe her. Who would go in and comfort that little girl? Apparently, they were still looking for family members. What if the nurses were too busy when she called for them?

Emma backed away from Noah's hospital bed and took a couple of tentative steps toward the door. It really wasn't her business. She didn't know Coral Butler or this child. She had absolutely no connection to them. Maybe the child's family wouldn't even want her getting involved.

She took another few steps. If it were Maya all alone in the hospital, having—maybe—just lost her mother, Emma would want someone who cared to check in on her. Besides—she glanced back at Noah, still unmoving on the hospital bed— maybe it wasn't true that she had absolutely no connection to the child.

Emma walked the rest of the way to the door and cast a brief glance down the hall. She paused, debating for one more moment, and then before she could change her mind, took a left, back the way she came.

She passed the room with the older couple again, and a second door that was closed.

Emma arrived outside the third room, the one situated right by the nurses' station. She hadn't peeked inside before, but it was exactly the room she would have chosen for an unattended child, where the nurses could keep an eye out. Except all the nurses seemed to be busy because, at the moment, nobody was sitting at the desk. Healthcare facilities were chronically under-staffed these days.

Emma glanced back at the door to the room. It hung open, but the curtain had been drawn, so Emma couldn't see past it. And then a breeze ruffled the fabric, and she spotted a toddler-sized pair of shoes lined up on the floor.

Her heart caught in her throat.

Was she in there? The mysterious child that had been in Noah's car?

At that moment, she heard footsteps behind her, and a woman's voice called out, "Excuse me."

Emma whirled around to find a younger woman approaching. She was dressed casually, in jeans and a button-up shirt, so she likely wasn't a nurse or hospital administrator. Could this woman be the child's relative?

"Can I help you?" the woman asked warily, stepping between Emma and the hospital room door. "You can't go in there."

"I'm sorry." Of course Emma looked suspicious. She was a

strange woman standing in front of an unattended child's room. "I—my husband is down the hall in a—" She took a deep breath. "In a coma. From a car accident. I heard there was a child in the car with him, and I was hoping to learn more about her condition. Are you a relative?"

"Oh." The woman's face registered understanding. She shook her head, her dark ponytail swishing. "No, I'm the social worker. We haven't located any relatives, yet." Her voice softened with concern. "How is your husband?"

"He's not great. We don't know if..." Emma trailed off. She took a deep breath and shook her head. "Anyway, I just wanted to see if the child is okay."

"She's fine. She's sleeping right now." The social worker gestured at a bench against a wall, a couple of doors down from the child's room. "Why don't we sit over here to talk?"

Emma followed her down the hall, and they settled onto the hard, plastic seats.

"I'm Kate Perez, a social worker from the child welfare agency."

"Emma Havern."

"Do you mind if I ask to see some identification?" Kate glanced at the door to the child's room and then shifted in her seat to look Emma in the eye. "I really don't feel comfortable sharing any information with you about the child until I know who you are."

Emma grabbed her purse to find her ID. "Of course." She pulled her driver's license from her wallet and handed it over. If the girl in the hospital room were her daughter, she'd want the social worker to be just as cautious.

"Thanks." Kate fished a file from her bag and flipped through it, occasionally glancing at Emma's driver's license and then back at the paper in front of her. After a moment, she nodded and then handed the card back to Emma. "Your information matches the name and address I have in my file for you."

Emma blinked for a moment, taking that in. "*I'm* in your file?"

Kate nodded. "You're listed as the next of kin for the driver of the car where the child was found. So, we're hoping you have some connection to her."

Do I have a connection to her? Emma had no idea.

"Now it's just a matter of figuring out what that connection is," Kate continued. "I understand from the police officer that you weren't acquainted with Ms. Butler, or the child."

"No, I wasn't." Emma paused. "At least I don't think so. But if they were with my husband, I suppose we could have some connection I'm unaware of. Maybe I've seen them around the neighborhood or at a school event, or something."

Another thought occurred to her, and she grasped at it like a lifeline. Maybe Coral had been Noah's neighbor at his new apartment building. That would explain why Emma wasn't acquainted with her. Maybe he was just being neighborly, offering them a ride, and it was nothing more than that.

"I suppose it's possible you'd know them from around town." Kate shrugged. "Though, the address on Coral Butler's driver's license wasn't in Grand Rapids. She lived in Millersville. And your husband was actually driving on Route 37 from that direction when he had the accident."

Emma took in this new development. Millersville was a small, rural community almost an hour away. They didn't know anyone there, and they'd never had any reason to go. "Is it possible Coral Butler recently relocated to Millersville from Grand Rapids?"

"It could be. I'll see if I can get that information from the officers. And we can peek in on Luna in a bit. See if maybe you recognize her from around the neighborhood."

"Luna? That's her name?"

"Yes. Is that familiar to you?" Kate looked hopeful. As a social worker, the child's welfare was her responsibility, and finding a qualified family member was probably her top priority.

"I'm sorry." Emma shook her head.

"Well, I hope the police officers will turn up some family members who can shed some light on Luna's situation."

"What if they go to the address and don't find anyone?" Emma glanced in the direction of the child's hospital room. Who would stay with her tonight? Kate? Or one of the nurses? But then what would they do with her tomorrow?

"The doctor is keeping Luna in for observation tonight, and that will buy us a little bit of time to find a family member who might be able to take her. I do suspect that Coral was Luna's parent, although I don't know that for sure."

Emma's eyes filled with tears. She hoped Kate was wrong, because that would mean that poor child had just lost her mother.

"If that *is* the case," Kate continued. "I'm hoping she has a father who can take her, or some other family—an aunt, some grandparents."

At the word *father*, Emma's mind drifted to her husband. What if Luna's father didn't turn up because he was asleep in the hospital room down the hall?

She shook her head. There was absolutely no evidence that Noah had been having an affair, except her suspicions and the fact that he'd grown so distant over the past two years. But maybe his distance had nothing to do with another woman, or a child. Maybe he just didn't love her anymore.

Except Luna is two years old, a little voice nagged in her head. *Could it be a coincidence?*

Emma pushed that thought out of her mind. "And if you don't find any family members, what happens then?"

Kate shook her head sadly. "Then, unfortunately, she'll have to go to foster care."

Emma's stomach churned at the thought. Some foster families were wonderful. But she'd heard plenty of horror stories, too. How could such a little girl possibly understand being thrust into a completely unfamiliar situation, with people who might not care for her properly? Emma's imagination formed the image of a small girl with sticky-uppy hair and a milk-mustache smeared across her upper lip, sitting up in a strange bed, calling for her mother.

Emma's tears spilled over, and she swiped at them with her palm. It was unbearable. Someone had to come and claim this child. A loving aunt or grandmother. Or maybe her mother was still out there somewhere. Emma hoped with all her heart that was the case.

Kate dug in her purse and pulled out an extra-large packet of tissues and a small bottle of water. Emma appreciated her presence in that moment. "Thank you," she murmured, wiping her eyes with a tissue. "I'm sorry I'm such a mess."

"You've been through an enormous ordeal today," Kate said. "If it will be too difficult to see Luna now, I can always stop back in later."

"No, I'm okay." Emma insisted. "I'm fine." Her problems were small compared to little Luna's. If she was able to identify the girl and help her to find her relatives—maybe she *had* seen Luna around the neighborhood—then she shouldn't delay another moment.

Emma pulled herself together and they made their way back to Luna's hospital room. Kate gently tugged the curtain aside and took a step into the dim room lit only by a small nightlight by the bed. She turned to Emma and motioned to be quiet, putting a finger to her lips.

When Emma stepped inside, her heart rocked in her chest.

About ten feet away, Luna lay curled on her side, eyes closed, her tiny body practically swallowed up by the enormous hospital bed. She clutched a stuffed elephant to her chest, one cheek resting on the furry animal's head. Emma was relieved to see her chest rise and fall rhythmically. Luna didn't appear to be in distress, but then again, maybe the trauma of it all had finally worn her out. Did she even understand what was happening? Emma longed to reach out and brush the dark lock of hair off her forehead, to tug the sheet up higher over her shoulder and make sure she wasn't too cold. But of course, she shouldn't. Emma had no connection to this child. And the last thing she wanted to do was wake her.

"She had a bit of a bump on the head from the accident, so the doctors said she might be sleepy for a day or two," Kate explained.

"But she was awake earlier—that's when she told you her name?" Emma whispered back.

Kate nodded.

"And she didn't say if the woman in the car was her mother?"

Kate shook her head. "I didn't want to push her to answer too many questions. The doctors said we should let her rest." Her gaze roamed over Luna for a moment, and then she turned back to Emma. "Does she look familiar to you at all?"

Emma blinked into the dim space. "It is okay if I go a bit closer?"

"Of course."

Emma tiptoed a few feet closer to the hospital bed. At that moment, Luna gave a little whimper and rolled onto her back. She dropped the elephant by her side and stretched her little arms out wide. For a moment, her eyes fluttered, and Emma held her breath, worrying that she'd disturbed her. But then they stilled again, and Luna settled back to sleep.

Emma's gaze roamed over her, taking in the shadows cast on her cheeks by her inordinately long eyelashes, the curve of her ears, the tiny purse of her lips. And then she backed up slowly, to where Kate waited with a hopeful look on her face. "What do you think?"

"Um," Emma murmured.

"Have you ever seen her before? Does she look like any of the children from one of the other families in your neighborhood?"

"I—" Emma's mouth felt like someone had filled it with sand, and she took a gulp from the water bottle Kate had given her. "She—no. No, she doesn't look like anyone from the neighborhood."

Kate's shoulders drooped. "Well, it was a long shot, I guess."

Dazed, Emma nodded and followed Kate back out into the hall. Her body was shaking now, shivering with cold and flushed with heat at the same time. She crossed her arms over her chest so Kate wouldn't notice.

Emma hadn't lied to the social worker when she'd said Luna didn't look like a child from one of the other families in the neighborhood. But she hadn't told the truth, either.

Because though Emma had never seen Luna before, she *did* recognize her.

Luna looked an awful lot like Noah.

5

On her drive to the high school, Emma turned the image of little Luna lying in the hospital room over and over in her head. Her initial reaction had been that the girl resembled Noah. But now that she had a little bit of distance, she started to talk herself out of it. Maybe it was only her imagination that Luna's dark hair flopped over her forehead the same way Emma's husband's did. Maybe it was only the shadows in the dark room tracing the curve of Luna's nose into a replica of Noah's.

Just that morning in her conversation with Alicia, she'd expressed her fears that Noah had been cheating on her. But Noah keeping an affair quiet for a couple of months was something altogether different than the possibility that he might have harbored *an entire secret family* for over two years, and that she'd suspected nothing. Could he have hidden a child from her? It just wasn't possible. She'd certainly felt a gulf between them for a while now, but Noah loved her.

Noah would never do that to her.

Emma pulled up in front of the high school and parked her car in front of the entrance. She'd called the school earlier to let them know she'd be picking Maya up today, since Maya usually took the school bus with her friends.

From somewhere inside the building, the final dismissal bell rang and, moments later, the double doors swung open, and students began pouring out. Emma scanned the crowd for Maya as kids filtered past. She finally spotted her daughter descending the steps chattering with Sam and Fatima, Maya's two best friends since elementary school. On the sidewalk, they stopped so Fatima could pull out her phone. The three of them leaned in together to snap a selfie.

Emma had seen her daughter toss her hair over her shoulder in this practiced pose dozens of times before. At sixteen, the teens were obsessed with social media. Emma and Noah had allowed it as long as they had full access to monitor Maya's account. But today, Emma paid extra attention to the curve of Maya's smile and the way her eyebrows arched when she laughed. Maya was tall and lean—just like her father—and she'd inherited his thick, wavy hair. There was no doubt that Maya was Noah's daughter. They used to joke that his genes must have been much stronger than Emma's. Emma was shorter than Maya, and there wasn't even a trace of Emma's curvier hips or thighs on her daughter's frame. And Emma had sandy-brown hair and blue-gray eyes, while both Noah's and Maya's were dark.

Had Noah passed those same traits on to a second child?

Emma did her best to shake off these thoughts. There was no point in speculating about Luna's parentage. For all she knew, they'd arrive back at the hospital to find that the girl's father had been located and was rushing to her bedside that very moment. Besides, she had other things to worry about. Like how she was going to tell Maya that her father was in a coma and might never wake up.

The back of Emma's throat ached as she watched her daughter laugh. Would Maya be truly happy and carefree like this again? Or did this mark the moment when her life changed, and her childhood ended forever?

Emma hesitated, giving her daughter another minute with her friends. But eventually, Sam and Fatima had to hurry to catch the bus, and Maya turned her gaze to the line of cars waiting at the curb. When she spotted Emma's car she waved and ran over to pull the door open.

"Did we forget that today's the follow-up at the orthodontist?" Maya asked, sliding into the passenger seat.

Emma wished that was why she was here. "No. That's in a couple of weeks."

"Oh." Maya shoved her backpack into the backseat. "So, why are you here, then?"

"Honey..." Emma trailed off. She should have rehearsed this on the way over. "I need to tell you something."

Maya reared back against the car door, her face stricken. "What is it?" she demanded, her voice rising with each word. "Is it Dad? You're leaving him for good, aren't you?"

Maya had been devastated when Emma had broken the news about the separation. While Noah had been physically present for the conversation, he'd remained silent and left Emma to do most of the talking. Which meant that Maya blamed Emma for making Noah leave.

"No, it's not about leaving Dad." Emma hesitated and then realized it would be worse if she dragged it out. "Honey, Dad was in a car accident."

Maya's face turned pale. "What do you mean, *a car accident*? Is he okay?"

Again, Emma wished she'd thought this through, or asked Kate the social worker for advice. She felt so ill-equipped to share this kind of news with her daughter. "He's in a coma."

"A coma?" Maya blinked. "Like, he's just lying there, asleep?"

"Yes, sort of like that." It wasn't exactly how the doctor had described a coma, but it was the simplest way to explain it to a teenager.

"When will he wake up?"

Emma wished she had more answers. "The doctors aren't sure. They're hopeful that he just needs a little time to heal and then he'll wake up."

"So, how did he end up in a coma? Did he hit his head in the accident?" Maya stared at her, wide-eyed.

Emma nodded. "And now there's some swelling in his brain. They're not sure how long it will take for it to heal."

"*Will* he wake up?" Maya asked, with a tinge of panic in her voice. "What if he doesn't?"

"We can't think that way, honey." Emma reached out and took her daughter's hand. "The doctors are hopeful that he just needs a little time, and then he'll be just fine." It wasn't completely true, and maybe Emma should be honest with Maya about Noah's prognosis. But Emma wasn't ready to let her own thoughts drift into the *what if* direction, and Maya was only sixteen. It wouldn't do her any good to dwell on the worst possible scenario. Emma needed to project positivity and hope for Maya's sake, and Noah's, too.

"Can I see him?"

"Yes, of course." Emma hesitated, remembering the bandages, bruises, and broken bones. "But I need to warn you that he looks pretty beat up."

Maya bit her lip nervously.

"He has some bumps and scrapes. A few broken bones. But the doctors said that all those physical injuries will heal. It looks worse than it is." *At least on the outside.*

Maya snapped her seatbelt into place, and Emma pulled the car out into the street, steering it toward the hospital.

"The doctors said the best thing we can do for Dad is to talk to him," Emma said, clicking on her turn signal. "Even if he doesn't respond, they think he'll be able to hear you."

"What am I supposed to say? Like, should I encourage him to wake up? Tell him he'll be fine?"

Emma glanced over at Maya, who was looking a little nauseous. "You don't need to focus on his injuries. Just tell him about your day. Tell him about the show you're working on. Anything. He just wants to hear your voice."

"Okay," Maya agreed quietly.

Emma pulled the car to a stop at a red light and reached out to rub a comforting hand up and down her daughter's arm. Should she tell Maya about the other part of the accident? That Coral Butler had been in the car? And Luna? Emma gave her head a shake. It would only raise questions she had no idea how to answer.

———

"How did this happen?" Maya turned to Emma with tears pouring down her cheeks.

Emma had been secretly hoping that she and Maya would arrive to Noah's hospital room to find him sitting up in bed smiling at them. But when they pulled aside the curtain, he was still lying there, as silent and still as ever. Maya had gasped and lunged to his bedside, her shoulders shaking with sobs.

"Where was he going when this happened?" Maya demanded.

"I'm not sure." Emma took a shaky breath to get her own emotions under control. It was as much of a shock to see Noah's deathly pale face mottled with scrapes and purple bruises as it had been the first time. "He was driving on Route 37 and was hit by an oncoming car."

"Route 37? Isn't that the road we take to get to his new apartment?"

"It does go by there, yes. He was probably on his way home

from somewhere. Maybe the grocery store or—" *Or Coral Butler's house?*

Maya's breath hitched with another sob. "That road is the worst. It has all that traffic that drives fast and blows through the lights. Dad called it an accident waiting to happen."

Emma reached toward her daughter. "The police officers said it wasn't his fault, honey."

Maya reeled backwards, away from Emma's hand. "Maybe it's your fault."

Emma froze. "What? How?"

"If you hadn't made him move out and move across town, he wouldn't have had to drive on that dangerous road every day."

"Maya—"

Maya cut her off. "If you'd let him stay home with us, he'd be safe right now."

Emma tried to remain calm and remind herself that Maya was in shock after seeing her father like this. Deep down, Maya had to know that Emma had nothing to do with Noah's accident. Something like this could have happened anywhere. And even if it was the fault of the dangerous traffic on Route 37, Emma hadn't rented that apartment for Noah. In fact, she'd been more than a little surprised when he'd chosen that particular place. It was across town, not remotely close to their house, and it wasn't terribly convenient to his job either. The apartment was a basic two-bedroom with a month-to-month lease, in a bland complex that had been built twenty or thirty years ago and hadn't seen an update since. As for the neighborhood, there was nothing but a few strip malls heading north out of town.

But it wasn't up to Emma to decide where Noah lived, even if it was inconvenient to drop Maya off there when she stayed with him every Saturday night. In her darkest moments, Emma had wondered if he'd chosen that apartment just to inconvenience her.

"Honey, Dad and I explained this—it was a mutual decision

for us to separate." But Emma was lying, and Maya probably knew it. Noah would never have moved out on his own. He would have just gone on traveling too much, missing important events, and doing whatever it was he was doing behind her back. But she couldn't say that to Maya. She couldn't bad-mouth Noah, especially now, with his recovery so uncertain. "You know that sometimes marriages are more complicated than kids can understand," she managed weakly.

"I understand plenty," Maya gasped, swiping at her wet cheeks with the back of her hand. "You made him leave. And now look at him."

"Maya—" Emma tried again.

"Just leave us alone," Maya yelled.

In normal times, Emma would never let Maya get away with talking to her like that. She'd ground her for a week or take away her phone. But this wasn't normal times, and if Noah didn't make it through, it might never be normal times again. So, Emma decided to give her a pass. "I'll be waiting out in the hall," she murmured, backing up toward the door.

With a quiet sob, Maya spun back around to face her father.

Alone in the hall, Emma's gaze was drawn a few doors down to the room where she'd seen Luna earlier. *Is Luna awake now? Is she calling for her mother?* Emma couldn't imagine how terrified and confused the little girl must be. Emma peeked back into Noah's room where Maya had settled into the chair next to the bed, murmuring to her father. Emma could hear the names "Sam" and "Fatima" and something about *My Fair Lady*, so Maya must have been telling Noah about her musical rehearsal last night. Maya seemed to have settled in for a while, so Emma turned back toward Luna's room and slowly made her way down the hall.

In the doorway, she took a couple of baby steps around the

curtain blocking the door. Luna had changed positions—now she was lying on her stomach—but she was still asleep.

"Hi," a voice whispered from the other side of the room.

Emma squinted in the dim light to find Kate sitting in a chair by the window with a book in her hands. "Oh," Emma whispered back. "I didn't see you there. I guess she still hasn't woken up?"

Kate shook her head. "The doctors think she might sleep until morning."

"I'm sorry. I know I shouldn't just be wandering in. But I can't help thinking about the poor girl all alone in here." Emma gazed hopefully around the room, but the other chairs were empty. "I guess you didn't track down any family members yet?"

"Unfortunately, no. But I'm still waiting to hear from the police officers in Millersville. Hopefully, they'll come up with something. Until then, I'm going to hang out here. Just in case she wakes up."

Emma had the strangest urge to sit down in the empty chair and wait it out with Kate. Just in case Luna woke up. But she had her own child down the hall, and despite her daughter's accusations, Maya needed her more than ever. Besides, as much as Emma wondered about her connection to this little girl, she was a complete stranger to Luna. So instead, she nodded and took a step backwards. "I hope they find someone soon. I wish I could have been more help in that regard."

"It's certainly not your fault." Kate looked at her with compassion. "This is a tough situation for you, and I appreciate you showing your concern for Luna, given the circumstances."

Emma bit her lip. Was Kate simply referring to the fact that her husband was in a coma? Or was this a veiled suggestion that Luna might be Noah's illegitimate child? Did everyone in the hospital suspect these "circumstances"?

And are they right?

Suddenly, Emma wished she could crawl into bed and sleep for a week. And that when she woke up, this nightmare would be over. "Well, I should probably leave you before we wake up Luna." She stumbled backward into the privacy curtain.

Kate nodded. "My colleague will take over tonight, but I'll be back here tomorrow if you want to stop and check in then."

"Thank you. I will." With one more uncertain glance at Luna's tiny back rising and falling with each breath, Emma turned and headed back into the hall.

6

NINETEEN YEARS AGO

A gentle breeze rustled the leaves overhead, teasing a lock of Emma's hair out of its messy topknot. Noah leaned across the small sliver of space between them and tucked it behind her ear. Emma smiled as she gazed through the tree branches up at the endless blue sky. *Could it be a more perfect day?*

Noah propped himself on his elbow so he could look into her eyes. "Thanks for inviting me on a picnic today," he said.

"Well, thanks for coming." Emma's gaze traced his face from the dark hair that always seemed to flop over his forehead to the five o'clock shadow on his jaw. Though his face had grown as familiar to her as her own over the last year, she never seemed to grow tired of looking at it. "Do you have any idea why I picked this spot today?"

They were sprawled on a blanket under a tree on the student union lawn. Emma tilted her head to look from Noah's face to the grassy area where a group of unfamiliar students kicked around a soccer ball. They reminded her of a group of fraternity guys she'd seen playing football in that same spot not so long ago.

By his expression, he remembered, too. He turned back to Emma with a grin. "This is where we met."

Emma nodded, laughing. "That's right. Any idea what day that was?"

Noah blinked. "Was it—?"

"It was exactly a year ago."

"So, this is our one-year anniversary?"

Emma had never dated anyone for more than a couple of months. And she'd certainly never felt about any of those men the way she felt about Noah.

Emma had initially been wary of getting involved. It wasn't just that he was a Theta Chi Delta, although that had been a factor at first. But it was also that she didn't have time for dating. She was working two jobs and needed to focus on finishing school. But Noah had been patient, waiting for her after she got off work at the restaurant to walk her home, and bringing her coffee at the studio when she had a project due. They usually ended up talking for hours, and he always asked a million questions about her artwork. Emma had kept it under wraps for most of her life—her parents had no interest in hearing her "drone on" about glazes and firing techniques—and it meant so much to finally be able to share it with someone.

"That's right." She flashed him a grin. "Happy anniversary."

"Best year of my life," he murmured, leaning down to kiss her.

It had been the best year of her life, too. Though her wealthy parents had showered her with material possessions as a child, they'd been miserly when it came to what she really longed for—their affection. Her father's world revolved around making money and then flashing it at expensive restaurants and country clubs. And when her mother wasn't jetting off to some exotic locale and leaving Emma with the nanny, she was more interested in gossip than she was in her own daughter. Emma had always known she was lucky to have everything she needed: clothes, plenty of food, and a beautiful, if sterile, home. But it didn't make up for how alone she felt.

Art had been Emma's escape. While the other kids spent their summers sitting around the country club pool, Emma would wander off alone to the stables to draw pictures of the horses.

Her father had indulged her interests in drawing and pottery at first, allowing her to enroll in art classes at the local museum. But once he realized that she was developing a reputation as the weird, artsy girl who didn't socialize with the other kids, he cut off the art classes and made her take tennis lesson instead. *It's a skill you'll actually use,* he'd said. *When you take over the company, you can hold business meetings over a game.*

Noah was the first person she'd ever met who didn't care that she was artsy and quiet. Who didn't mind that she spent half her time up to her elbows in pottery clay or that she showed up to meet him for dinner covered in paint. He never pressured her to attend his fraternity parties or social events if she didn't want to.

"Noah," she murmured when they broke off the kiss. "I have something to ask you."

He cocked his head. "Anything."

"Well..." Emma hesitated. "Would you come home with me this weekend to meet my family?"

Emma had rarely been home since she went away to college, and she'd seen her parents even less frequently since they'd stopped paying her tuition because she'd pursued art education against their will. But her mother had called and guilted her into agreeing to come home that weekend. Emma's best guess was that her mother probably didn't have any upcoming trips and needed something to do.

Emma dreaded the inevitable comments about her appearance, the pressure to be seen at the country club, the snide remarks about her career choices. If Noah came along, maybe her parents would tone it down a little. Or maybe not. But knowing that he was by her side and supported her choices would make her parents' criticisms hurt less.

Noah hesitated, raising his eyebrows, and Emma immediately regretted asking. He knew all about her parents. She'd explained how they'd wanted her to go into the family business and had cut her off when she'd chosen art instead. So, of course he'd hesitate. Who would want to give up a weekend to hang out with some stodgy rich people? Especially when her family sounded so completely opposite from his own loving parents. Noah had lost them in a fire the summer after high school, and it had completely crushed him. He still couldn't talk about it without choking up. When he'd first told her, Emma's eyes had filled with tears, too. It was so cruel that Noah had lost his family, his entire support system, just as he was starting out in the world. And in such a terrible way.

"Never mind," Emma mumbled, scrambling to a sitting position. "Forget I said anything."

"Hey." Noah grabbed her hand and pulled her back toward him. "I'd love to go with you. If I paused, it's just that I'm little surprised. I know your relationship with your parents isn't easy."

"It's not. My dad will probably grill you about your job prospects, and my mom will be silently judging what you're wearing. But having you there will make the weekend bearable. Less..." She trailed off. "Lonely..." Emma finally admitted.

He gazed at her across the narrow space with an affectionate smile. "Thank you for inviting me. I'd love to come."

"Yeah?" Emma bit her lip. "Are you sure? It won't be fun or anything. My parents are—a lot to take."

"Emma." Noah's face turned serious. "I don't care if your parents are difficult. I'm not going to their house to be with them. I'm going to be with you."

Emma's heart flipped. If she thought she was falling for him before, now she completely fell. "Noah. I love you."

For a moment, he froze, and the only indication that he'd heard her was the amazement playing across his face. Finally, he leaned in and took her face in his hands. "Emma, I love you, too." His voice crackled with emotion. "I've never loved anyone..." Noah trailed off, shaking his head. "Not like this. I never could have imagined it." And with that, he tugged her down on the blanket next to him and pressed his mouth against hers.

She kissed him back, feeling the strength of his arms around her and the weight of his body half-leaning onto hers. She'd never loved anyone like this, either. As a child, Emma used to picture what it would be like to meet someone who felt this way about her. Someone who could love her with no reservations or conditions. Someone she could love the same way. It was so much more than she could have ever imagined.

"Noah," Emma murmured, when they finally broke apart. "Tell me something about your family. About what it was like for you growing up." They'd talked endlessly about her family, her lonely childhood, but he rarely opened up about his own past. It was still too painful, he'd say. Too raw. He hadn't had any other family, so when his parents passed, they'd left him on his own.

A dark shadow passed across Noah's face, and Emma reached up to smooth the lines from his forehead. "I know you don't like to talk about your parents, but—"

"It's not that I don't like to talk about them. The truth is—" Noah took a deep breath and blew it out slowly. "Emma, the truth is that I grew up really differently than you."

Emma nodded. "I know, and I'm so glad." She gave him a sad smile. "It breaks my heart that you lost them, but I take comfort knowing you had such a wonderful family."

Noah opened his mouth and then closed it. Finally, he nodded. "Me, too. Yeah, I was really lucky."

"Maybe it will hurt less if you share some of the good things about your childhood. If you let me in, just a little," Emma prompted. "For example, you could tell me—" She paused, searching for a topic that might be easiest for Noah to start with. Something that wouldn't be too painful. "Tell me about where you grew up." By the relieved look on Noah's face, Emma knew it was the right question.

"Okay, sure." Noah rolled to his side and pulled himself to a sitting position. "I was born in Northern California, at the hospital at Stanford University, and I grew up in Palo Alto."

Emma nodded in encouragement. "What was that like, growing up in Palo Alto?"

"It was..." Noah gazed out across the lawn at a couple of kids about ten years old riding their bikes on one of the walking paths. "It was a college town, sort of like this one, so we had lots of interesting places to roam."

Emma watched the darker-haired boy yank his bike back into a wheelie and then pedal off. If she squinted, he could be a ten-year-old version of Noah. She loved the idea of a childhood with so much freedom and adventure. Although her parents weren't around much, they'd made sure to schedule her in a dozen different activities. Tennis, piano, ballet. She couldn't imagine having been allowed to just ride off on her bike. Or where she would have even gone in the gated community where she lived. "And your parents didn't worry about you?"

"It was a really safe place... Idyllic, in a lot of ways. And my parents were always waiting for me when I got home. They were...the best." A wistful expression drifted across his face, and for a moment, he was quiet. Probably remembering.

"Didn't they want you to apply to Stanford and stay in California?" Emma asked, thinking of her own parents who'd told her exactly where she ought to go to college. Noah's mom and dad had died the summer before he'd come to Cartwright. If they'd been so close, why had he chosen a school all the way across the country?

"I'd spent my whole life in California, so they were excited for me to have new adventures. And now..." Noah lifted a shoulder. "It's probably for the best that I didn't go to Stanford. Cartwright isn't full of old memories." He sat up abruptly, brushing off his hands, and flashed her a grin. "But it *is* where I'm going to make new memories." Before Emma could answer, Noah stood up and reached down to help her to her feet. "Let me take you somewhere nice for dinner tonight."

A bit dazed by Noah's sudden burst of energy, Emma nodded, leaning over to fold up the blanket. She wanted to ask him more, but it sounded like he'd had enough of sad talk for one day. And besides, if Noah wanted to look ahead to their future, she certainly wasn't going to argue.

———

Noah met her at the train station wearing a perfectly pressed pair of khaki pants, a Ralph Lauren Oxford shirt, and a navy-blue blazer. Emma almost didn't recognize him. When they'd hung out after class or work, Noah usually wore a pair of a jeans and a T-shirt, often with Theta Chi Delta's Greek letters across the front, or occasionally Cartwright University's logo. In colder weather, he'd throw on his Lawrence Academy sweatshirt from the private high school he'd attended in California. It was one of the few things that had survived the fire at his parents' home.

"Wow," Emma said, stopping in front of him as her gaze slid from the Sperry loafers on his feet all the way up to his dark hair combed back off his forehead and held in place with some sort of gel. "My dad is going to *love* you."

Noah smoothed a hand down his shirt. "Do you think so?"

Emma blinked. It hadn't occurred to her that he'd be

nervous to meet her parents. It wasn't like he needed to impress them. "I do, actually. But it's really okay if he doesn't." She gave him a wry smile. "My dad doesn't even like me, so no pressure whatsoever on you."

"That's not true. I'm sure your parents love you." He flashed her an affectionate smile. "What's not to love?"

"Let's see..." Emma held up her fingers, counting them off. "My college major... my disinterest in working in the family business... my haircut... my sense of style, or lack thereof... that's just off the top of my head."

Noah grabbed her hand and tugged her toward the train platform. "I'm sure they just want what they think is best for you, even if it's misguided."

Noah had grown up with a family who'd loved him unconditionally, so he wouldn't know what it was like to have his parents meet him with disapproval at every turn.

Emma hurried to hop onto the train, teetering in her high-heeled pumps. She had no idea why she'd even bothered with the shoes, or the black designer dress she was wearing. Her mother would comment that they were last year's styles, and her father could barely look at her ever since she'd made the decision to switch majors.

Thank God Noah is here.

With Noah sitting across from her at dinner and sleeping down the hall in the guest room, Emma could cheerfully smile her way through this visit. It didn't matter if her parents couldn't accept her. Noah did. Noah knew her and loved her just the way she was. And that's all that really mattered.

Emma's father sent his car and driver to pick them up at the station and take them to the estate. When they stepped into the entryway of the house with its 20-foot vaulted ceilings and marble and wrought-iron staircase winding up to the second level, Noah's eyes widened, but he remained silent, taking it all in.

"I know it's a bit much," Emma whispered. From what little Noah had shared about his family, she got the feeling he grew up comfortably, but not even close to this kind of wealth. The truth was that the whole thing embarrassed her a little. Why did a family of three—a family of two now that she lived at Cartwright—need an eight-bedroom house with a separate guest cottage and four-car garage? Why did anyone?

"No." He smiled at her, smoothing his face into a neutral expression. "It's great. Very beautiful."

Emma appreciated that he was willing to play along for her sake.

A pair of heels clicked on the floor above, and a moment later, Emma's mother appeared at the top of the stairs. "Darling, you're home!" Despite her three-inch heels, Celine descended the staircase as gracefully as if she were barefoot.

Emma shifted in her own uncomfortable pumps and wished with all her heart she could kick them off and leave them by the front door. Instead, she slapped a smile on her face and stepped toward her mother. "Hi, Mom."

Celine embraced Emma in a cloud of Chanel No. 5, and then stepped back, her regal gaze sweeping down from Emma's aching feet up to her face. "It's an absolute delight to have you here." She reached out to tuck a lock of hair behind Emma's ear. "Every time I see you, I'm taken aback by what a gorgeous young woman you've grown up to be."

Emma gave her mother a warm smile. It had been a while, and maybe it *was* nice to be home.

And then Celine brushed an invisible piece of lint from Emma's shoulder. "Feel free to borrow any of my dresses to change into before dinner. And my make-up is in the top drawer of the vanity."

Emma's shoulders slumped. There it was. The dig about

her appearance, her clothes, the suggestion that she should be trying harder. She'd been hearing it her whole life, and somehow, she never got used to it. "I think I'm just going to stick with what I'm wearing."

"Well." Celine blinked. "I suppose if you're comfortable in that old thing..." Her mouth stretched into a wide smile—quite a feat, Emma knew, considering all the Botox and fillers she'd had injected there—and turned to Noah. "You must be Noah."

"I am. It's nice to meet you, Mrs. Lockhart." He held out a hand to shake hers. "Thank you so much for inviting me."

"Call me Celine." She gave him an appraising look and Emma knew that at least her mother couldn't find fault with Noah. If Theta Chi Delta had a handbook for meeting the parents—*which, come to think if it, they might actually have one* —Noah could have jumped right from the pages of the section on 'what to wear.'

Noah held out a bottle of wine. "This is for you and Mr. Lockhart. I hope you like red."

Celine looked at the label, her face registering surprise. "We do, and this is Thomas's favorite. What a coincidence."

Emma checked out the bottle of Bordeaux. This was no coincidence. They'd once shared half a bottle of this wine when he'd picked her up after work, after a wealthy patron and his date had left without finishing it. Emma had mentioned it was her father's favorite. At the time, they'd laughed at how these expensive wines really didn't taste any different than the $10 bottles of Pinot Noir they picked up at the mini mart to share over cups of ramen noodles. Noah must have written down the name to remember for a situation just like this. Emma was touched that he'd make that kind of effort. But... there was something about it that nagged at her, just a tiny bit. That bottle cost the equivalent of her tips for an entire night. They had rolled their eyes at the price, marveling at all the other things you could buy with that kind of money. Like a week's worth of groceries. There was no need for Noah to waste his money like that. But he'd probably just been nervous about the trip.

"Come this way," Celine urged, waving Emma and Noah in the direction of one of the house's several sitting rooms. "Thomas just got home, so we'll have a cocktail before dinner."

They followed Celine to a large, airy room in the back of the house with stiff white couches arranged around a glass coffee table and facing an imposing fireplace. An enormous chandelier hung overhead with thousands of twinkling crystals that, as a child, Emma used to be terrified to sit underneath for fear that it would fall on her head and cut her into teeny, tiny pieces.

Against one wall sat a vintage bronze bar cart, where her father stood pouring a glass of bourbon. Thomas turned to face them when they walked in the room and, for a moment, Emma was struck with the thought that she was dating a man who looked an awful lot like her father. Not necessarily in coloring or facial features—her father was blond once and now graying, with a higher forehead and wider nose than Noah. But they were both tall with a slightly commanding presence, the kind of men that people noticed when they walked into a room. And at the moment, both her father and Noah were dressed eerily alike, down to their leather topsiders. Maybe there really was a Theta Chi Delta handbook.

"Darling." Celine waved a manicured hand at Thomas. "Come over and say hello to Emma's new boyfriend, Noah. And look at this wonderful wine he brought for us."

"Hello, sir," Noah said, straightening his shoulders. "Thank you so much for having me."

Thomas crossed the room to shake Noah's hand and subtly look him over. Just like Celine, Thomas appeared to be slightly impressed and more than a little taken aback by what he saw. "You're a Cartwright student, son?" Thomas asked.

Noah cleared his throat and gave Thomas a stiff nod. "I am, sir, yes."

"Major?"

"I'm in the undergraduate business program. Hoping to get my MBA when I finish."

Thomas's gaze shifted to Emma, and she could guess what he was thinking. She'd defied all of their wishes to become an art major. When she'd called last week to tell them she was bringing a boyfriend home, they probably hadn't been expecting a business major wearing Ralph Lauren and offering a 1996 Bordeaux.

And honestly, she'd hadn't been expecting that either.

"Are you a member of a fraternity, Noah?"

"I'm a Theta Chi Delta, sir." Noah paused for a moment, and then added, "And proud of it."

"A Theta." Thomas's voice was positively jolly now. "Emma, why didn't you tell me you were dating a Theta?"

Maybe because being a Theta wasn't even in the top-ten list of things she loved about Noah. Or maybe because she knew Thomas would react like this. He was smiling at her for the first time in years, just because she was dating a man he deemed acceptable. For a moment, her father looked so happy, Emma half wondered if he was going to call his attorney after dinner and have her written back into his will.

No thank you. She'd made it this far on her own.

"I guess I forgot he was a Theta," Emma finally managed.

Thomas gave her a familiar look of disapproval, and Emma almost laughed. *There goes the will.*

"I would have made dinner reservations at the country club," her father admonished. "Introduced Noah around a bit."

And to Emma's surprise, Noah nodded eagerly. "I'd love to meet your friends at the country club. Especially other Thetas."

Thomas slapped Noah on the back. "Well, Celine has already arranged for our chef to make dinner here tonight, but do you golf?"

"I do, yes."

He does? Emma squinted at Noah. How did she not know that?

"Why don't I set something up for tomorrow morning? We can play a round and then have lunch in the clubhouse?"

Emma had been planning to take Noah into the city tomorrow. He'd never been to Boston, and they were going to play tourists, walking the Freedom Trail and visiting the art museum. But instead, he was nodding along to her father as the two of them wandered over to the bar to pour another glass of bourbon.

Emma took a deep breath and let it out slowly. So what if Noah had forgotten about their plans tomorrow? They could always go another time. It was sweet that he was making such an effort to impress her parents, particularly her father. She needed to let this go and be grateful she'd met such a great guy; one who obviously cared about her, or he'd never be going out of his way like this.

Emma slapped a smile on her face and took the glass of Bordeaux her mother held out to her. "Delicious," she murmured, taking a gulp.

7

Emma and Maya grabbed a quick sandwich in the hospital cafeteria on the way out, but neither of them ate more than a few bites. On the drive home, Maya had resisted Emma's attempts at conversation, resting her head against the window and closing her eyes. It was well after dark by the time Emma pulled the car into the driveway.

Maya grabbed her bag from the backseat and ran into the house.

Emma followed more slowly, locking the door behind her and heading into the kitchen to clean up the breakfast dishes she'd never gotten around to loading into the dishwasher that morning. Upstairs, she heard doors swinging open and closed, and then the sound of the shower turning on and then off. Emma shuffled around the kitchen, wiping down the counters and tossing an empty carton of milk. She was too keyed up to sit down and rest, but too exhausted to do anything productive like work on a piece for her upcoming pottery show.

The bathroom door upstairs swung open again, creaking on its hinges. She need to remember to pick up some WD40 the next time she was at the hardware store. It was the sort of thing

Noah used to take care of on the weekends. A large house like this required all sorts of projects and maintenance. Emma wondered fleetingly if she should consider moving to a smaller place, especially if Noah wasn't coming back home.

With that thought, Emma's stomach twisted. When she'd asked Noah to leave, part of her had always believed he'd be back, that they'd work out their marriage problems and go back to the way they used to be. But what if Noah didn't wake up and they never had the chance now?

Luckily, the sound of Maya's footsteps on the stairs dragged Emma from her dark thoughts, and a moment later, she heard Maya call out, "Mommy?"

Emma's breath caught. Maya hadn't called her *Mommy* for a long time. Maybe not since last year when Maya'd had a terrible case of bronchitis and had ended up in the ER with pneumonia. Usually, Emma was "Mom," said by her daughter with an eyeroll and toss of her hair.

"Yes, honey?" Emma called up.

"Can you come up and sit with me for a minute?"

Emma glanced around the kitchen. She needed to run the dishwasher and make sure they had enough bread for Maya's lunch tomorrow. But she wasn't about to pass up this moment if her daughter needed her.

She hurried up the stairs to Maya's room and found her daughter slowly climbing into her double bed and flopping back against the pillow. Emma moved to Maya's side and tugged the mint-green striped duvet to her shoulders. When Maya's eyes met hers, Emma could see that they were red and swollen from crying. Emma's heart constricted. For all her attitude and bravado, Maya was still just a kid. Seeing Noah lying so still in the hospital had been awful for her.

"Oh, honey," Emma murmured, sinking down on the bed and putting a hand on Maya's arm.

"What if he doesn't wake up?" Maya whispered, gazing up at her.

"It's early days," Emma said, with as much confidence as she could muster. "The doctors said his brain needs time to heal. So, we just need to keep going in and talking to him. If there's anything that will wake Daddy up, it's hearing your voice."

"Do you think he could die?"

Emma's eyes pricked with tears. As much as she wanted to promise that Noah would wake up, she couldn't lie to her daughter. "I don't know, honey," she finally managed over the lump in her throat. "I wish I knew."

"If he does wake up, will you let him come home again?"

"I—" Emma sucked in a breath at the memory of Luna lying in the hospital room, her brown hair flopping over her forehead, so much like Noah's that it hurt to look at it. What secrets had Noah been keeping from her? "I know our separation has been hard on you. I love your father very much, but marriage is complicated, and I just don't know how things will play out. Right now, I'm just focused on helping him to get better."

Maya nodded. "Yeah." She looked defeated. "Okay."

Emma gave the duvet another tug. "Try to get some rest."

Maya grabbed her hand. "Will you stay with me until I fall asleep?"

Emma pushed a lock of Maya's dark hair off her forehead. "Of course I will."

Maya was asleep in less than five minutes, worn out by all the emotional energy she'd expended that day. As Emma tiptoed out of her daughter's bedroom, she was tempted to turn left down the hall and fall headfirst into her own bed. But even though she'd gotten used to sleeping without Noah when he was traveling these past few years, and especially since he'd moved out, it somehow felt different tonight.

There were still so many reminders of him around the house. A book he'd been casually reading before he'd left still sat on his bedside table, next to one of his pairs of reading glasses. Most of his clothes still hung in the closet. He'd only taken one suitcase with him. They'd agreed to discuss what to do with the rest once they'd sorted out their future.

Though Emma had laundered the bedsheets a few times since Noah had moved to the apartment, she hadn't been able to bring herself to wash his pillowcase. Sometimes, late at night, she'd roll over and clutch it to her chest, breathing in the familiar scent of the man she'd fallen in love with all those years ago.

Now a sense of panic enveloped her. What if those small reminders—a half-read book, an unwashed pillowcase—were all she had left of him?

What if he was gone long before he'd moved out?

Emma thought about Luna in that hospital bed again, and the mysterious Coral Butler. She wished she'd given Kate her phone number and asked her to call immediately if they found any new information about the deceased woman's identity. Or if any of Luna's family members had stepped forward. But it was too late now. She'd have to wait until morning.

Emma knew the best thing for her was to go to sleep and forget about it all for a while. But, as if they had a mind of their own, her feet took a right down the hallway, toward the small bedroom that Noah used as an office in the back of the house.

She pushed the door open and stepped inside. Noah hadn't packed up his things in his office yet, either. He'd taken a small folding table from the garage that Maya reported he was using as both a makeshift dining table and desk in his new place. Emma didn't like to think about him spending his days on an uncomfortable kitchen chair in that stark, outdated apartment:

the image was so far from this beautiful office space with its built-in desk-and-cabinet combination painted a soothing dark gray, ergonomic chair, and a framed collection of Emma's paintings on the wall.

Noah had always said the best part of the office was the window overlooking the garden. He loved being able to peek out when he was on boring conference calls and see Emma through the studio window with her head bent over her pottery wheel. It reminded him of why he worked so hard: to support her dream of being a full-time artist.

If only he'd understood that she would have happily given up the backyard studio and gone back to teaching in exchange for a husband who was home every night, and who loved her more than his job. Emma sighed and sank down into Noah's desk chair. *A husband who loved me more than who or whatever kept taking him away from me and Maya.*

She knew she shouldn't snoop. They'd never been the kind of couple to look through each other's phones or search histories. But they'd never been the kind of couple to keep secrets from each other, either. Secrets like a mystery woman and child traveling in his car in the middle of the day.

Emma yanked the top drawer to Noah's desk open and stared inside at a collection of pens, more reading glasses, and a handful of change he'd probably unloaded from his pockets. She had no idea what she was even looking for. Love notes? Photos? A diary confessing that Noah was having an affair?

She slammed the top drawer shut and turned to her right. Inside another drawer, she found a neat row of manila folders, labeled with the names of their electricity provider and mortgage company. She slid her hand to the file with the name of their cell phone company and pulled out a statement. But as Emma stared at a list of Noah's call history, she quickly realized that cell phone records would only help her if she knew Coral Butler's number.

Shaking her head, Emma stuffed the pile of papers back into its folder. The calls listed on the bill could have just as easily been made to Noah's clients as to his potential mistress.

Her fingers continued to flip through the files. Car insurance... life insurance... their tax returns for the past seven years. Emma was about to slam the drawer shut when her hand stilled on a file labeled *Noah Checking Account*.

When she'd married Noah, they'd made the decision to combine their finances. It made the most sense given that they wanted to buy a house and eventually have kids. But they'd also kept their own separate checking accounts, too, for personal expenses; things like hobbies and stops at the coffee shop. They never asked what the other spent their personal money on. That was the whole point of separate accounts. Emma didn't want to consult Noah every time she bought a new pair of shoes, and she had no interest in monitoring his Starbucks habit.

But now, she wondered if maybe she should have paid closer attention. Could there be anything in his checking account statements that would explain his behavior lately?

Emma pulled the file out of the drawer and spread the statements across the desk. She'd switched to electronic statements years ago, but Noah still liked to have hard copies. This had always surprised her, given that his parents had died in a fire that had also burned all their old paperwork and records. But he didn't like to talk about the fire much, so she'd never pressed him.

Emma grabbed Noah's first checking account statement from the pile, the one from last month, and scanned the list of charges. Like she'd expected, Noah frequented the coffee shop over on Main Street and the salad place on Fifth. He'd ordered a few things from Banana Republic—probably work clothes—and what looked to be a couple of small items from Amazon. There was nothing notable there.

She was about to toss the statement to the side when her

eyes focused on a charge at the very bottom of the page, and suddenly the room started to spin.

Payapp to Coral Butler: $2,500

Emma grabbed the next statement in the pile and scanned the page looking for that now-familiar name. After a moment, she found it.

Payapp to Coral Butler: $2,500

One by one, Emma sifted through Noah's statements and, one by one, she found the $2,500 payment he'd sent to Coral every single month dating back at least two and a half years.

A whisper of the same thought had gone through her mind earlier, but now she held on to it: if she traced the timeline back to when she first began to notice Noah's increase in travel at work, his distance from their family, the way he'd seemed so distracted all the time... It had started about two or three years ago. The police officers had told her that Luna was about two years old. And now she'd discovered that Noah had been sending Coral Butler thousands of dollars a month for that same period of time.

She grasped for an excuse that could explain this all away... but what could it possibly be? Was there any conclusion she could draw, other than the fact that Noah had been having an affair with Coral Butler, and had fathered a secret child?

Emma lunged to her feet and paced across the room and back.

How could he do this to her?

How did she end up such a cliché?

And why hadn't she listened to her instincts and confronted him when he was still able to answer for his actions? When she had the chance to tell him how much she hated him for doing this to her, and to their family?

She spun on her heel, and on her next trip to the other side of the room and back, she stumbled to a stop in front of a frame hanging on the wall. Their wedding photo.

Noah, looking young and handsome in a dark gray suit gazed down at her, an affectionate smile tugging at his lips. Twenty-five-year-old Emma, wearing a simple white dress, looked up at him in awe, amazed that she'd found this kind, thoughtful man to share her life with.

How did they evolve from that young, loving couple to Noah in a hospital room and Emma clutching a bank statement with evidence of his infidelity? When did he start keeping secrets from her?

Was everything she'd ever believed a lie?

8

EIGHTEEN YEARS AGO

"Oh, Emma. I wish you'd gone with the Marchesa," Emma's mother murmured. "But still..." In the reflection in the mirror, Emma watched Celine lift a shoulder. "... you look very pretty."

Emma sighed and pushed her chair back from the curved vintage vanity where she'd been checking her hair one last time. Only her mother would find a way to subtly insult her about her fashion choices on her wedding day. Celine had been pushing for Emma to choose a designer gown with a fitted jeweled bodice and four tiers of ivory lace. Celine's stylist had recommended it, and apparently all the brides were wearing Marchesa. This particular dress cost almost $4,000.

Emma couldn't imagine shelling out that kind of money for a garment she'd wear for eight hours total. Especially when she'd just started her job as an art teacher and her student loans had just come due. Thanks to his connections in Theta Chi Delta, Noah had gotten a good position at a finance firm, but Boston was an expensive city and they'd just paid their first month's rent and security deposit.

Celine had offered to buy the Marchesa, but Emma had

refused. To her mother's mortification, Emma had chosen a simple satin sheath she'd found on sale at Nordstrom for $200.

Her parents had refused to pay her college tuition, but as soon as Emma's engagement was announced, they couldn't wait to start throwing money at their only daughter. Her mother had insisted they hold the reception at the country club. Her father had drawn up a list of his business associates to add to the guest list. Emma had resisted it all, vowing that she and Noah would elope before she'd allow her parents to take over her wedding. Noah had finally talked her into letting them be involved, gently suggesting that she'd regret it someday if her parents missed her wedding. Emma knew he was thinking about his own parents who'd passed away over half a decade earlier, and she'd given in. But the wedding had to be a small, intimate affair, she'd insisted. Just close friends and family, and absolutely no business associates.

So how did it happen that, eight months later, she was getting married in the towering, 200-year-old Sacred Heart Cathedral and hosting a 300-person reception in the country club ballroom?

Emma sighed, standing up and gazing into the full-length mirror. At least she'd put her foot down about the dress. And, ultimately, the location and guest list really didn't matter, as long as she was married to the love of her life by the end of the night.

Emma turned to face her mother. "You don't want me to dress like every other bride this season anyway. It would be so... *tacky*," she said, lifting her flower bouquet to her nose to hide the amusement on her face.

Celine flinched and clutched a fist to her chest. There was nothing she hated more than people who were tacky. "Well," she said breathlessly, composing herself again, "I suppose we'll have to agree to disagree. But no matter. The ceremony is about to start, and your father should be outside the door waiting to walk you down the aisle."

The wedding ceremony was a blur. Emma hadn't grown up religious—the church had been chosen by her mother for the photo opportunities and because that's where the governor's daughter had gotten married—so all of the prayers and scriptures didn't mean that much to her. But what did matter was the man standing across from her, more handsome than she'd ever seen him in an elegant black tuxedo with a pale pink peony— her favorite flower—pinned to his lapel. His usually floppy hair was styled back off his forehead, which made him look older than his early twenties. When she met his eyes, they sparkled with mischief, as if to let her know he didn't care about all this pageantry either, and he couldn't wait to get her alone. And when he slid the ring on her finger and promised to stand by her side for better or worse—*forever*—Emma could hardly believe it.

After they'd headed out of the church, arm in arm, Emma and Noah lined up with Emma's parents to greet their guests. It seemed to take forever for the hundreds of people to shuffle their way past, giving cheek-kisses to Emma and her mother, and pumping Noah and Emma's father's hands in congratulations.

Finally—*finally*—the guests dispersed, headed over to the country club for the reception, and after another eternity of photos snapped on the steps of the church, Emma's parents took off in their car, too. Emma and Noah's limo—her parents had insisted—pulled up next, and Noah took Emma's hand to help her down the stairs in her heels.

"Can we just skip it and go right to the hotel?" she asked, fluttering her eyelashes at him in a promise of what was in store for him back at the hotel.

Noah raised an eyebrow and cleared his throat, letting her

know exactly how he felt about that possibility. But then he shook his head. "I'm afraid not, sweetheart. All these people showed up for us. We really ought to at least make an appearance."

Emma sighed. "I know." Of course, she'd been joking about going straight to the hotel. They could never skip out on their own wedding reception. But of the three hundred guests who'd headed to the country club after the ceremony, only a handful of them were Emma and Noah's friends who had come to celebrate their marriage. The majority were there to network with Emma's parents, and they probably wouldn't even notice if the bride and groom no-showed.

"How about this?" Noah tightened his hand around hers as she teetered down another step. "I'll slip the DJ a hundred to move us quickly through the dances and toasts. We'll be in and out in under two hours."

Emma nodded. "Okay. But you promise? *Two hours*."

"I promise. It will be good for me to make the rounds with your dad's friends. But then we're out of there."

Emma grabbed the handrail and stopped to face him. "Why do you need to make the rounds with my dad's friends?"

Noah shrugged. "You never know. Someone might have a job opportunity for me."

"But you already have a job." Emma looked at him sideways. "You don't want to work for my dad's friends—do you?" She couldn't imagine Noah in her father's world, hanging out at the country club, networking over a round of golf. She couldn't imagine herself gossiping next to the pool like her mother and her friends, either.

Emma didn't want to imagine it. That was exactly the sort of life she'd been evading.

"I'm just keeping the doors open," Noah said. "We said we want to buy a house and start trying for a baby. I'm just thinking about our family's future."

Emma leaned in earnestly. "You know we can do all of that without having to live in my parents' world, right? We don't need a huge house, and lots of people who aren't rich have babies."

"Look." Noah took her arm and tugged her closer. "Let's not worry about it. Like you said, most of the guests are here for your parents, not for us." His lips curved into a grin. "Two hours." He leaned in closer. "Two hours and then you're all mine."

"I cannot wait." Emma reached up and wrapped her arms around his neck. Noah bent his head and pressed a kiss to her mouth. She pulled him closer, deepening the kiss, and when they finally broke apart, Emma was pretty sure that, in that moment, she could have convinced him to head directly for the hotel. It was tempting.

Noah led her the rest of the way down the steps and waved away the limo driver when he came around to open the door. Instead, he helped Emma inside himself. The door was halfway closed when he froze and cursed under his breath.

"What?" Emma leaned partway out of the car. "Noah? What is it?" She looked up to find him staring out across the roof of the limousine, anger slashed across his handsome face. Her head swung in the direction of his gaze.

Standing across the street, about a hundred feet away, was a man she didn't recognize. It was hard to see him through the tinted limousine windows and cars zipping by, but she could just make out that he had dark wavy hair streaked with silver, and he wore an ill-fitting gray suit and black shoes that had lost their shine.

Her head swung back to Noah. "Who is that?" Something about Noah's hard expression as he stared the man down sent a shiver running up her spine. "Noah?" she repeated.

Noah tapped the roof of the limousine. "I'll be right back."

And then, to Emma's complete astonishment, he swung her

door closed, rounded the limousine, and crossed the street to where the man shifted from one foot to the other, almost as if he were nervous.

Emma slid from her side of the car to the other so she could peer out the window and get a better look at Noah and the mystery man. Noah hopped up on the opposite curb and stood directly in front of the man, right in her line of sight, so all she was able to make out was Noah's tuxedo-clad back, straight and rigid, and his hands clenched in fists at his sides.

Emma's heart began to rap painfully against her sternum, and she searched the corners of her mind for some idea of who this man could be. He looked too old to be any of Noah's friends from school, and he certainly wasn't dressed the part, either. None of the Theta Chi Deltas would be caught dead in a suit that wasn't custom-tailored, or a scuffed pair of shoes. And most of the people Noah had kept in touch with from Cartwright were over at the country club waiting for them to arrive for the reception. *Could he be someone from Noah's new job?* Emma quickly shook her head. That was as unlikely as him being a Theta Chi Delta.

She watched Noah's hand wave in what seemed like an angry gesture. What could they possible be arguing about on her wedding day? Emma reached for the door handle. There was only one way to find out. But before she could step out into the street, the man stepped back, away from Noah, and then turned and headed down the street. Once again, Emma strained to catch a glimpse of his face, but his back was to her and all she could see was that his suit was in worse shape than she'd thought, and his thick hair—in desperate need of a cut—curled over the back collar.

The mystery man turned around the corner just as Noah made it back to the car.

Emma slid over to make room for him. "Who was that?" she asked.

"It's—" Noah closed his eyes and shook his head. "It's a homeless guy."

Emma searched his face for answers. "How do you know him?"

"He—uh." Noah busied himself smoothing the folds of her dress so he didn't sit on it. "He hangs around outside my office asking for money. I gave it to him once, and now he keeps coming back and asking for more."

"I don't understand what he's doing here." Emma gave her head a shake, trying to work it all out. "Your office is across town."

Noah met her eyes now. "I know." He shrugged and gave a little laugh. "Weird coincidence, isn't it?"

"But—"

The sound of a window rolling down between the front and back seats cut her off. "You ready to head to the country club?" The limo driver flipped on his turn signal.

"Yep," Noah answered, his voice buoyant. "We're ready."

Emma pitched to the left as the limo driver pulled the car out into the street, and her shoulder bumped Noah's. He tugged her closer to his side.

"Sorry to leave you sitting here like that," he said, giving her a rueful smile. "I just feel bad for the guy, you know?"

Maybe they weren't arguing after all. Emma pushed her worries from her head. Noah was a good guy who cared about people. It was one of the things she loved most about him. "You were sweet to help him."

And with that, the limo headed down the street, away from the church and toward their new life together.

9

"Emma, oh my God, how *are* you?"

Emma looked up from the magazine she was pretending to read to find Alicia standing in the doorway of Noah's hospital room. She lunged out of her vinyl chair, and Alicia ran across the room to sweep her up in a hug. Emma felt her eyes tear up as the familiar scent of Alicia's perfume wafted across her.

"I'm so sorry about all of this." Alicia backed up, holding Emma at arm's length to search her face. "It's a real shitshow, isn't it?"

Emma swiped at her wet cheeks with the back of her hand and let out a half-laugh, half-sob at her friend's accurate assessment of the situation. "It sure is."

"First things first." Alicia gazed across the room at Noah laid out on the bed, his chest rising and falling along to the beeps and whooshes of the monitors above his head. "Is there any change to his condition?"

Emma shook her head. "None. The doctor was in earlier and said that everything looks essentially the same as yesterday. So, it's just a waiting game now."

"And—the girl?"

"Luna." Emma had called Alicia last night to fill her in on the whole story. Well, as much as she knew of the whole story. There were some very big holes in the plot. Like why Noah had been transferring over two thousand dollars a month to Luna's mother. "I'm waiting for the social worker to stop by. She'll know how the girl is doing and if they found any more information about Luna and her family."

"And you?" Alicia tugged Emma back over to the chair she'd vacated moments ago and then pulled another one to face her. "How are *you* holding up?"

Emma's eyes pricked with tears again as she sank down into the chair. There was one fundamental issue she kept coming back to: "I thought I knew him, you know?"

"I thought so, too." Alicia sat in the other chair and leaned forward. "I wish I had some explanation to offer you that would rationalize everything that's come to light. And maybe there is something." Her gaze turned back to Noah. "I just hope he'll wake up soon and tell you."

Emma grabbed for Alicia's hand. Thank God her friend was there, because suddenly, the reality of the past twenty-four hours swept across her, and Emma was exhausted. Alicia was one of the few people she'd always been able to count on, and the list of people she could count on seemed to be growing shorter by the minute.

Emma and Alicia had met at Maya's kindergarten orientation over a decade earlier. Emma had been dressed in yoga pants and a sweatshirt, thinking this would be a casual affair focused on the children. She hadn't expected the other moms to show up with blowouts and expensive, trendy jeans, looking every bit like the sorority girls she'd always avoided back in college. Emma had hovered around the periphery, listening to them talk about all the activities they'd signed their kids up for over the summer to help them get a leg up.

"A leg up for *kindergarten?*" Emma had murmured. "I thought this was public school."

"Right?" came a voice from beside her, and Emma had turned to find a woman in a regular pair of jeans and a T-shirt, rolling her eyes. "This isn't a fancy private school where Junior needs to speak four languages before first grade or you might as well brand him a failure."

Emma had shuddered. She'd gone to those competitive private schools and had wanted a more normal childhood for Maya. Had they made a mistake in moving here? "I hope not."

"I'm Alicia, by the way." Alicia had held out a hand. "And don't worry. We're not all signing our children up for polo lessons and sending them to Florence to study Michelangelo over the summer. Those are just the PTA moms over there." Alicia had nodded at the group vying for the teacher's attention so they could discuss their child's gifted educational plans. "Steer clear, and you'll be fine."

Emma had seen a couple of those PTA moms around her new neighborhood, the gated community Noah had picked out when he'd landed the job in Grand Rapids. He'd loved the area and how safe it was for Maya to play outside. But it had turned out that most of the other kids had been too busy with their extra lessons and sports to roam the neighborhood freely.

"Why don't you come sit with the normal moms over here?" Alicia had cocked her head toward a table of regular-looking women—*no designer labels in sight*—and Emma's anxiety had dissipated.

A rap on the doorframe reverberated through the hospital room, dragging Emma back to the present. She spun in her seat to find Kate, the social worker, peeking through the curtain.

"I'm sorry to interrupt. Can I come in? I have some things to tell you."

Emma jumped back to her feet, and Alicia followed. "Yes, of course. Come in."

"Hi," Kate said, easing into the room. Her gaze flitted to Alicia for a moment and then she turned back to Emma. "Is it okay to talk here, or do you want to speak privately?"

Whatever Kate had to say, Emma didn't want to be alone to hear it. "No, no. It's okay. This is my best friend, Alicia."

"Hi," Alicia said, with a little wave in Kate's direction.

Kate gave her a nod and then focused on Emma. "Well, first of all, I have some information about Luna."

"Okay." Emma took a shaky breath. Alicia's hand found hers and gave a squeeze.

"The police went out to the address on Coral Butler's driver's license last night," Kate began. "She lived in an apartment complex in Millersville. While they were knocking on the door, a man from the apartment next door came out, and they were able to ask him some questions."

Kate gazed past Emma at the wall over her shoulder, sadness drifting across her face. "Unfortunately, the man confirmed that Coral was Luna's mother."

Emma blew out the breath she'd been holding as her heart folded in on itself. It was the worst possible news. Luna's mother was dead. The poor baby was lying there in her hospital room, waiting for her mother, and her mother wasn't going to appear. Emma didn't realize how much she'd been hoping that some other woman would come forward to claim Luna until it was confirmed that she never would.

"What about other family members?" Emma asked, desperately. There had to be someone who would step up to care for that poor girl. *A grandmother, or an aunt.* "Were they able to locate anyone?"

"The neighbor reported that he's only seen one other person coming and going from Coral's apartment—" Kate hesitated, and her expression turned almost contrite, like she hated to be the one to break the news. "The neighbor reported a tall, middle-aged man with dark hair."

Emma's gaze flew to Noah, who fit that description perfectly. But then again, so did half of the state of Michigan. She should *not* start jumping to conclusions.

"On a hunch, the police officers pulled up your husband's driver's license photo, and the neighbor was able to confirm the man he'd seen coming and going was Noah."

Emma's shoulders slumped. Of course it was Noah. At this point, nothing should surprise her. "How often did he say Noah has been there?"

"He said he's seen Noah about once or twice a week, at least since Luna was born." Kate cringed. "I'm sorry to tell you this, but the neighbor also said he was pretty sure that he's seen Noah coming in the evening and leaving the next morning."

Emma pressed a shaking hand over her mouth. Noah had been going to see a strange woman and child *once or twice a week for two or three years?* He'd been staying overnight? How was it possible Emma had gone so long without having any idea? When did Noah even go? He often worked from home. There were certainly days where she'd been so wrapped up in her pottery that she didn't even look up to take a breath for hours at a time. Was it possible Noah had managed to sneak out of the house and drive all the way to Coral's place, almost an hour away, and then back again, without Emma noticing? Or had he gone when he was running errands on the weekend? And then, the overnights certainly explained all the work trips he'd been taking, didn't they?

Kate held out a comforting hand. "I take it that comes as a bit of a surprise?"

Emma nodded dumbly. "It does. Yes."

Alicia stepped forward. "So, did this neighbor say anything else about this guy who looks like Noah? Did he seem like he was close with the kid? Was he—I don't know—affectionate with her? Or Coral?"

Kate shook her head. "The officers didn't go into that level of detail."

"Well, could they go back and ask this guy for more information?" Alicia asked sharply. "I mean, a neighbor seeing a guy who maybe looks like Noah swinging by this woman's apartment every now and then isn't really a lot to go on."

Emma appreciated what Alicia was doing—trying to protect her. But she was afraid it *was* a lot to go on. Especially since the guy's wife had absolutely no idea he'd been swinging by a strange woman's apartment.

Emma focused on Luna because it was easier than thinking about Noah. "Did the officers find anything else that might help locate a family member?"

Kate nodded. "Nobody answered when the officers knocked on the door, so they used the key they found in Coral's purse to enter the apartment. They did a search and managed to dig up some important paperwork that Coral had saved. They found Luna's birth certificate, which confirmed that she was the girl's mother."

Emma held her breath. Was this the part where Kate told her that Noah's name had been listed as the father? Was this when the bottom officially dropped out of her life? "And? What about the father?"

"The space where the father's name should go was blank. Coral didn't name a father."

"Can you do that?" Alicia demanded. "Is that legal?"

"In Michigan, it is."

"So, Luna's father could be... anyone," Alicia waved a hand.

At that moment, Kate's phone rang. She grabbed it out of her purse and checked the name. "Excuse me, I'm going to need to take this. I'll just be out in the hall for a second." Kate swiped to answer as she headed for the door.

Emma sank down into her vinyl chair. "Oh my God. How did he keep this from me for all this time?" She studied her husband's face. Even with the cuts and bandages, she still found him as handsome as she always had. That face had been more special to her than just about anyone's except Maya's for over half her life. She'd spent two decades with Noah, she'd trusted him, and now it had been all but confirmed that he'd betrayed her. A wave of nausea rolled over her.

"Alicia," Emma whispered, weakly. "Is there any way that Noah didn't cheat on me? Is there any possible way this child isn't his?"

Alicia shook her head sadly. "Oh, honey. I wish I could tell you that there is. And I suppose maybe there is some sort of wild explanation for all of this—Noah's visits to Coral and Luna, the car ride, the child not having a father listed on her birth certificate. But given those monthly payments Noah has been making, and the neighbor talking about him staying overnight..." She held up her hands, palms up. "Anything I could come up with would be pretty far-fetched."

"She looks like Noah." Emma's gaze traced Noah's face. "Luna. She looks just like him."

"I could kill him for doing this to you."

Emma choked out a sob. "You may not need to. There's a very good chance he'll never wake up, and I'll never really know."

There was nothing to say to that, Emma knew. So, Alicia didn't say anything, she just pulled Emma in for a hug.

Kate returned to the room, tucking her phone back into her purse. "That was the police officers. They've continued to sort through Coral Butler's belongings in search of any evidence of next-of-kin."

Emma dragged herself out of her hole of self-pity. How could she forget poor little Luna in the hospital room down the hall? If no family members were located, Kate had said she'd have to go to foster care. Emma prayed that the officers had found a grandmother or someone familiar to Luna who would take her in.

"Unfortunately, nobody has turned up yet. But the officers did find something." Kate hesitated, and Emma's anxiety rose yet higher.

"What is it? Just tell me."

"Well." Kate sighed, as if she didn't want to be doing this any more than Emma did. "It seems that Coral had a will drawn up around the same time that Luna was born. In it, she named a legal guardian should anything happen to her."

Emma held her breath.

"Emma." Kate's face twisted into a grimace. "Coral Butler named Noah Havern as Luna's legal guardian."

10

SEVENTEEN YEARS AGO

Emma paced from the living room to the kitchen and back again, listening for the sound of Noah's key in the lock. She'd been waiting all afternoon, staring at the clock as each minute that slowly ticked by felt more like an hour. It was summer vacation, which meant she didn't have her job as an art teacher to distract her, and her pottery—usually the activity she could get completely lost in—wasn't holding her attention today.

This was the biggest news of her life—the biggest news of both her and Noah's lives—and she was desperate to share it with him.

Emma was half-heartedly digging through the vegetable drawer in the fridge for something to make for dinner when she heard the apartment door swing open and Noah's keys drop on the table. "Wife!" he called, playfully. "I'm home!"

They'd only been married for a couple of months, so the novelty of calling each other "Husband" and "Wife" hadn't worn off, yet. Emma hoped it never would. She swung the refrigerator door shut and made her way into the living room.

Noah stood by the front door sorting through a pile of junk mail she'd dumped on the table when she'd come back from a walk earlier that day. Her heart fluttered at the sight of him, and she hoped that would never wear off either. Before Noah noticed her, Emma took a moment to study him, her gaze skating from his broad shoulders beneath his blue Oxford shirt to his dark hair flopping over his forehead, finally landing on his dark eyes crinkling at the corners just as they slid up to meet hers.

"Hello, gorgeous." Noah dropped the mail on the table and was in front of her in three steps. He slid an arm behind her back and pulled her in for a kiss. When they moved apart, he gave her a grin. "How was your day?"

"Well." Suddenly nervous, Emma clutched her hands together to keep them from shaking. They'd wanted this. They'd been trying for this. Still, it meant everything was going to change. And things were so perfect right now. "It was good. Great, actually."

"Yeah?" He took her hand and tugged her over to the couch and sat facing her. "Can you show me your latest creation?"

Emma couldn't help but smile. He was expecting to see a vase or a sculpture. "Actually, my latest creation won't be available for viewing for about nine months."

Noah's eyebrows knit together. "Nine—" Suddenly, it dawned on him, and he sat up straight in his seat. *"Emma."* He reached a hand toward her midsection. "Are you saying...?"

Emma laughed and pressed his hand to her stomach. "You're not going to feel it kicking yet, silly."

"But there is a baby in there?" His eyes softened as a look of wonder drifted across his face. "You're pregnant?"

"Yes. I took the test this morning."

"We're having a baby?"

"Yes!"

"This is amazing." Noah pulled her against him. "We're having a baby," he repeated. "I'm going to be a dad." When

Emma slid out of his grasp, he sat back to study her. "Why do you look so nervous?"

Emma looked down at her hands. "Well, you've met my parents. They haven't exactly been the best role models." She shook her head. "They were always so cold and distant, and I was lonely as a child." Emma could still remember wandering the echoing corridors of that big house with nobody to talk to. Waking up to nightmares and calling for her mother, who was in Rio or Bali. Eventually, it was the housekeeper who came in to console her. And she was pretty sure her father hadn't shown up for a single school event unless there were going to be someone there he could network with.

"Just because you didn't have great parents, it doesn't mean you're doomed to repeat their mistakes."

"I want our child's life to be different than that." Emma grabbed Noah's hand. "I want game nights and family dinners and beach vacations at regular old American beaches. Not even the fancy ones. I want our family to eat ice cream cones and play silly ring toss games on the boardwalk of the Jersey Shore."

"I think we can arrange the Jersey Shore." Noah smiled. "Is that all?"

Despite herself, Emma felt her own lips tugging upward. "You know what I mean. I want us to spend quality time together as a family. And—" She gave his hand a squeeze. "I want us to be there for our child. For parent-teacher conferences and doctor's appointments and when they wake up from nightmares. I want them to know they can count on us, and we'll always be there."

"I want that too," Noah said, staring down at the couch cushions. Did she imagine that waver in his voice?

Emma ducked her head to meet his eyes, and noticed his were red. "Oh, honey, I'm sorry."

"What do you have to be sorry for?"

"I know this brings up painful memories for you." Emma

leaned closer. Even three years into their relationship, Noah still never talked about his family. "But—we're having a baby now. Can you tell me a little bit about your parents?" Emma asked, cautiously. She hadn't asked about his family this directly for a long time. Not since before they were married. "Please? Shouldn't we tell our child about his or her grandparents? Wouldn't your mom and dad want us to keep their memory alive?"

Noah gazed over her shoulder at the opposite wall, his eyes strained, as if the memories played out there. Finally, he seemed to shake himself out of it. "It was exactly like you described." Noah gave her a sad smile. "Family bike rides and vacations and backyard barbecues. We did everything together. My parents were wonderful."

Emma's heart broke for him. To have had that and to lose it all.

"It's exactly what I want for our child." Noah said. "We'll be that kind of family, and our child will have two parents who are always there for them. I promise."

After finding out Noah had been sending Coral money each month, Emma didn't think he could possibly shock her any more than he already had. But apparently, she was wrong. Her mouth dropped open, but no words came out.

"Are you okay?" Kate finally asked.

"I—" Emma shook her head weakly, and thank God, Alicia was there, because she stepped forward to fill the stunned silence.

"Excuse me." Alicia waved a hand in the air. "Did you say that this Coral Butler person left *a small child* to Noah in her will?"

Kate shook her head. "Well, it's not really that she left her to Noah the way you'd leave a piece of china or something. Coral Butler named Noah the guardian in the event that something should happen to her..." She turned to Emma, her head cocked and shoulders raised. "Which, unfortunately, it has."

"But— Noah is—" Emma realized she might be stating the obvious. "Noah is in a coma," she finally managed to blurt out.

"He is," Kate agreed. "For now."

"Well, maybe she meant to leave Luna with Noah just until

another guardian was arranged?" Alicia asked. "Surely you can sort something else out."

Kate raised her eyebrows. "Generally, when you name someone as the guardian for your child, you mean for it to continue until they're of legal age. Coral named Noah for that role."

Emma nodded. She and Alicia both had children, and they knew how it worked. She never would have named a guardian for Maya who she didn't trust completely to care for her daughter until she was eighteen, or even beyond that.

"So, Coral's dying wish was for Noah to raise Luna to adult-hood?" Alicia reached out and took Emma's hand. "Oh, Emma, honey. There's only one reason why she would pick him."

Emma hands shook. *Coral would only have picked Noah if he was the child's father*.

Emma had suspected, of course, but having the facts laid out like this...

It was devastating.

"I can't speak as to why Coral picked Noah as the guardian of her child," Kate said, gently. "But I can tell you that Noah's signature was on the paperwork. He knew she'd made this choice, and he'd indicated that he was okay with it."

Emma's breath caught in her throat. How could he do this? How could he agree to something that would affect their family —their own child's life—in such an immeasurable way, and do it behind her back?

"Obviously, none of this is legally binding," Kate was quick to add. "Luna's case will still have to go in front of a judge. But deceased parent's and intended guardian's wishes will carry a lot of weight. Especially given how much time it seems Noah spent with Luna. This is a situation where her comfort and familiarity with her new guardians will be very important."

"But—" Emma waved her hand at Noah's sleeping form. "Noah might have agreed to take Luna, but these are obviously extenuating circumstances. We don't even know for sure if or when he'll wake up."

"I realize this is all a bit of a shock to you. And of course, it would be ideal if Noah could participate in this discussion. But since he can't..." Kate gestured at Emma. "You're his next of kin."

"Wait," Alicia cut in. "Are you suggesting that Emma should take the child?"

Kate raised her hands, palms up. "I'm only telling you Coral's wishes and what the options are. Coral wanted Noah to take guardianship of Luna. Obviously, Noah can't be consulted right now, so it's up to Emma to decide what to do."

Emma's mouth dropped open. "How could it possibly be up to *me*?"

"If Noah agreed to take on the responsibility of raising Luna," Kate continued, "it's quite possible Coral knew you'd be involved. That she'd made the decision knowing that you would be raising her child, too."

Had she, though? Emma wondered. *Or had Noah hidden his first family from Coral the way he'd hidden his second family from me?*

"But..." Emma shook her head as if that would somehow help her clear through this chaos. "I wasn't listed in the will. They have no idea if I'm fit to care for Luna." There was also the issue that Kate didn't know anything about her and Noah's separation. But why would she? He'd barely moved out when all of this had occurred. He wouldn't have changed the address on his driver's license or any other paperwork. All his mail still came to the house. "Would social services just hand a child over to me? I'm essentially a stranger."

"Of course we'd have to arrange for an emergency custody hearing, and it would only be temporary until a permanent adoption could be arranged."

Emma's head spun. Custody? *Adoption?* Two days ago,

she'd been working on her next piece for a pottery show in the fall, dealing with her teenage daughter's attitude, and hoping her marriage could be saved. And she'd thought that was a lot to juggle. But suddenly, she was making decisions about a two-year-old's future. A two-year-old who was likely her husband's secret child.

"But to answer your question," Kate continued. "Yes. It's very likely a judge would send a little girl who just lost her only parent home with a woman who is already a mother, who is an upstanding member of the community, and whose husband was named the child's guardian. Especially because the alternative is to hand her over to an overcrowded foster care system. And nobody wants to see that happen."

Who knew how long it would take to find Luna a permanent, stable, loving home in the foster system? What if she was bounced around between different families? How could a situation like that possibly equip her to handle the fact that her mother had just died?

And could Emma live with herself if she made that decision? Especially if it went against Coral and Noah's wishes for the child.

But it wasn't as simple as Kate was implying. Maya was a teenager who'd be out of the house in a couple of years. Emma's days of parenting a toddler were long gone. And what about the real possibility that Noah might never wake up? Wouldn't it be better to find Luna a family that wanted to adopt her?

"What does Luna understand about her mother?" Emma asked. "Does she know she died?"

"A two-and-a-half-year-old is too young to understand the concept of death," Kate explained. "It's really not until they're a few years older that children can grasp that sort of permanence. So, we've just told Luna that her mother can't be here right now, and that the nurses are here to care for her. As she gets older, Coral's death can be explained in an age-appropriate way."

Emma nodded. Despite Emma's strained relationship with her mother, Celine had adored Maya when she was little, and Maya had loved her too. Celine had died of cancer when Maya was close to Luna's age. Though Emma and Noah had read Maya books to help explain the concept of death, it wasn't until her first-grade class hamster had passed away that Maya seemed to really grasp what had happened to her grandmother.

"The most important thing is to make sure that Luna is placed in a stable, loving home," Kate continued. "That's the best thing we can do for her right now, and—" Her eyes cut into Emma. "Coral Butler believed that stable, loving home was yours."

What if Coral was wrong? How could Emma provide a stable home for Luna when her whole life was in upheaval?

Look," Kate cut in, clearly grasping Emma's indecision, "I've talked to the doctor, and he said he can put in an order to keep Luna here one more night for observation. We also need time for the emergency custody hearing. Go home and sleep on it. Talk it over with your family and friends." She nodded in Alicia's direction. "We'll check in again tomorrow."

"I will, thank you." Emma nodded, grateful for the reprieve. "It's all just been a bit of a shock."

Kate's face softened. "I know. And I'm so sorry for that. You haven't even had a moment to grieve over your husband's condition before I sprung this on you."

"No, it's not your fault. It's—" Emma moved over to the hospital bed and stared down at her husband. Had he thought he'd just continue on with his secret family, and that she'd never find out? Or maybe he didn't think about her at all. Maybe he only cared about himself. And now she was left to pick up the pieces.

Vaguely, from somewhere far away, she heard Kate tiptoe out the door and Alicia move up beside her.

"Emma, honey," Alicia said. "What do you need from me? How can I help?"

Emma took one more look at Noah. She hated that, even now, even when she knew who he was, her heart still beat a little bit faster at the sight of him. She'd always thought he was one of the most attractive men she'd ever seen, and through it all, that hadn't changed. But he'd lied to her, and betrayed her, and she'd never forgive him for that.

Emma closed her eyes and turned away. "Talk to him." She pushed away from the bed. "The doctors said it's good for him to hear our voices, that it might help him to come out of this. I can't be in here with him another second. So, can you just—" Emma waved in his direction.

"Of course. Is it okay if I tell him what a selfish jerk he is?"

Emma let out a watery laugh. "Absolutely. I'd expect nothing less."

Alicia nodded. "I'll call you later, okay?"

Emma nodded. "Thanks."

She turned and headed out into the hall, grateful she still had one person she could count on.

Emma headed for the elevators, but halfway down the hall, she stumbled to a stop. Where was she going? It was the middle of a weekday. Normally, she'd be working on her pottery, but there was no way she was going to be able to focus today. After a lot of negotiating, Emma had convinced Maya to go to school and then play rehearsal afterward. The doctor was right. If Maya got behind in her studies, it was going to be a nightmare for her to catch up, especially in her junior year with college applications around the corner. And Maya loved play rehearsal and had worked hard to land her part. *Dad wouldn't want you to miss it*, Emma had argued.

But it meant that Emma didn't have to be home for hours,

and she wasn't quite sure what to do with herself. She supposed she could drag Alicia to lunch, but Emma was pretty sure she couldn't choke down a thing. Besides, it *was* good for Noah to hear voices. She hoped Alicia would really lay into him.

Emma found herself nearing the nurses' station across from Luna's door. Was Luna awake now? Was she all alone in there?

Brittany was on duty, and she looked up from the computer as Emma approached. "Emma Havern, right?"

"Yes, hi." Emma was surprised the nurse remembered her name. There must have been several dozen patients on the floor.

Brittany smiled. "Are you here to see little Luna?"

Emma hesitated. "Am I allowed to see her?"

"Sure." Brittany clicked around on the screen in front of her. "Kate just stopped by and put you on the visitor's list. So, you can pop in for a few minutes if you want."

Emma cocked her head. How did Kate know she'd end up here at Luna's room again? Probably because the social worker was good at her job. Kate was trained to read people, and Emma's heartbreak over Luna's situation was probably obvious. She shouldn't go inside, though. Despite what Coral's will stated, Luna wasn't her responsibility, and it probably wasn't a good idea to let anyone believe otherwise.

But Luna was a child, a little girl who could barely comprehend what was happening to her. She might be all alone, and scared. Emma couldn't bear the thought of turning and walking away; of leaving a child in need when she had the ability to offer a little bit of comfort. What could it hurt to just stop in for a minute?

"I'll go and say hello," Emma said to Brittany, and before she could lose her nerve, Emma stepped inside the hospital room.

She pushed aside the curtain to find Luna sitting up in bed playing with her stuffed elephant. Luna looked up and when her eyes met Emma's, Emma's heart leapt from her body.

Those eyes. If she'd had any doubts that Luna was Noah's, they flew out the window when she saw the little girl's beautiful dark brown eyes. Those were Noah's eyes. And Maya's, too.

Oh, God. This is really happening.

"Hi," Emma said gently, forcing herself to get it together for the child's sake.

Luna stared back at her.

"I'm Emma. I'm—" *Who am I?* A friend of your father? Did this child even know that Noah was his father? "I'm your Mommy's friend." It was the best she could come up with.

At that, Luna perked up. "I want my mommy."

"Oh, honey." Emma's feet automatically pulled her into the room and next to the bed. "I know you do. Your mommy can't come right now, but—" Again, what could she say? She didn't want to promise the poor child that Coral would be there soon. Kate had told her that Luna was too young to really understand that her mother was gone forever. "But she sent me."

Emma's gaze swept around the room. She wished she'd thought to run to the gift shop for something for Luna to play with. On the side table, she found a pile of children's board books. *Little Blue Truck* sat on the top. It had been one of Maya's favorites as a little girl. She'd loved when Emma would read it to her and exaggerate the animal noises. Usually Maya, drama queen that she was, would end up imitating the chicken and duck sounds even better than Emma could. She smiled at the memory. "Can I read you a book?"

Luna nodded, and Emma picked it up. The nurses had pulled up both handrails on the bed so Luna wouldn't fall out. It took a moment to figure out how to lower one down, and another moment to raise up the head of the bed so she could lean back on it next to Luna.

The child settled against the pillow next to her, and Emma opened the book. Just like Maya had, Luna giggled at Emma's *moo* and *peep* noises, and clapped at her extra-loud *Vrooooom* when a dump truck rolled in.

When Emma was finished reading, Luna reached for the side table. "Another one!" she demanded. So, Emma read *Green Eggs and Ham*, and *Corduroy*, and *The Very Hungry Caterpillar*. She'd forgotten how much she'd loved some of these old stories. It had been years since Maya had wanted her to read anything except a permission slip to go on a field trip, and she missed it.

Halfway through *The Snowy Day*, Luna's little body slowly began to tilt toward Emma until her head rested on Emma's shoulder. Emma slid an arm around the girl so she could lean more comfortably against her side. A moment later, Luna's little chest rose and fell with a contented sigh.

Unexpected tears sprang to Emma's eyes, but she quickly brushed them away before Luna noticed. This poor little girl's life had been tossed completely upside down at such a young age. She wished she knew what Coral Butler had been like. Was she a good mother to Luna? Would Luna remember her someday?

And now, Emma thought, her heart aching, Luna might lose her father too. As much as she hated Noah in this moment, he'd been a good dad to Maya. If Noah was Luna's father, she prayed that Luna would have a chance to grow up knowing him.

Emma sighed and reached for another book. Halfway through *Goodnight Moon*, Emma glanced down at the little girl nestled in against her chest and found Luna asleep.

Emma was gently sliding her arm out from under Luna's head, trying not to wake her, when the curtain by the door moved, and Kate popped her head in.

"I thought I'd find you here," Kate whispered with a smile

in Luna's direction. "It looks like she's grown pretty comfortable with you."

Emma didn't respond. She knew what Kate was trying to do, encouraging her to spend time with Luna, and she understood why. Emma imagined it was hard to have a job placing kids in foster care, and Kate must grow weary of dealing with all the flaws of the system. When Kate found a stable, suitable family for a child—or in Emma's case, at least one that appeared that way—she probably felt like she'd won the lottery.

Emma slid off the bed and followed the social worker into the hall. Kate waved her back to the bench they'd sat on yesterday.

"I wanted to stop by to apologize for the way I presented the news about Luna earlier," Kate said when they were settled in their seats. "I know this had all been an enormous shock, and with your husband in a coma, of course you can't make a decision about taking on the guardianship of a child you just met."

Emma nodded, her shoulders finally relaxing. "Thank you. You're right... it's overwhelming."

"But..." Kate began, and Emma's heart sank. "... the reality is that Luna has to go somewhere tomorrow." Kate shifted in her seat to look Emma in the eye. "The doctor is already pushing it by letting her stay here tonight. One way or another, that's going to end up being a short-term foster placement until we can establish a suitable permanent situation." The social worker leaned in. "I'd like you to consider taking Luna, just as a temporary placement."

Emma held her breath.

Kate lifted a hand, as if to say *hear me out*. "It would just be for a few weeks. And hopefully by then, Noah will be awake and you two can make some decisions together. Or another family member can be located. I wouldn't be pushing for this if I didn't think it was in Luna's best interest."

Emma could still feel the pressure from Luna leaning

against her side as she read her a book, still feel the little girl's soft hair brushing against her arm. Would Luna's temporary foster family read to her, and cuddle her until she fell asleep? How would they respond when Luna cried that she wanted her mommy?

For what felt like the hundredth time that day, Emma's eyes filled with tears. "Can I have the night to think about it? I'm not the only person in this equation. I have a teenage daughter, and I can't possibly decide something like that without discussing it with her first." *Not like Noah did.*

Kate nodded. "Of course."

"I'll let you know in the morning."

12

"Maya, I need to talk to you about something."

Emma picked up her coffee mug and moved over to the kitchen island, where Maya was engrossed in her phone as she absently ate a bowl of cereal.

"Mmmm?" Maya murmured, flipping to the next photo in her Instagram feed.

Emma reached out and gently pressed a palm to her daughter's hand. "Maya, it's important."

Maya looked up now, wide-eyed, and slowly set the phone on the counter. "Is it Dad?"

Emma hated that waver in her daughter's voice, hated that Maya couldn't just be a normal teenager today, worrying about her English test and spending too much time on social media. She hated that she had to have this conversation.

"Dad is fine." Emma gave a quick shake of her head. Well, he wasn't really *fine*. As soon as she woke up, Emma had rolled over to check her phone, just in case she'd missed a call from the hospital last night. *No new calls.* She wasn't sure if she should be disappointed that Noah hadn't showed any improvement, or happy that at least he hadn't declined either. She'd dialed the number for the hospital—in the list of favorite numbers in her phone now—and spoken to the nurse on duty who'd reported that Noah's condition was unchanged. He'd kept his voice positive, as if she should view that as good news.

Emma borrowed that same upbeat tone now. "He's the same. So, he's really hanging in there."

Maya gave her a narrow-eyed stare. "But he didn't improve, either? So, he could just stay... asleep... forever. Couldn't he?"

Emma sighed. She missed the days when Maya believed everything she'd said without question. The days when the tooth fairy and Santa Claus were real, and Emma could do no wrong in her daughter's eyes. "Yes. It's possible. But the doctors aren't remotely ready to start thinking in that direction. It's only been a few days, and it will take time for the swelling in Dad's brain to heal."

Maya nodded. "Okay, so what do you need to talk to me about?"

"Well..." Emma hesitated. She'd rehearsed how to say this in the shower this morning, but somehow it all flew out of her head the moment Maya was sitting in front of her. She didn't want to lie to her daughter, but she couldn't tell the truth either. Not when Emma was still sorting the truth out herself. "It turns out that there was a woman in the car accident with Dad."

Maya's eyebrows knit together. "The driver of the truck that hit him was a woman?"

"No... the woman was in Dad's car. She was a—" Emma did her best to keep her voice neutral. "A work colleague." She had decided to tell this lie for the moment. It was important they keep focused on Luna for now. And though she had her suspicions, Emma didn't actually *know* the truth about who Coral really was. "Dad was giving her a ride when the accident happened."

"Is she in a coma too?"

"No." Emma took a deep breath. "Unfortunately, she died."

"Oh." Maya stared down at her cereal bowl. "Oh, wow. That's awful."

"Her name was Coral, and she had a two-year-old daughter named Luna."

Maya looked up, stricken now. "Oh, God. Don't tell me Luna died too."

"No." Emma gave a vigorous shake of her head. "Luna is just fine."

Maya pressed a hand to her chest and blew out a breath. "Jeez. You scared me. You should really lead with 'the little kid didn't die' next time."

"I'm sorry. You're right."

"But—" Maya's mouth twisted into a frown. "I guess she lost her mom, right?"

Emma nodded. "She did."

"So, is she with her dad now?"

"Well." Emma leaned into the counter. "Luna didn't have a dad, so they're trying to locate her other family members. Maybe some grandparents. There's a social worker involved."

Maya's shoulders drooped. "God, that poor kid."

"Yes. Well, the social worker suggested that until they can locate Luna's other family, maybe—" Emma clutched her coffee cup more tightly. "Maybe *we* could take Luna for a while."

Maya's eyes widened. "We're going to take a two-year-old kid? Like, she'll move in here with us?"

"Well, I'm not sure. That's why I wanted to talk to you." Emma held her breath. Maya's parents had just separated, and her father was in a coma. She'd been through a lot already, and Emma hated to add to it. But what other choice did she have? Luna could very well be Maya's sister.

Emma's hands shook. *Maya has a sister.*

"How long will she be with us?"

One step at a time, Emma told herself. "It's not completely clear. Hopefully, they'll locate her other family members at any moment." Emma prayed it was true. The police were still searching for aunts and uncles. Grandparents. Someone could turn up at any moment.

"So, until they do, we're just going to babysit her?" Maya's face scrunched up. "Do *I* have to babysit her?"

Suddenly, the gravity of the situation hit Emma. She'd have a toddler in her home. Twenty-four hours a day, seven days a week, with no reprieve. Toddlers required constant attention, and they got into everything. Their house hadn't been toddler-proofed in over a decade. There were exposed outlets, cleaners under the sink, a glass coffee table.

How could she take on the responsibility of a toddler?

But... how could she not?

Emma slumped against the counter. "I know you're busy with school, and this is a hard time for you right now. But I hope you'll help out a little."

"What about play rehearsal? What about visiting Dad in the hospital? I can't be a babysitter, too."

Neither can I! Emma wanted to scream. But this situation wasn't Maya's fault. The person Emma really wanted to scream at, the person who'd left her with this enormous responsibility, was lying asleep in a hospital room, blissfully unaware of the complete upheaval he'd left behind.

"I know, honey. It would only be temporary, and we'll figure it out." Emma took a shaky breath. "The truth is that Luna doesn't really have anywhere else to go right now."

Maya's eyes filled with tears. "That's so sad."

Emma reached out to take her daughter's hand and give it a squeeze. She was encouraged by the fact that Maya didn't pull away. "So, what do you think? It wouldn't be fair for me to agree to this if you're not on board with it."

Maya swiped at her eyes with the hem of her Hamilton T-shirt. "I don't think we have a choice, do we?"

Emma shook her head. Thanks to Noah, they didn't have much of a choice at all.

13

FOURTEEN YEARS AGO

Emma adjusted two-year-old Maya's wiggling form on her hip with one arm while wrestling her hair out of her daughter's grasp with the other. "Ouch. Maya, honey. You're hurting Mommy." She followed Noah into the bathroom where he was packing up his travel kit with a toothbrush and sample-sized shaving cream.

"Do you really have to go this week?" Emma asked from the doorway. Maya clutched the neckline of her shirt, pulling it sideways so it was practically choking her. She yanked it back. "Maya, stop please."

Noah threw a small bottle of shampoo into his kit and then eased past her into the bedroom. "I'm sorry, but the boss wants me to be at this meeting."

"Can't you say no to the boss?" Emma asked. Maya was wiggling again, so Emma put her on the bed, where she immediately lunged for Noah's suitcase lying open by the pillows. "You said yes last week. I thought that was your last trip for a while."

"Can you please take her out of here?" Noah waved at Maya as she picked up one of his carefully folded shirts and tossed it on the floor.

"*You* take her out of here," Emma snapped back. "You're her father, and I'm supposed to be finishing my sculpture right now."

"Look, I can't just say no to my boss because my wife has some art to finish. It doesn't work like that. Someone has to pay the bills."

Emma reeled backwards and bumped into the dresser. "*Really?*"

Noah sighed and pressed a hand to his temples. "Emma, I didn't mean it like that—"

"Don't." She cut him off. "Don't act like my art is some silly hobby. We talked about this. You're the one who pushed for me to stop teaching so we didn't have to put Maya in daycare." Her gaze found her daughter, who'd discovered Noah's socks in the suitcase and was pulling them out of their neatly rolled balls. "You're the one who said I should focus more on my art. I would have happily kept teaching."

"It didn't make sense for you to keep teaching. The hours were completely inflexible."

"Fine, but when I quit to spend all day with Maya, you promised that you'd take her in the evenings so I could work. How am I supposed to do that if you're in Atlanta again?"

"Can't you just put her on the floor with some crayons? Is it really such a big deal?"

It was a completely unreasonable suggestion and Noah had to know it. "Do you really think I can be at my pottery wheel, covered in clay, and Maya is going to sit calmly on the floor and color?" As if to emphasize Emma's point, Maya began pitching Noah's socks on the floor, one by one. "Maya, honey, please stay out of Daddy's suitcase."

Maya unearthed a cough drop from a side pocket. "Candy!" she yelled, holding it up.

"That's not candy." Emma took the cough drop. "That's a choking hazard."

Maya held up her now empty hand and started to wail. "I want candy!"

Noah heaved a sigh as he surveyed the mess on the floor. "Can you just please get her out of here so I can finish packing? And then we can talk about this."

Emma leveled a glare at him. If he was going to finish packing, there really was nothing to talk about, was there? Noah was obviously going to go on this trip whether she liked it or not. She scooped up their daughter. "Come on, honey. It's bedtime. Let's find your *Goodnight Moon* book, okay?"

Noah looked relieved, seemingly oblivious to his wife's ire. Or maybe he just didn't want to deal with it. "Thanks. I'll be out in a minute to kiss her goodnight."

Deliberately turning her back to him, Emma carried Maya out of the room, pulling the door shut behind her with extra force.

Emma changed Maya's diaper and took her into the bathroom to brush her teeth, but all the while, she could hear Noah's voice in her head.

I can't just say no because my wife has some art to finish.

Can't you just put her on the floor with some crayons? Is it really such a big deal?

Noah's dismissive tone was an echo of her father's. Her art was a silly hobby, a distraction from what was really important. Her art didn't matter.

And neither did she.

"Look." Noah's voice cut into her thoughts a few minutes later as she smoothed Maya's blanket over her shoulders. "I'm sorry for what I said earlier. I didn't mean that your art isn't important. I know it's important—that's why I always encouraged you to do it."

Emma turned around to find him leaning against the doorframe. She motioned to keep his voice down—she'd just gotten Maya to sleep—and slipped past him into the hallway. "I know you have, Noah," Emma said when they were back in their own bedroom. "But lately, it seems like you have a one-track mind that's completely focused on work. You don't see anything else around you."

"I do. I promise I do." Noah sank down on the bed next to his suitcase. "That's why I'm working so hard. We always wanted a house with a studio for your pottery. And a neighborhood where Maya can go to a good school. That's what I'm working toward."

"I appreciate that, Noah, I do."

"I'm so close to this promotion." He reached out a hand to tug Emma down to the bed next to him. "Once I get it, we'll be able to afford all of that. And maybe we can hire a regular babysitter so you can work during the day. One of the guys at work just got an au pair for his two kids, and he says it was a game-changer. He and his wife have so much more time now."

The suitcase was in Emma's way, so she gave it a shove. "Don't you get it, Noah? I don't *want* an au pair for Maya! I grew up with nannies and au pairs while my father worked, and my mother flitted around the globe." Her voice wobbled. "I wanted something different for our child. I wanted two parents who would be here—*all the time*. I thought you wanted the same thing."

"I *do* want the same thing." Noah gave a heavy sigh. "But I also want her to have security. To have what she needs in life. A stable home, a good school. Every opportunity."

"She can have that, Noah. You had that kind of security, and you didn't need au pairs or fancy houses. You had two stable parents who loved you."

Noah looked down at the bedspread, but not before Emma saw the pain in his face. She reached out to squeeze his hand. He'd lost his parents so young, it had to be what was coloring Noah's decisions now.

Noah finally met her eyes. "I promise I'll be around more.

As soon as I get this promotion, I can tell them I want to travel less and spend more time with my family."

Emma shook her head. She wanted to believe him; she really did. But her childhood memories were painful too.

"I love you, Emma. I'm just trying to do what's best for our family."

14

The next morning, Emma arrived at the hospital to find Noah sitting up in his bed. For a moment, she stood in the doorway, rooted in place.

Oh my God.

Emma hurried into the room and ran to Noah's bedside.

"Noah?" Emma pressed a hand to his cheek. And then louder this time. "*Noah?*"

His chest continued its rhythmic rise and fall, and his eyes remained closed. Emma's gaze darted around the room looking for some sign of Noah's condition. Had he woken up? Had he sat up on his own? Why hadn't they called her?

She was about to turn and run into the hall, looking for a nurse, when the curtain in front of the door rustled, and Dr. Woodward walked in.

"You're here bright and early," he said with a smile when he saw Emma standing there. "How are you holding up?"

Emma stared at the doctor. "Noah is sitting up." She waved a hand in her husband's direction. "What does this mean?"

Dr. Woodward's eyes slid to Noah and then back to meet

Emma's. "Ah. Yes. I suppose we should have warned you about this. Noah's condition is unchanged."

At the word, *unchanged*, Emma's heart dropped.

"The nurses have been adjusting his position to vary the pressure on different parts of his body," Dr. Woodward continued. "So, you may come in and find him lying on his side or sitting up like this. It's just to keep the blood flowing."

Emma pressed her hands to her face and blew out a breath.

"Hey," Dr. Woodward stepped toward her. "Are you okay? I'm so sorry, I imagine that when you walked in and saw..."

"I thought he'd woken up."

"Of course you did. And again, I apologize for that."

Emma's shoulders drooped. "So, he's the same? Nothing's changed at all?"

"He's the same."

"It's been forty-eight hours." Emma swung around to face the doctor. "Shouldn't we have seen some improvement by now?"

"Maybe. Maybe not." Dr. Woodward shrugged. "Unfortunately, with these sorts of injuries, recovery times really vary. Some people might show improvement quickly, while others take a little bit longer to heal."

"And some don't improve at all."

Dr. Woodward pressed his lips together and nodded his head. "Yes," he finally answered. "Some don't improve at all. I don't want to candy-coat your husband's condition. But the good news is that we're not seeing any declines."

Was that actually good news? Or was the doctor just telling her what she wanted to hear? After all, Noah's score on the Glasgow Coma Scale was at rock bottom.

Dr. Woodward performed a quick exam and then tucked his stethoscope back into the pocket of his lab coat. "Keep talking to him," the doctor urged, before he headed out the door.

After Dr. Woodward left, Emma turned back to her

husband. She knew he was still in a coma, but somehow, she had more trouble believing it with him sitting up like this, the way she'd seen him sitting up in bed thousands of times over the past twenty years.

"You look just like you do when you're sitting up in bed next to me, Noah," Emma said, keeping her voice low. It felt strange to talk to him when she knew he wouldn't answer. But the doctor seemed to think this would work. And she was willing to try anything. "I know I sometimes complained about the light from your e-reader, but I secretly liked you reading next to me when I went to sleep at night." She'd felt comforted by his sold presence as she'd drifted off, often scooting a little closer until her hand was touching his thigh or her back was pressed up against his side.

"I miss having you in our bed, Noah. And—" The house felt so empty lately, with Maya busy at play rehearsal and nothing but silence coming from Noah's office. Sometimes, she still listened for his key in the lock, even though she knew he had his own place across town now.

"Remember how much fun we used to have cooking together?" When Maya was little and they hadn't felt comfortable leaving her with a babysitter yet, they used to have date nights at home. Emma would find recipes in *Gourmet* magazine, and they'd open a bottle of wine and cook them together. The most successful recipes went into a sauce-splattered binder to be made over and over again for holidays and birthdays. After Noah had moved out, Emma had sat up late one night flipping through that old binder and crying over photos of lemon pasta and shishito peppers.

"What happened, Noah. How did we end up like this?" Emma paused, waiting for him to answer, but his face remained unmoving, and his eyes stayed closed. "Are you still in there?"

No answer.

"Were you *ever* in there?" Emma swallowed hard. "Or were you a stranger all along?"

Noah's chest rose and fell in the same rhythm.

Frustrated, Emma pushed away from the bed. "Fine, just lay there and sleep while I pick up the pieces of the mess you made!" And she turned and marched out of the room.

On her way out, Emma peeked into Luna's room and found Brittany there. She had the pile of board books in her lap and was working her way through *The Very Hungry Caterpillar*.

Emma stepped into the room. "Hi. Is it okay if I come in?"

At the sound of her voice, Luna looked up from the book, and her face broke into an enormous grin. "Hi!" she said, waving at Emma across the room.

Emma gave her an exaggerated wave in return. "I just wanted to check in on Luna," she said to Brittany.

"It looks like Luna is pretty happy to see you," Brittany said, with a smile. She slid off the bed and held *The Very Hungry Caterpillar* out to Emma. "I should go check on your husband. Maybe you'd like to take over reading duties?"

"Sure." Emma took the book and perched on the bed next to Luna. "Is this one your favorite?"

Luna nodded. "Caterpillar."

Emma flipped open the book. "What's this he's eating?"

"A leaf!" Luna declared.

"That's right, a leaf." Emma turned the page, and she and Luna examined each page, identifying the objects and colors of the caterpillar's extensive meal. When they got to the end of the book, Emma set it on the bed and reached for the pile. "Let's see... oh, here's a new one. It's called *Are You My Mother?*"

The moment the words were out of her mouth, Emma froze in horror.

Who'd put this book in the pile? What had they been thinking? *Are You My Mother?* was the story of a baby bird whose mother went missing. The bird ventured out in the world looking for her, interrogating a broken-down car, a bulldozer, and a whole host of other objects as to whether they were his mother. Emma remembered that when she used to read to Maya, *Are You My Mother?* always made her a little sad. But now, that sweet children's book was absolutely heartbreaking. At the conclusion of the story, the little bird was reunited with his mother, but real life didn't always have a happy ending.

"I want my mommy," Luna said, looking up at Emma with wide, innocent eyes.

Emma's battered heart broke open. "Oh, honey. I know you do." Emma smoothed a lock of her hair off her forehead. "I'd do anything to get her for you. But, unfortunately, she can't be here right now."

Thankfully Kate arrived at that moment. "Hi, Luna," she said, flashing a wide smile at the girl. "And Emma! I'm so happy to see you here, too." Her gaze roamed over the two of them on the bed. "You're reading together and getting along so well. Wonderful!"

Emma nodded. "Yes, Luna and I are both big fans of *The Very Hungry Caterpillar*."

"I love that one, too."

Emma hopped off the bed. "Kate, I'm wondering if we could talk out in the hall for a minute."

"Of course."

Emma reached for the bag she'd left on the chair, digging around to find a metal lunchbox full of colorful wooden blocks. She'd found it in the basement, in a drawer full of Maya's old toys that she hadn't been able to make herself give away. "Luna, do you want to play with these while I talk to Kate for a minute?"

Luna was already reaching for the lunchbox.

Emma followed Kate out into the hall. She leaned back

against the wall next to the door and turned to meet the social worker's eyes. "Look, I'm just going to be really honest with you. I know this probably won't come as a surprise, but I think there's a very good chance that Luna is Noah's daughter."

Kate nodded. "I can't say the thought didn't cross my mind."

"If Luna *is* Noah's daughter, it makes her Maya's sister."

"It does."

"There's no way I can send her to foster care if there's even a chance that she's Maya's sister. And as much as I want to walk into that room down the hall and wring my husband's neck for —whatever it is he's been doing—and for keeping these secrets from our family, the kids shouldn't be the ones to suffer for Noah's..." His what? His indiscretions? His betrayal? Finally, she settled on "... lapses in judgement." Emma sighed. "I owe it to Maya and Luna to sort this out."

"That makes perfect sense," Kate agreed. "How would you like to move forward?"

"Well, first of all," Emma continued. "I'd like to get a DNA test for Noah and Luna. I'd like to know for sure if Luna really is Noah's child. Can that be arranged?"

"There will be some paperwork involved, but I'm sure we can work it out. Especially if you're granted temporary custody of Luna." She tilted her head. "It sounds like that's something you're still considering—?"

Emma had decided that she would take Luna for the time being. She and Maya had agreed on it. But somehow, when she opened her mouth to let Kate know, terror overtook her, and all she could manage was a nod.

Kate reached out and gave her arm a squeeze. "It's all going to work out."

Emma nodded again, but she wasn't convinced. "My daughter is a teenager, and I haven't spent any time with small children in a long time."

"You seemed to be doing just fine in there."

"Reading a couple of books is different than full time."

"I know," Kate said, in a reassuring voice. "Especially with everything else you're dealing with right now. But I promise you, this is the absolute best thing for Luna. She's clearly comfortable with you and, at this point, other than me and the nurses, you're the only person she's familiar with in the world. It would be very traumatic for her to go to a foster home."

Emma worried the social worker was getting ahead of herself. "Look, I can't promise that this will be permanent, especially with Noah's prognosis so up in the air. Coral left Luna to Noah, not to me, so, ultimately, I'm not sure this is my decision. I'm still hoping that you'll find some members of Coral Butler's family who would be suitable guardians. But I'm willing to do this while we sort it all out."

"I completely understand. I'll contact my office and get the paperwork started for both the temporary custody order and the DNA test. We should be able to have Luna ready to go with you in a few hours."

Oh God, a few hours. Emma would be taking a toddler home in a few hours. But what choice did she have? Luna was leaving the hospital today, one way or another.

"And how long will the DNA test results take?" Emma prompted.

"That might take a few days to arrange, and then maybe another week to ten days to get the results back."

"Hopefully Noah will be awake by then. If not, I suppose we'll just have to see what the results say."

But Emma was afraid she already knew what they would reveal.

15

That afternoon, Emma steered her car toward home with a trunk full of toddler clothes provided by the social services agency, and Luna strapped into a car seat in the back. It had taken Emma a few tries before she managed to install the car seat and click Luna into the five-point harness. Emma had worried for a moment that it would upset Luna to get back in a car so soon after the accident, but it seemed she didn't even remember it.

Emma took a short detour to Target to stock up on other things a small child might need—diapers, a high-chair, a portable crib for sleeping. Then she filled the rest of the cart with all the gadgets she could find to toddler-proof the house.

Emma zipped through the store as fast as she could before Luna grew restless in the cart. For a moment, she was transported back to the days of shopping with toddler-aged Maya, remembering the stress of trying to get her shopping done before the meltdowns and begging for candy started. Luckily, Luna was entertained by her stuffed elephant and a bag of pretzels Emma had grabbed on the way in.

When they arrived home, Emma gave Luna a sippy cup of

milk and put her on the couch in front of *Sesame Street* while she frantically ran around clearing out the guest room and shoving plastic blockers into electric sockets. There was probably something she was forgetting, but she'd done her best on short notice.

Emma peeked in on Luna, who seemed perfectly content to binge-watch TV, and was just about to head into the kitchen to figure out dinner—*What am I going to feed a toddler?*—when Maya arrived home from play rehearsal.

"Mom!" Maya called, as she dumped her backpack by the stairs and walked into the living room. When she spotted Luna, she stumbled to a stop. "Oh." She took a tentative step toward Luna, as if she were an exotic animal in the zoo. "Oh, wow. She's... you really brought home a toddler. I guess I didn't totally believe it."

Emma nodded, because Maya was only saying what she was thinking. Emma didn't totally believe it, either. "Maya, this is Luna."

At the sound of her name, Luna looked up, and her wide eyes snapped to Maya.

"Hi," Maya said, taking another step forward.

Luna continued to stare.

"I guess you must be Luna."

She nodded but didn't speak.

"She's met a lot of new people lately," Emma explained. "I'm sure she's a little overwhelmed."

"Yeah, I get it," Maya said, an overexaggerated nod in Luna's direction. "When I was a kid, I was a little shy about meeting new people, too."

Emma smiled because Maya had never been shy a day in her life. At Luna's age, she was chatting up every shopper in the grocery store, and as a teenager, she was literally singing show tunes on public transport. But it was sweet that she was trying to make Luna feel comfortable.

"I'm Maya." She took another step forward. "Welcome to our house. I live here too." Her gaze shifted to the wooden train in Luna's hand. Luna had found it in the box full of blocks and hadn't let it go since. "Ohhh, what do you have there?"

Luna held it up. "Train."

"I used to have one like that. You know what I liked to do with it? Build it a train station." Maya picked up the box of blocks on the end of the coffee table and pulled out a couple of colorful shapes. She stacked them up into a makeshift wall. "Want to help me?"

Luna scooted to the end of the couch and picked up a block. She set it on top of Maya's pile. "It's to park the train!"

"That's right. We'll park the train here."

Emma caught Maya's eye and mouthed, *Thank you.*

Maya shrugged and waved her away.

Emma headed into the kitchen to dig through her cabinets for something a toddler might eat for dinner. As she boiled pasta and steamed frozen peas, the sound of Maya's lilting soprano and Luna's little kid voice singing the 'Choo Choo Train' song drifted in from the living room.

Emma's heart squeezed. Did Maya sense that Luna might be her sister? Did she feel some sort of unconscious genetic connection to the little girl? Or was she just being kind because Luna had lost her mother? Maya could be a difficult teenager sometimes, but she was also a really good kid, especially when it counted the most.

After dinner, Maya's friend, Fatima, picked her up to drive her to the hospital to visit with Noah. They had a math test the next day, and Maya had the idea that they could study in Noah's room. "He always used to help me with my math homework, so maybe he'll like listening to us talking about it. Or maybe he'll hear how bad I am at geometry and wake up to lecture me about how to find the circumference of a circle."

"That's a great idea, honey." Emma had the feeling that

Maya and Fatima would spend as much time chattering about who was dating who at school as they would about their test tomorrow. Which could also motivate Noah to wake up just to beg them for some peace and quiet.

After Maya headed out with a promise to be home by ten, Emma carried Luna upstairs for bed. She'd already assembled the portable crib next to the bed in the guest room and set a moon and stars night light on the side table. She'd had to Google whether Luna was old enough to use a pillow without the risk of SIDS, because she couldn't for the life of her remember, and next to it in the crib, she'd set Luna's stuffed elephant and the wooden train.

It seemed to take forever to get Luna ready for bed. She refused to stand still when Emma tried to help her into her firefighter pajamas, was more interested in the bathroom cabinets than she was in brushing her teeth, and then went in her diaper about a minute after Emma had changed her. They finally made it back to the guest room and Luna chose *One Fish, Two Fish* as her bedtime story.

Halfway through the book, Emma found herself yawning and her voice growing hoarse. She'd forgotten how long and drawn-out this book was, and with all the tongue twisters, she actually had to concentrate on what she was reading. After what felt like an hour, she finally folded the book shut and peeked down at Luna.

The little girl was fast asleep with her cheek against Emma's arm. Her mile-long lashes left dark smudges under her eyes from the shadows cast from the dim light, and as usual, her hair flopped over her forehead.

Emma desperately wished she had a baby photo of Noah to compare to this child lying next to her. But they'd all been lost in the fire. And the truth was that the more time she spent with Luna, the less proof Emma needed that the girl was Noah's. It was clear not just from her appearance, but her smile and mannerisms, too.

The responsibility of it all felt like a boulder sitting on her chest. Just one day of caring for a toddler had left her aching and exhausted at 8 p.m. How could she fathom doing this for days at a time? And what about Maya? She'd been lovely to Luna today, but Maya also thought the girl was a visitor staying with them for a few days. What would it do to her to learn that her father had betrayed them, and Luna was the result?

Emma sighed and slid her arm out from under Luna's head. *I'll worry about it tomorrow.*

She leaned over, gathered Luna in her arms, and gently placed her in the crib. And then she tiptoed out the door and headed for her own bed.

———

Emma woke to the sound of a child's screams. Shaking, she sat up straight in bed. What time was it? Did Maya need a bottle? Or a fresh diaper? Disoriented, she fumbled on her bedside table for the lamp and switched it on.

Squinting in the light, it hit her. Maya was a teenager, not a baby, and those were Luna's cries she was hearing from down the hall.

Emma lunged to her feet and ran for the guest room. She found Luna on her feet, clutching the side of her portable crib with one hand and her stuffed elephant with the other, her mouth open wide in a wail.

"Oh, honey." Emma ran for the crib and picked her up. "It's okay, I'm here."

But Luna didn't want Emma. She wiggled and squirmed, her wails growing louder. "Mommy! I want Mommy."

Oh, God. Of course she wanted her mommy. The poor baby had woken up alone in a strange room, and when she cried for her mother, she got Emma instead. "I know you do, honey. I know." She shifted Luna on her hip as the girl's little arms flailed, and one hand nearly connected with Emma's eye. "It will be okay. I'm here to take care of you."

"Mommy." Luna repeated over and over, tears pouring down her cheeks as her fists pummeled Emma's chest. "Mommy."

Emma felt her own eyes fill with tears. This was an absolute nightmare. She wasn't equipped to care for a traumatized child who'd just lost her mother. Maybe if Noah were here, he could help. It sounded like Luna had at least spent time with Noah. But Emma was a stranger to her. And Noah wasn't here.

Noah had left her entirely on her own, well before that car accident.

"I know, honey. I know. It will be okay." Emma paced across the room and back, bouncing on her heels and hoping the rocking motion might calm Luna the way it had calmed Maya as a baby. "I'm here for you."

Luna flung her stuffed elephant to the floor, and Emma bent over to pick it up, still holding the wiggling child and nearly throwing out her back in the process. God, this had been so much easier when she was in her twenties. She was too old for this. Luna needed a caregiver who had the energy to chase a small child around, whose back wasn't perpetually sore from decades of sitting bent over a pottery wheel.

She needed someone who'd signed up for this. Someone who was cut out for this.

What was she going to do if that DNA test came back positive, and Noah didn't pull through? For about the hundredth time since she heard about the circumstances of his accident, Emma's chest burned with anger. How could he *do* this to her?

Emma paced back and forth again and again, still rocking Luna and murmuring soothing words. Eventually the girl's cries faded to whimpers and her wild movements settled. Shifting

Luna in her arms, Emma eased back onto the guest bed next to the portable crib and leaned on the headboard with Luna pressed against her side. Luna gave one more half-hearted, "Mommy," and then finally quieted.

Emma reached up to stroke her silky hair, feeling it slide through her fingers, and Luna took a deep, shaky breath and then blew it out.

"I'm sorry, Luna," Emma murmured. "You don't deserve any of this. And I wish there was something I could do to make it better."

Luna sighed again, and Emma had a feeling that the girl wasn't really listening to her, but Emma kept talking because the sound of her voice seemed to soothe the child. "We're going to figure this out." Emma looked down to find Luna's eyes fluttering closed and her chest rising and falling in an even rhythm.

"No matter what, you'll be okay." Emma continued, sliding down the headboard until she was lying on the pillow with Luna's head on her chest. "You'll be better than okay."

With one more sigh, Luna's eyes closed completely, and Emma felt her own growing heavy.

"Luna," Emma murmured. "I promise that you'll find a family who loves you, and you'll be so happy." And her final thought before she drifted off to sleep was that she hoped she'd be able to keep her promise.

16

Emma was awakened by Luna driving a wooden train up her back and singing 'Choo Choo Train' at full volume. She opened her sandpapery eyes and blinked into the darkness. *What time is it?*

She rolled onto her side and checked her watch. *Oh, God. Five o'clock.* She'd forgotten the part where toddlers wake at the crack of dawn, ready to party. Now, Maya would sleep later than anyone if Emma didn't drag her out of bed to get to school on time. But of course, it would be years before Luna was a grumpy teenager pulling the pillow over her head and begging for five more minutes.

"Good morning, sweetie," Emma murmured, stretching her aching back. She must have slept at an odd angle on the guest bed, and of course, Luna had been draped across her for half the night.

"Hi!" Luna had clearly forgotten her distress of the night before because she seemed happy to see her.

Emma rolled out of bed, and she and Luna headed downstairs in search of coffee and Cheerios. Once she was properly caffeinated, Emma realized her next problem. She was desperate for a shower, but she couldn't very well leave Luna on her own. Maybe she could put her on the couch with *Sesame Street* again, but what if Luna got bored and wandered off? And besides, she probably shouldn't be plunking a two-year-old in front of the TV every time she needed a minute to herself. The problems seemed to pile up on each other.

Thankfully, at that moment, Maya stumbled into the kitchen half-asleep and with her hair sticking up on one side. "Hi," she murmured, staggering over to the coffee pot.

Emma stared at her daughter. She couldn't remember the last time Maya had gotten out of bed on her own on a school day. "What are you doing up?"

"Couldn't sleep."

"Oh?"

Maya hitched her chin at Luna. "It might have been the Choo Choo song on repeat."

"Sorry about that." Emma smiled and slid her coffee mug across the island into Maya's hands. "Here, take mine."

"Thanks." Maya took a sip and then sank down on one of the bar stools, laying her head down on the counter.

"Maya!" Luna clapped her hands, delighted. "Choo Choo song!"

Maya's head popped back up. "Maybe later, okay? It's a little early."

Emma put some new grounds in the coffee pot and set it to start. "How was Dad last night? Any change?"

"No. We tried singing him all the best songs—*Wicked, Phantom of the Opera, Les Miz.*" Maya shook her head. "Nothing worked, but we were a hit with the nurses."

"What about math? Did you get any studying done?" Emma didn't want to put too much pressure on Maya when her father was in a coma. But at the same time, what if Noah stayed in the coma for weeks, or even months?

Maya heaved a dramatic sigh. "Who cares about math if Dad doesn't wake up?"

"Well, I know it's a tough time right now, but eleventh grade is the year that colleges put the most weight on grades. If you feel like you're getting behind, we should talk to your teachers."

Maya shrugged. "I may not even go to college. Sam, Fatima, and I might just move to New York City and get an apartment together."

Emma blinked. "When did you decide this?"

Maya shrugged. "I don't know. A while ago."

"You'll only be eighteen. How are you going to afford to live in New York?"

"Restaurants are always looking for servers. Then we'll have flexible jobs so we can go on auditions."

"What about Carnegie Mellon?" They had one of the best theater programs, and it had always been Maya's dream to go.

Maya gave another indifferent shrug. "Maybe I don't want to spend four years learning about theater when I can, like, go *do* theater instead."

Emma pressed a hand to her temples. Unlike Emma's own parents, she and Noah had always encouraged Maya to follow her passion, but they still expected her to go to college.

She could not face this today. She'd kill Noah if he died and left her to deal with these kinds of problems. Emma pushed away from the counter. "Can you watch Luna for a few minutes? I need to go take a shower." She took off before Maya could answer.

———

Three hours later, Emma and Luna dropped Maya off at school and then headed for the hospital. In the elevator from the parking garage, it occurred to her that Luna might feel traumatized to go back there again, but when they arrived on Noah's floor, all the nurses who'd cared for her the past few days came running with juice and snacks and hugs.

Five minutes later, Luna was settled in the corner of Noah's hospital room drinking a carton of juice one nurse had given her, eating a package of cookies from another, and scribbling in a coloring book that had been offered by a third. Satisfied that the child was entertained for the moment, Emma turned to her husband.

The nurses had removed the bandages from Noah's face, revealing a tic-tac-toe of black stitches across his forehead. His bruises had faded from bright purple to more of a yellowish tinge, and someone had switched out the plaster cast on his ankle for a soft plastic stabilizer. Something about these external changes had Emma's anxiety rising. While Noah was slowly healing on the outside, on the inside nothing had changed. He was still locked in a place she couldn't reach, and with each passing day, Emma began to worry that she never would.

"Emma, Luna, good to see you again!" A voice cut into her thoughts, and Emma didn't have to turn around to know it was Dr. Woodward who'd entered the room. That bothered her, too. She didn't want to recognize the doctors in this place. Dr. Woodward was only being friendly, but in Emma's opinion, it would be good to *never* see him again.

She turned around to find the doctor high-fiving with Luna.

"Ouch!" The doctor shook his hand out, pretending that Luna had hit him hard. "You're a pretty strong kid," he said, making Luna giggle.

His face turned more serious as her turned to Emma. "How are you holding up?"

"Fine." Emma sighed. "I guess."

"The social worker—Kate—arranged for the DNA test you requested. The nurse swabbed Noah's cheek earlier today. I can send her in to do Luna's as well."

Emma's face flushed. Did everyone on the floor know that

her husband had cheated on her and likely fathered a child? "Great," she managed. "Thanks."

"It's a lot, I know." Dr. Woodward gave her a sympathetic look. "First your husband, and..." He hitched his chin at Luna. "You're a good person for taking her in."

In that moment, Emma didn't want to be a good person. She just wanted her old life back. "Doctor, it's been several days, and nothing's changed with my husband's condition. I know you said that he might just need time to heal. But isn't there anything that can be done? Some other medicine you can give him to reduce the swelling? A surgery? *Something?*"

Dr. Woodward shook his head. "Believe me, if there was something else we could do, we'd be doing it. I know it's really hard to hear this, but the best thing for Noah really *is* rest and time."

Emma sagged against the wall.

"But like I mentioned the first day, there is quite a bit of research that hearing voices of loved ones can helps awaken coma patients' unconscious brains and speed recovery. Your daughter and her friends put on a quite a show yesterday, so keep them coming." He smiled. "I think they were good for the staff's morale too, to be honest."

Emma would have to let Maya know the doctor had prescribed more show tunes.

"I know you have your hands full with Luna now, and won't be able to be here all the time, but are there other friends or family members you could call to come by and talk to Noah?"

"Noah's parents are gone, and he didn't have any siblings..." Emma knew she should call her own father and let him know about Noah's condition. But his reaction when she'd told him that she and Noah had separated was too reminiscent of the day when he'd cut her off for choosing art school over business. He'd acted like her marriage troubles were a personal affront meant to humiliate him. He'd actually said the words, *What am I supposed to tell people?* Although they didn't see him often, Noah had always gotten along better with her father than she had, but Emma knew she'd have to call him eventually. *Not today, though.* "... and my mother passed years ago," Emma added, weakly.

"What about friends of his?" the doctor asked.

Alicia was already doing so much. There were neighborhood families they sometimes socialized with, but with all the traveling Noah had been doing lately, he'd missed out on the block parties and backyard barbecues more times than not. It was the same with the parents at school: many of them wouldn't even recognize Maya's father if he actually showed up for one of her performances.

Emma thought harder. Noah had mentioned some guys at work, but there were none he'd seemed particularly close with.

She must have hesitated for longer than she thought because Dr. Woodward cocked his head. "College friends, maybe? Or high school?"

In college, Noah had been popular with his fraternity brothers. Many of them had been at their wedding. As far as she knew, Noah hadn't seen any of them in a while, but maybe she ought to let them know about his condition. "I could call some of his college friends. They're scattered all over the country, though."

"Well, even if they can't come for a visit, maybe they'd like to do a video call, or just send a message you could play for him." Dr. Woodward gave a nod in Noah's direction. "Anything helps."

"Okay, I can do that. Good idea."

"And you can do the same with high school friends, too. Sometimes hearing voices from people the patient was close to in the past can jog memories in their unconscious brain. So, even if he hasn't seen them in a while, they could still have a positive effect on his condition."

Noah still didn't talk much about his life before she'd met him, but he was well-liked in college, so he'd probably had lots of good friends in high school, too. Even if they'd lost touch over the years, they might want to know about Noah's condition and have a chance to send him a message.

Especially... Emma thought, her stomach lurching, *especially if he's not going pull through.*

17

Emma and Luna headed home for a lunch of grilled cheese sandwiches, and then Emma put Luna down for a nap. After loading the dishwasher and wiping down the counters, Emma puttered around the house picking up stray blocks and stuffed animals. When she passed the French doors that opened up onto the patio, she stopped and gazed with longing at her pottery studio across the yard. She hadn't been back there in days, not since the police officers showed up in her garden and set off a bomb in her life. Her gallery show was only a couple of months away. She'd been planning to use every spare minute between now and then to get her exhibition ready. Of all the things she'd expected to get in the way of her work—Maya's latest musical, PTA meetings, doctor's appointments—caring for a toddler hadn't been on the list.

She cocked her head in the direction of the staircase and was met with silence. Could she just sneak out to the studio for half an hour while Luna napped?

Emma shook her head. What if Luna woke up and called for her mother, and Emma wasn't there to hear it? It would be too cruel to take the chance, especially after everything the child had been through. Besides, her work wasn't the sort you could pop out and do for half an hour. Just measuring out the right amount of clay would take her fifteen minutes.

Emma turned back to the living room and eyed the couch as exhaustion overtook her. Maybe she ought to lay down for a few minutes while Luna slept. What was it people used to tell her when Maya was little? *Sleep when the baby sleeps.*

Emma quickly shot down that idea. A nap would be amazing after the night she'd had, but she had a million other things to do. If she didn't tackle them now, she certainly wasn't going to have a chance once she was chasing a toddler around the house. With one more look of longing at the couch, Emma turned on her heel and headed back upstairs to Noah's office.

Noah kept an old-school address book with people's names and phone numbers scribbled inside. Like his paper records of their bills and statements, it had always seemed a bit odd for someone who'd lost everything in a fire, but when she'd pointed it out, he'd said he liked the information to be easily accessible. She was glad for that now, since his phone had been lost in the accident.

Emma took out her cell phone and typed in the numbers of several of Noah's college friends, quickly firing off a group text letting them know about the accident and asking if they'd be willing to send a video or schedule a call. Immediately, her phone lit up with good wishes for Noah's speedy recovery and commitments to send videos later.

Heartened by that response, Emma decided to see if she could track down any of Noah's high school friends, too. She knew she was unlikely to find old high school yearbooks or an address book from when he was younger—all of that would have burned up in the fire—but she poked around in Noah's drawers and dug through a few boxes on his bookshelf.

As expected, Emma came up empty-handed. So, instead, she turned back to her phone. Like many of the kids who ended up at Cartwright, Noah's parents had sent him to a private high school. He didn't talk about it much, but he still had an old, tattered sweatshirt with the name of the school on it that he mostly wore to do repairs around the house. Emma Googled that name now—Lawrence Academy—and the website for the school popped up.

On a whim, she clicked the link that said, "Alumni" and was directed to a page with options to read a newsletter about notable alumni achievements, to follow the alumni association on social media, and to donate to the school. Her gaze skated past all that and settled on a link titled, "Alumni Memories."

Emma's eyes widened as the page loaded with archives of school yearbooks from classes dating back to the 1950s. It was more than she could have hoped for. Maybe Noah would be in photos for clubs he'd belonged to, or even just in candid shots smiling with other kids. If Emma could find some names, she could try to hunt down those people on social media.

She clicked on the link for the year Noah was a senior, and a PDF of an old yearbook opened up. Emma flipped past the individual headshots to the section that showed off photos for clubs and events that had taken place at the school. She carefully examined each photo, squinting and zooming in to look for Noah among the other kids in their red and black private-school uniforms. At the end of the document, Emma went back and searched again. As far as she could tell, there weren't any photos of Noah among the debate club, the school newspaper staff, or any of the other clubs. He didn't show up at the homecoming dance or talent show, either.

Maybe Noah had been there and just didn't happen to end up in the photos. Or maybe he hadn't participated in that sort of thing in high school. Emma flipped to the section of the yearbook where the kids' individual class photos were displayed, and flipped to the letter H. Haden... Halliwell... Harrison...

Emma paused. The next photo after Harrison was a kid named Alexander Imler. There were no other H last names...

There is nobody here named Noah Havern.

Emma closed the yearbook and clicked on the one for the year that Noah would have been a junior. She skipped the candid shots and club photos and flipped straight for the eleventh-grade headshots. Again, there was no Noah Havern. She turned to the tenth graders and then the twelfth graders. Was it possible she'd gotten the year wrong? But Noah didn't show up in *any* photos in the yearbook, or in any for five years before or after.

It was like he'd never gone to Lawrence Academy at all.

Emma was sure this was the school he'd said he'd attended. In college there had been friendly rivalries between students who'd gone to some of the more exclusive private high schools. Noah's wasn't a top school like Phillips or Trinity, and it was all the way out on the West Coast, so he hadn't been a target for much of the trash-talking. But she'd definitely heard him mention this particular school. It was in Palo Alto. And besides, he had that sweatshirt.

Emma clicked away from the yearbooks. Maybe Noah simply hadn't gotten his photos taken. She couldn't imagine why he would have missed it for all four years, but it was possible there was an explanation she hadn't considered.

Scrolling down to the "Contact Us" section of the school's website, Emma clicked on the phone number listed there, opening up her phone's call function.

"Hello, Lawrence Academy," came the voice of a friendly, older woman through the phone. "How may I help you?"

Emma blinked at the sound of the person on the other end of the call. She probably should have thought through what she was going to say first.

"Uh, hi," Emma stuttered.

"Hello?" the woman said again. "Is there something I can help you with?"

"Actually, yes." Emma took a deep breath. "I'm calling because my husband is an alumnus of your school."

"Oh, wonderful!" the woman answered warmly.

"Yes. He—" Emma fiddled with a pen on the desk in front of her. "He speaks so highly of it."

"I'm so glad to hear it."

"And the reason I'm calling is because—well, I don't know how else to say this—he was in a terrible car accident."

"Oh, my goodness. I'm so sorry."

The woman really did sound sorry, and Emma straightened her shoulders, encouraged. "I really appreciate that. I'm reaching out to you because he's in a coma, and the doctors said that the best thing for him is to hear voices of friends and family. They said I should have people come in and talk to him, or to send audio messages. It could reach his unconscious mind and help wake him up."

"Oh, that makes perfect sense."

"So, I was thinking it would be great to reach out to some of his old high school classmates. By the time I knew him, he'd lost touch with people—you know how it is—so I don't know who to contact. But I thought maybe it would spark something to hear their voices."

"Well, it doesn't hurt to try, does it?"

"That's what I thought."

"So, you're hoping I can help you track down some of your husband's classmates?"

"I don't need you to give me their contact information," Emma was quick to say. "I know that's probably a violation of privacy. But if you could help me figure out who he might have been friends with—if there's some record of clubs or activities or something—then maybe you'd be willing to reach out and give them my information?"

"Well, give me his name and I'll see what I can do. The first thing I'll do is to look him up in our system and see what information I have about him."

"Noah Havern," Emma said, and then added the year of his graduating class. "I think."

"Okay, let me just sign into the computer."

Emma blew out a relieved breath. "Thank you so much." She stood up and walked out into the hall, listening for sounds of stirring in Luna's room. All she heard was the click-clack of typing through the phone, so she headed back into the office.

"Hmmm," the woman murmured. "Let me just check the spelling on that."

Emma slowly spelled out Noah's first and last names.

"Hmmm." More typing. "H-A-V-E-R-N, you said?"

Emma's pulse picked up speed. It wasn't that complicated of a name. "Yes. Is there a problem?"

"Not necessarily. Can you hold please?"

And before Emma could answer, the woman's voice cut off and the bland tones of an electronic keyboard playing a slow jazz ballad drifted to Emma's ear.

Emma dropped down in the chair and stared at her phone, watching the clock tick while she waited for the woman to return. This was getting weirder by the minute. Why hadn't Noah shown up in any of the yearbooks? And what could the woman have found in Noah's file that would have caused her to run off like that? Emma's head spun as she scanned through the possible scenarios for what Noah could have been up to in high school that would explain this strange series of events. Had Noah been a troublemaker? A bully? Had he cheated on exams?

She couldn't imagine Noah having done any of those things, but then again, a few months ago, she couldn't have imagined that he'd cheat on her and hide a secret family. So, at this point, anything was possible.

After what felt like ages, the elevator music clicked off, and the woman's voice came back through the phone. "I'm so sorry about that."

"Oh, no problem," Emma said, shakily. "Did you find any information on Noah?"

"Well, that's the thing..." The woman sounded perplexed. "I didn't find a file for him in our electronic records."

"Oh." Emma's eyes widened.

"So, I went and checked in our file room," the woman continued. "Twenty years ago, we would have kept paper copies of student records. We only made the switch to fully digital maybe eight or ten years ago."

"I see. So, you looked in the file room?" Emma prompted.

"We do keep very thorough records, but mistakes happen, so I thought perhaps his file fell through the cracks when they converted everything to the new system."

"Oh." Emma breathed out a sigh. "Of course." Maybe there really *was* an explanation.

"So, I searched the file room for *Havern*, and then again for *Noah*, just in case someone filed your husband's records in the wrong place."

Emma's stomach gave a slow roll as she realized where this was going. No yearbook photos... No electronic records... No paper record under Noah's last name...

"I'm so very sorry to have to tell you this," the woman continued, "but I didn't find any record whatsoever of your husband having attended this school at any point in the past sixty years."

The phone slipped from Emma's hand and clattered on the desk. Noah had never attended Lawrence Academy. Just like so many other things he'd told her about his life, it had been a lie.

"Hello? Ma'am are you there?" The tinny sound of the woman's voice carried across the space.

With shaking hands, Emma picked up the phone and

adjusted it against her ear. "Yes. I'm sorry. Yes, I—" She straightened her shoulders. "You know, I think I must have gotten it wrong. I've been so distressed by my husband's condition that I'm just not thinking straight. Now that we're talking, I believe I Googled the wrong school."

"Well, that's completely understandable," the woman soothed. "What a difficult time it's been for you. I hope you'll be able to track down the correct school and find some of your husband's friends."

"I hope so, too."

"I'll put you and your husband in my prayers tonight."

"Thanks," Emma said. They weren't religious, but at this point, she could use all the help she could get.

As soon as they said goodbye and hung up the phone, Emma stood up and paced across the room. Noah hadn't gone to the high school he'd claimed he'd attended. She already knew he'd been lying to her for at least two years, about Coral and Luna. So, what else had he lied to her about?

Emma walked back across the office and yanked open Noah's file drawers again. She didn't know exactly what she was looking for, but there had to be *something* about the man she'd married in these files. She flipped past the tax forms and bank statements—she'd already gone through those—and kept digging. Noah had kept a file full of old photographs from college— those were the days before smartphones, when they used to actually print pictures in order to share them—but there was nothing surprising among the shots. She recognized most of the men from his fraternity and a few of the women from Theta Chi Delta's "sister" sorority.

Emma paused for a moment at a photo of twenty-year-old Noah sitting on a couch with a couple of pretty college girls. A few months ago, she wouldn't have even blinked at that: she was never the type to get jealous of his female friends. But now Emma couldn't help but wonder if he'd ever cheated with anyone else. If he was capable of going behind her back with Coral Butler, what else was he capable of?

She shoved the photo back in the file. At this point, it didn't really matter if Noah had cheated with some random girl in college or not.

Emma continued to dig through the drawer, but nothing else jumped out as suspicious. She was about to give up when her hand landed on the last file. She'd almost missed it; it wasn't hanging on the metal rail like the other files but shoved in the very back of the drawer as if Noah had intentionally wanted to hide it.

Nervous now, Emma pulled out the file and flipped it open. Her gaze skated past their marriage license—she had her own copy of that—and his social security card. The next document was a birth certificate. The names of his parents were in line with what he'd told her—Gary and Delia Havern. And then she looked at the place of birth.

The words on the paper blurred and, for a moment, Emma thought she might faint.

Because right there in black and white, Noah's birth certificate declared that he had not been born in Palo Alto, California, as he'd always told her. No. Instead, Noah's birthplace was listed as Millersville, Michigan.

Millersville, Michigan.

The same town where Coral Butler had lived, right up until her death earlier this week.

Emma's heart pounded and her chest squeezed. Nothing she'd believed about the man she'd spent half her life with was true. For every lie she peeled away, she found two more beneath.

If Noah wasn't from Palo Alto, and he didn't go to school at Lawrence Academy... Was anything she'd believed about him real? And if it had all been a lie... *Who is the real Noah Havern?*

18

TWELVE YEARS AGO

"Daddy!" Maya yelled, barreling into the kitchen to wrap her little arms around Noah's waist.

Emma looked up from the vegetables she was chopping, and her heart tugged at the scene. Four-year-olds could be a challenge sometimes, but you couldn't beat their enthusiasm or unconditional love. Noah had only been on his work trip for two days, but Maya treated his homecoming as if he'd been away at war for years.

"Hi," Noah said, giving Emma a smile over the top of Maya's head.

"How was your day, dear?" Emma joked.

"Great, it was great." Noah leaned over to plant a kiss on her lips and then he snatched a pepper slice from the cutting board. "Actually, it was better than great. I have some news." He took a bite of the pepper and gave Maya a pat on the head. "Maya, why don't you go and set up your trucks in your room? As soon as I talk to Mommy for a minute, I'll come in and we can play until dinner's ready."

Never one to give up the opportunity for a playmate, Maya

ran off, her little feet pounding down the laminate floor of the apartment's hallway to her room.

"No running!" Emma called, but she knew it was useless to rein Maya in. Most of the time she admired her daughter's boundless energy, but in a small apartment with thin walls, the neighbors weren't always quite so charmed by it. "The downstairs neighbors are going to start pounding on the ceiling with the broom again."

Noah stole another pepper. "Well, maybe we won't have to worry about that for much longer."

Emma lowered her knife to the cutting board and took a long look at her husband. There was something about his energy that reminded her of Maya as he shifted his weight from one foot to the other and seemed to be trying to hold back a smile.

"What is this news you're talking about?"

"Emma." Noah shuffled back and forth again. "I got a new job."

"What?" Her eyes widened. This was the first she was hearing of another job possibility. "You didn't tell me you were applying for a new job!"

"I didn't want to say anything until I knew it would come through." Noah held up his hands. "But it did, and it's a fantastic opportunity. More money, and it should be less travel, too."

Emma perked up at the words *less travel*. It seemed like Noah had been traveling endlessly lately. He kept promising it would end with each new promotion, and while he'd been successful at moving up the ladder, the work trips seemed to continue. "Oh, honey, that's great. Tell me about the job."

"It's a high-level management position at a start-up company that builds fully electric cars."

Emma bit her lip. "A start-up? Isn't that risky?"

"It would be, but they've just secured a quarter of a billion dollars in venture capital funding. And they already have several large contracts overseas." Noah grinned. "The pay is triple what I'm making now, and the best part is, I won't need to travel anymore."

"At all?" Emma asked. "You'll just work here in an office in Boston?"

"Well, no. Not exactly."

Emma cocked her head at him. "So, where will you work?"

"Well..." Noah cleared his throat, and his eyes shifted past her to the striped curtains she'd hung in the apartment's kitchen window when they'd first moved in.

Emma felt a twinge of apprehension. "Noah, what is it?"

"The job is in Grand Rapids, Michigan," he finally blurted out.

"*What?*" Emma took a step backward. "Grand Rapids? Why there?"

"Well, they're an automobile company, and they wanted their headquarters based near their factories. They'll be taking over several General Motors plants that shut down a few years ago and modernizing them for their production. There are plenty of workers looking for jobs."

"But—you don't know anything about cars."

"But I know business, and that's what the venture capital firm wanted. They encouraged the company to hire me."

"Who is the venture capital firm?"

"Technology Enterprises."

Where had Emma heard that name before?

And then it came to her. The country club. "You got a job working for a company that my dad's friend Allen's firm is investing in? Is that why you've been spending so much time at the country club? So Allen would get you a job?"

It shouldn't have bothered Emma that Noah had been spending more time at the club, had been playing golf with her dad, and even taking private lessons on his own. *I guess he was networking with my dad's friends, too.* "Noah, I can't under-stand why you didn't tell me about this before."

"I guess... There wasn't a point on dwelling on it if I wasn't going to get it. Allen was putting in a good word, but..."

Emma blinked at that. Did he really believe that? "Allen gave this company 250 million dollars. Did you really think they weren't going to give you the job if you wanted it?" And that bothered her, too. Her father's friend, and her father by association, was buying Noah a job. In an indirect sort of way, it felt like her father was trying to control her again.

Besides, Noah was one of the smartest people she knew. He didn't need to get hired this way.

Noah seemed to register that she wasn't completely thrilled with this news because his smile faded. "I haven't accepted it yet."

But he wanted to. He'd planned to.

"We don't know anyone in Michigan."

"We'll meet people." He pressed his hands against the counter, leaning forward. "We'll make friends. I'd never suggest we move somewhere without researching it first. There are some really nice suburbs with good schools for Maya, and neighborhoods full of other families like ours. With the salary I'd be making, we could get out of this cramped apartment and buy a house."

Emma hesitated. They *were* starting to outgrow this apart-ment, and it would be nice for Maya to have a backyard and some friends in the neighborhood. The schools in this area weren't great, either. They'd chosen this apartment back before Maya was born because it was convenient to Noah's office. That was before they'd known he'd spend half his time on the road.

As if sensing an opportunity, Noah rounded the island and took Emma by the shoulders. "We might even be able to find a place with a little carriage house you could use as a studio in back."

Emma definitely liked the sound of that. Especially with Maya starting kindergarten next year. She could finally focus on her art and maybe show in some galleries instead of just the occasional summer art fair.

"My dad is here in Boston," Emma pointed out. "I know he's difficult, even more since my mom died, and he hasn't always been supportive of me. But I hate to take Maya away from her family."

"We can get a direct flight from Grand Rapids to Boston. Your dad can certainly afford to fly in. And he doesn't see her more than once a month now."

Noah wasn't wrong about that. Her father enjoyed visits with Maya, and he certainly made more of an effort than he had with her. But his real loves were still work and the country club.

"Your dad might actually get more quality time with Maya if he flies out for longer visits than he does having us for dinner at the club every few weeks."

Emma's shoulders relaxed an inch. If she were really honest about it, she hated those dinners. Hated going back to that soulless country club, nibbling on an overpriced salad, and trying to rein in Maya's energy at the dinner table. Maybe if her father was forced to come and visit them, they'd all get more quality time together.

"Emma, you know I love you," Noah implored. "I'd never suggest something that I didn't think would be good for our family. And I know it's a lot to suggest moving cities. I'm sick of traveling, too, and I want to be home with you and Maya more often." He reached out and pulled her close, wrapping his arms around her. "I think this could be it. This could be the place where we settle down and Maya gets to grow up in a nice neighborhood with lots of kids. Grand Rapids is such a great community. She'll have the typical childhood that you always wanted."

Emma pressed her cheek against Noah's chest. "The kind of childhood that you had."

Noah was silent for a moment. "Yes," he finally said, and Emma could hear the emotion in his voice.

Emma pulled back to look up at him. "I want Maya to have that."

Noah cocked his head. "So, what do you think?"

"I think you should take the job."

19

As Emma cleaned up the dishes from dinner that evening, she glanced out the kitchen window. It was a beautiful spring evening. Maybe if Luna got a little more exercise, she'd sleep better tonight. And Emma could stand to get out too. After her latest revelation about Noah, she kept feeling like the walls of this house were closing in on her.

"Maya comes too," Luna declared, as Emma wrestled the girl's little feet into sneakers.

"Maya might have things she needs to do, sweetie." Emma didn't want Maya to feel obligated to entertain Luna. She'd already done plenty of babysitting, and her life was in enough upheaval. If she wanted to sneak off after dinner and message with her friends, Emma didn't want to make a big deal about it.

But to her surprise, Maya took her jacket from the hook by the back door. "Sure, I'll come."

Luna reached up, grabbed on to one of Maya's fingers, and they headed for the door together.

Something about the image of her daughter walking hand-in-hand with this little girl had Emma's heart squeezing. She and Noah had talked about having another baby, but the timing had never been right. In the years right after Maya was born, Noah had traveled too much for her to even consider taking on the care of another baby. By the time they were settled in their house in Grand Rapids, Maya was almost six, in full-time kindergarten and, thanks to Emma's ability to focus more on her work, she was starting to gain attention in their local art community. Neither she nor Noah had been eager to go back to the sleepless nights and constant exhaustion a baby would bring.

It had been the right choice for their family but, over the years, Emma had sometimes worried about Maya being an only child—like she and Noah were. If she'd had a sibling, maybe her childhood would have been less lonely. And if Noah had grown up with a brother or sister to support him through his parent's death, he might have had an easier time of it.

Was it possible Maya had ended up with a sibling after all? Emma realized that despite the circumstances, something about the idea comforted her. If Luna were Maya's sister, they'd always have each other, for the rest of their lives. Even if something happened to her or Noah, the girls could count on each other.

Emma watched Luna and Maya slowly shuffle down the sidewalk and gave a quick shake of her head. She was getting way too ahead of herself, imagining this connection between these girls. And if Luna and Maya really were related, it would only be because Noah had betrayed their family. Could Maya welcome Luna with open arms after that?

Could Emma?

Emma focused on the toddler in front of her and hurried to catch up. Luna still wasn't completely steady on her feet and needed extra help stepping on and off the curb at intersections. Emma and Maya each held one of Luna's hands and swung her into the air while she squealed with delight.

They continued on at a snail's pace, with Luna stopping to examine everything in her path: bugs, rocks, and flowers were all equally interesting to her. Emma had to admit it was fun to look at the world through the eyes of a child again; for the past few years, Maya had seemed to make a point of sighing with boredom over just about everything.

Emma glanced at her daughter, and mentally took back that thought. Maya seemed to be getting into the spirit too, pausing to point out the shimmering colors on a butterfly's wings.

"Bug!" Luna yelled, running after the insect and waving her finger wildly as if to coax it to land there.

Maya laughed and followed Luna into the neighbor's grass. "You have to stand still, silly. Like this. Pretend you're a tree." Maya struck a pose with her body straight like a tree trunk and arms outstretched to imitate branches.

"Luna a tree, too," the little girl said, trying to copy Maya's graceful pose with her chubby little limbs. She was only able to stand for about two seconds before she wobbled and toppled backwards onto her diapered butt.

Luna sat frozen in the grass, her eyes wide, and Emma knew that look well. It was the expression of a child who was deciding whether or not this was something worth crying over.

Before Emma could react, Maya broke into wild applause. "Yay! Excellent landing! Ten out of ten!"

Luna giggled and clambered to her feet, toddling off to chase another butterfly. Emma and Maya exchanged amused glances, and Emma felt a wave of gratitude for this moment of connection with her daughter.

When the butterfly flew off, they turned a corner and headed down the next street. Just ahead, Emma spotted a woman powerwalking toward them in head-to-toe Lululemon and a pair of trendy sneakers. Her long, blond hair flowed behind her, as if she'd styled it just to go out for a walk, and she wore full make-up.

Emma looked around, hoping she and the kids could veer

off in a different direction, but it was too late to hide. She sighed and slapped a smile on her face. "Hi, Connie."

Connie was one of the PTA moms Emma had first encountered back when Maya was in kindergarten. Despite Emma's post as the secretary of the PTA, she'd never really ended up fitting in with that crowd. Especially after Connie's daughter had teased Maya on her first day of school because Emma had dressed her in clothes from Target instead of the stores at the local upscale mall.

"Oh, Emma," Connie called as she approached. "I was *so sorry* to hear about Noah's accident. How is he?"

"He's hanging in there." Emma wasn't ready to start telling the neighbors the truth about Noah's condition. She was still processing it herself and holding out hope that Noah would wake up soon.

"It's just so tragic," Connie lamented.

"Well, hopefully not," Emma managed.

"I'll be praying for him." Connie reached out a hand to give Emma's arm a squeeze.

"Thanks."

"And, oh, my goodness! Who is this little darling?" She crouched down to Luna's height. "Well, hello there!"

Luna clutched Maya's hand and half-hid behind her leg. *Smart kid.*

"This is Luna. She's—staying with us for a bit."

"Oh." Connie stood back up, pressing a manicured finger to her glossy lips. "Come to think of it, when the local news reported the accident, I *did* see that there was a woman and child in the car with Noah. I heard the woman died. So sad." She bowed her head.

"Yes, it is."

Connie's gaze snapped back to Emma's. "Is *this* the child?"

Emma hesitated, but without being rude, there really was no way to dodge the question. Besides, Emma didn't want Maya to catch her lying, or she'd get suspicious. Better to pretend like everything was perfectly normal. "Yes. Coral was—a family friend."

"And you've just... taken in her child? For how long?"

What could Emma say to that? "Well..." Maybe it hadn't been a great idea to parade Luna around the neighborhood like this. But what was she supposed to do—keep her locked inside? Her gaze shifted to Maya and Luna, and she was relieved to see they'd wandered off into the next yard to pet the neighbor's cat. "It's just temporary."

Connie gave an exaggerated tilt of her head. "You know, when I first saw you walking down the street, I honestly thought to myself, 'Did Emma have a baby and somehow I missed it?' She looks so much like Maya, doesn't she? And, of course, Maya looks so much like your husband. Was Luna's mother any relation to Noah?"

"Nope." Emma took a step backwards. "Well, we really should be going. It will be Luna's bedtime soon." She forced a smile and a wry roll of her eyes. "You know how toddlers are. One minute they're fine and then next it's meltdown city."

"Oh, I remember those days. You're a saint to take this on, especially with Noah..." Connie cringed. "You know."

"I'm really not," Emma said, backing up another step. "Well, it was nice to see you. Come on, girls!"

"Text me if you need *anything*," Connie insisted.

For a moment, Emma was tempted to call Connie's bluff and ask her to watch Luna so she could get some work done. But the woman might actually say yes if for no other reason than to gather more gossip. Emma would never put the poor child through an afternoon with that awful woman.

"Thanks, I will," Emma murmured, with a plastered-on smile. And with that, she turned and headed into the neighbor's yard to get Maya and Luna before Connie could say anything they might overhear.

———

"Mom, I'm leaving for Fatima's." Maya knocked on the door of the bathroom where Emma was giving Luna a bath. Last time they were at Target, she'd forgotten to buy bath toys, but Luna seemed content enough to splash around in bubbles Emma had made with her favorite moisturizing body wash—the one she'd splurged on at Sephora for her birthday—and some plastic baking tools from the kitchen.

"It's open." Emma reached for the same body wash to scrub into Luna's hair. She'd forgotten to buy baby shampoo, too. This thirty-dollar body wash seemed unlikely to burn if a child accidentally got some in her eyes.

Maya popped her head in, and when she spotted Luna in the tub putting the measuring cup on her head like a hat, her hair sticking out in every direction from the soapy lather, she burst out laughing. "Oh my God, she's so cute. Like an adorable clown."

"You used to love baths at this age. You'd bring in your trucks and play for hours while I'd sit on the floor and read a book." Emma remembered those days of constant exhaustion. Maya's baths had been one of the few times she'd been able to sit still.

"Really? I don't remember that. I haven't taken a bath in forever. I'm usually so busy."

Emma held up her expensive body wash. "Well, if you want to give one a try, I just discovered this stuff makes excellent bubbles." Who cared about the price if it gave Maya some happiness?

"Maybe I will this weekend. Especially if it's going to be as much fun as she's having." Maya giggled again as Luna tossed bubbles into the air.

Across the bathroom, Emma met her daughter's eyes in silent agreement over the cuteness of it all. She never would have imagined that Luna would bring her and Maya together like this. Usually, Maya would have yelled goodbye from down the hall and been out the door by now.

"Home by eleven, okay?"

Maya nodded and gave Luna a wave. "See you later."

Luna lowered her measuring cup into the bath. "Maya." She reached out her chubby little arms. "Maya stays here."

"Oh, honey." Emma smoothed the soapy hair out of Luna's face. "Maya has to go see her friends. But you and I are going to rinse off these bubbles, and then we'll go read a book, okay?"

Luna's big brown eyes filled with tears. "I want Maya."

"I'll see you tomorrow morning at breakfast." Maya gave Luna a wide smile. "Tomorrow is Saturday. Maybe Mom will make us bunny-shaped pancakes."

Luna's mouth opened as wide as it would go, and a second later, she let out an ear-piercing wail.

Maya flinched, and her gaze swung to Emma. "What do we do?"

"Luna," Emma said calmly but firmly. "Maya has to go."

Luna's cries intensified, and she clutched the side of the tub with one hand, trying to pull herself to her feet while she reached for Maya with the other hand. Emma grabbed the girl's arm to keep her from slipping.

Maya's phone chimed and she pulled it from her pocket. "Sam is here to pick me up. What should I tell him?"

Emma cursed Noah for the distressed look on their daughter's face. Maya was only a sixteen-year-old girl, and this wasn't her problem. But Noah had managed to dump his responsibilities on everyone but himself. When he was sleeping around behind everyone's backs, had he even stopped to consider their daughter and what this might do to her? He'd clearly been thinking with only one part of his body, and it wasn't his brain.

"Go," Emma urged Maya, still gripping Luna as the girl tried to wiggle out of her grasp. She needed to rinse off the soap and get her out of the bath before she slipped and hit her head. "Go with Sam. It's okay. I've dealt with toddler tantrums many times before."

Maya glanced down at her phone one more time, her face twisted with uncertainty, and then back to Emma. "Are you sure?"

"Yes, go and have fun."

"Okay." Maya hesitated for one more second, and then she turned and bolted out of the room, clearly relieved to be free.

Luna's wails increased in volume as she repeated, "I want Ma-yee" over and over. It occurred to Emma that she couldn't quite tell if the girl was saying, "I want Maya," or "I want Mommy." Her words were slurred with sobs, and tears streamed down her cheeks.

Emma's heart ached for her. That's what all this was really about. Luna wanted her mother. She'd probably transferred her attachment onto Maya because the teenager had distracted Luna from her sadness for a while. And now Maya had left, too. Luna didn't have the cognitive ability to understand that Maya would come back; that this wasn't like the situation with her mother at all. The poor baby was suffering, and Emma didn't know how to help her. She'd managed toddler tantrums before, but not with a toddler who was dealing with the soul-crushing loss of her mother.

Emma's own eyes filled as she pulled Luna out of the tub and wrapped her in a towel. She was still soapy, and dripping water everywhere, but in that moment it didn't matter. Emma held Luna against her chest and rocked her like she had the other night. "It's okay, baby. It's okay." She felt like a liar. She had no idea if it *was* okay. No idea if Luna's life would ever be okay again. But she was doing her best in that moment. Hot tears streamed down her face and mingled with the water and soap on her soaked T-shirt as her own body shook with sobs. "I'm sorry, sweetie. I'm sorry."

Eventually, Luna's crying quieted, and she rolled over in Emma's arms to look up into her face. Reaching up, she put one soapy little hand on each of Emma's cheeks. "Emma no cry." She shook his head and repeated the words. "Emma no cry."

Emma let out a soft laugh and brushed the tears from her eyes. "Okay. How about we both agree to stop crying now and get ready for bed?"

"*Goodnight Moon.*"

"*Goodnight Moon* it is." Emma put Luna back in the bathtub to quickly rinse off the bubbles.

When the child was clean and dry, Emma carried her to the bedroom where they read books until Luna's little eyes began to droop and her mouth opened in a yawn. By the time Emma had laid her gently into the portable crib and switched on the night-light, Luna was asleep.

Emma was just pulling Luna's bedroom door shut when the doorbell rang. She jumped at the sound. It had to be close to 8 p.m. Who could be at her door at this hour? Her anxious brain snapped to the police officers who'd showed up to let her know about Noah. What if it was Maya this time? What if someone had crashed into Sam's car on the way to Fatima's house?

Emma barreled down the stairs, swung the door open, and then sagged against the doorframe. "Oh my God, you scared me to death. I thought it might be the police."

"I'm so sorry." Alicia eased past her into the house with a bottle of wine and a box from the local bakery. "I texted you about five times, but you didn't respond."

Emma had no idea where she'd even left her phone. "It's bath night."

Alicia eyed Emma's drenched T-shirt. "I can see that. Was it a bath for you or for Luna?"

Emma swung the door shut and then closed her eyes, leaning back against it. "Alicia, I'm not sure I can go back to having a toddler full time. I don't know if I have it in me."

"Listen." Alicia took her by the shoulders. "All you have to do is tackle today. And tomorrow, you can worry about tomorrow." Her friend tugged her away from the door and gave her a gentle shove toward the stairs. "Now go upstairs and change, and I'll open the wine."

Five minutes later, Emma was seated on the living room couch with a glass of wine in her hand and a plate of cake on the coffee table in front of her. She'd changed into a pair of comfy pajama pants and an old T-shirt, and had shoved a pair of fuzzy slippers on her feet. "Thanks for coming," she said, taking a sip of her wine. "You have no idea how much I needed this."

"Are you kidding? I wish there was something more I could do." Alicia sloshed some more wine in her glass. "I stopped by to see Noah on my way over here, by the way."

"I assume they would have called me if there'd been any change."

"They'd rolled him on his side, but no change in his condition." Alicia shook her head slowly. "I sat there and looked at him, and despite the bruises and cuts, he still looks like the same Noah. The guy who helped me move when Josh left me, and then later came over to fix my dishwasher and help me assemble my new furniture." She ran a finger around the mouth of her glass. "I know this isn't about me, but I really thought he was my friend, too, you know? I just feel so shocked by the whole thing. So *deceived*. I can't even imagine what you're feeling."

She had called Alicia earlier that day to fill her in on what she'd learned about Noah's birthplace and the fact that he hadn't attended Lawrence Academy. Emma nodded now. "I keep going over and over it in my head. How did he hide all of this stuff from me for twenty years?"

"It's an awfully strange coincidence that he was born only an hour from here when he told you he was born in Palo Alto." Alicia cocked her head. "And if he didn't go to the high school he said he did...where *did* he go?"

"I don't know. Luna woke up from her nap, and I didn't get that far."

Alicia sat up straight. "Where's your laptop? Why don't we Google the names of his parents and where Noah said they died in the fire? Maybe some part of the story is still true. Maybe you just got confused with the timeline of events."

Emma doubted it. She'd been certain Noah was born in Northern California. He'd told her so little about his past, but she could clearly remember him saying he'd been born at Stanford Medical Center and lived his whole life in a house in Palo Alto—the one that had burned in the fire. And of course, he'd had such fond memories of roaming the Stanford campus as a child.

But Emma wanted to believe that it was all a misunderstanding, so she grabbed her laptop and quickly Googled 'Gary and Delia Havern', 'Palo Alto', and 'California'. Scanning the search results, Emma found lots of links to people named Gary, Delia, or who had the last name of Havern, but none with the first and last names together. "Nothing." She turned back to the keyboard and typed 'Gary and Delia Havern fire'. Again, nothing.

"Try 'Palo Alto' and 'fire' with the year Noah said they died," Alicia instructed, sliding closer to look over her shoulder. "See if there were even any fires that could have been related."

Emma typed in the words and slowly scrolled through a list of building fires—a store in a strip mall where a worker had been smoking in the storage room, faulty electrical wiring in an apartment building—but nothing that could have been the fire that had killed Noah's parents stood out to her.

They kept digging, searching thought obituaries, marriage announcements, and real estate records. Emma's eyes began to cross, and her head ached. Finally, she snapped the laptop shut and tossed it aside. "What if Noah's parents aren't even dead? What if he lied about that, too?"

Alicia poured some more wine in their glasses. "What about Millersville?"

Emma blinked. "What about it?"

"It's less than an hour from here." Alicia shrugged. "And it's a small town. People know each other in small towns. People talk."

Emma peered at Alicia over the rim of her glass. "What are you saying? That I should go to Millersville and..." She scrunched up her face. "And ask around? How would I know who to talk to?"

"That's exactly what I'm saying. Pop into local shops. Try the library." Alicia sat up in her seat, clearly warming to the idea. "You could even ask people on the street in a small town like that." She shrugged. "At this point, it can't hurt."

Emma stared across the room, her gaze settling on her wedding photo. Her marriage was a lie and the man she thought she'd known for two decades had turned out to be a stranger.

If she went poking around a little... well, what more did she have to lose?

20

Welcome to Millersville, Michigan. Population 10,235

Emma slowed the car and stared at the painted wooden sign. A week ago, Millersville, Michigan was just an exit she'd driven past on the highway going north, and now it was a landmine that could blow up her life at any minute.

Earlier that morning, she'd snuck off to Noah's office and called Kate on her cell phone. Emma had hated to bother the social worker on a Saturday, but she could argue that this constituted an emergency. She and Alicia had decided that the best place to start her search was the apartment complex where Coral had lived. All she'd needed was its name.

"Can you look in the police report and find it for me?" she'd asked Kate.

"I'm not sure if I'm really allowed to..."

"Please, Kate?" Emma had begged.

"What are you going to do with it?" Kate had asked warily.

"I'm going to go there and poke around."

"I'm not sure that's a good idea."

"Why not?" Emma had grabbed a pen from Noah's top

drawer and scribbled on a Post-it note to get the ink flowing. "What harm could it do?"

"I don't know. Technically, Coral Butler's apartment is still part of the police investigation."

"And I'm caring for Coral Butler's daughter." Emma had slapped the pen down on the desk. "I'm running into her room at night when she has nightmares, I'm hearing her call for her mommy, I'm drying her tears. I just want to see if I can find out more information."

"The police already searched Coral's apartment."

"I'm not going to go inside. I'm just going to ask around to the neighbors. See if anyone knows anything they didn't tell the police. Or anyone the police didn't question."

Down the block, someone shut off their lawnmower, and the sudden quiet had underscored Kate's silence on the other end of the phone. Emma had sensed her wavering. "Please, Kate. You're asking me to care for Luna, maybe for the rest of my life. Don't I deserve to know the real story here? Doesn't Luna deserve to know it? If Noah dies, we might not have another chance."

"Let me think about it, okay?"

Emma sighed in irritation. "Look, you know I can get it myself. Police reports are public record. It will just take me a week to do what you can do in an hour, and that's an extra week that we could be doing something more to help Luna. An extra week that a family member could be out there."

At that, Kate had sighed. "Okay. Give me a few minutes and I'll get you the name. Promise me you won't get into any trouble. Or get arrested. Think of where Luna might end up."

"Kate, I'm a middle-aged woman. Nobody is even going to notice me."

Half an hour later, a text had come in with the name and address of an apartment complex. Emma had checked in with

Maya, who had plans to go back to the hospital with Sam and Fatima later that morning.

As much as Emma hated to dump more responsibility on her daughter, she'd asked Maya to take Luna along with her. Emma had used the excuse that she needed to run some errands. There was no way she could take Luna back to the old apartment where she'd lived with her mother. She'd think she was going home again, and Luna would be devastated when Coral wasn't there. Emma hated lying to Maya about her plans, but how could she explain the truth, especially when she didn't know it herself?

Now, Emma found herself driving down a two-lane road that led into a small, slightly rundown town with a mix of secondhand stores, mini-marts, and empty storefronts lining the main street.

Emma took a right at the Dollar General and followed Third Avenue for another mile or so, past a row of small 1950s bungalows that varied in how much care had been put into maintenance over the years. The road ended at a three-story apartment building with green and beige aluminum siding that looked like it had been painted based on whatever colors had been on sale that week.

Emma parked her car and got out, gazing up at the building. So, this was where Luna had lived, and where Noah had been visiting weekly for the past few years. This was where he'd kept his secret family. The building had a set of exterior stairs leading to the upper floors. Even from all the way across the parking lot, Emma could tell the paint on the railings was peeling off, revealing flaking orange rust beneath. The doors to the apartments were dented in places, showing them to be made of cheap metal.

It was another world from the upscale suburban community where Noah had lived with Emma and Maya for the past decade.

For a moment, Emma felt an irrational pang of guilt about the obvious differences in socio-economic circumstances between her and Coral. Emma remembered the $2,500 a month Noah had been transferring into Coral's account. Had that money been enough for Coral to support Luna? Had the other woman ever worried about buying food or paying her bills? And had she known about Noah's other family living in a four-bedroom house with a yard and separate art studio, less than an hour away?

Emma had been hoping to run into a neighbor outside the building, but though it was a beautiful Saturday morning, nobody was sitting on the plastic chairs set out in the grass or riding bikes in the parking lot. She checked Kate's messages for Coral's apartment number—206—which must be on the second floor.

At the top of the stairs, she made her way along the walkway to the apartment that used to be Coral Butler's.

Emma hesitated here, remembering Kate imploring her to please not get herself arrested. Technically, the contents of this apartment belonged to Luna now, and she was the child's guardian. At least temporarily. But Coral hadn't owned the apartment itself. Would it be trespassing to go inside? Emma settled for cupping her hand against the small side window and peering inside through a crack in the curtain. The room was dark, but as Emma's eyes adjusted, she was able see that the apartment was laid out with a small kitchen at one end and a living area with a slightly worn couch, coffee table, and TV at the other end. The room looked tidy, or at least tidy for someone who had a toddler. A box of crayons was scattered across the brown carpet and several stuffed animals sat on the couch, but the magazines were stacked neatly on the coffee table and clean plates were lined up in the dish drainer.

Emma stepped back from the window and looked right and left down the walkway, then she checked the parking lot for anyone who might be walking to their car. Way off down the road, a car was headed in her direction, but it made a left at an intersection a few blocks away. Emma swung back toward the door, and before she could talk herself out of it, she grabbed the door handle and twisted.

Locked.

Damn it.

She took one more look behind her and then bent over and flipped the doormat, hoping to find a key. But there was nothing but some dirt and a brown, crumbling leaf that had gotten trapped there.

"Can I help you?"

Emma bolted upright and swung in the direction of the voice.

And older woman stood on the welcome mat in front of the next apartment over, peering at her over a pair of reading glasses. "Are you looking for Coral?"

Emma pressed a hand to her heart. "Oh, gosh. You scared me."

"Well, *you* scared *me*. I heard scratching out here, and I thought we had another raccoon problem. I was about to call the landlord and tell him he needed to call animal control."

"Not a raccoon. Just me." Emma held up her hands to show she was harmless, and the woman didn't need to call anyone.

"Coral isn't here, I'm afraid." The woman shook her head sadly.

"I know." Emma bit her lip. "I wasn't looking for Coral. Just —some information about her."

"Are you with the police? I heard Bernard in apartment 205 talked to them last week."

"No, I'm not with the police. I—I have Coral's daughter. I've been her guardian since... Well, I assume you heard Coral passed away?"

"I did hear that, bless her heart. And bless yours, too, for taking in that sweet girl of hers. Poor baby. Are you a foster parent?"

"No, I'm—" *Who am I?* "—I'm sort of a family friend. My husband Noah knew Coral well. Apparently."

The older woman's eyes widened. "Noah is your... *husband*?"

Emma nodded. "You know him?"

"I do. But I thought Noah and Coral were..." She trailed off.

"You thought Noah and Coral were a couple?" *Of course she did.*

"Well, I assumed. Since he was here so often. And he and Coral seemed so..." The woman grimaced.

Emma sighed. "It's fine. You can say it."

"Well, they seemed *close*. Noah, Coral, and Luna... they seemed like a family."

Emma didn't think her heart could ache any more, but she was wrong. Because up until that moment, she hadn't let herself believe that Noah had actually cared about Coral. She'd imagined the other woman to be sort of a mistress—a seductress—someone who Noah turned to for physical gratification, but not someone he'd actually... *loved*. "I guess they *were* a family," Emma finally managed.

"So, you and Noah. You've taken Luna in?"

"Well, sort of. Noah was in the car accident with Coral, and he's been hospitalized ever since."

"Car accident?" The other woman blinked, pressing a hand to her heart. "Coral died in a car accident?"

"Yes." Emma looked at her sideways. "Noah, Coral, and Luna were all in the car accident. I thought you said you knew."

"Bernard told me that Coral had passed. But he didn't say how. I just assumed..." She trailed off.

"What did you think she'd died of?"

"Well, to be honest—" The woman's shoulders drooped. "I'd assumed Coral overdosed."

"Overdosed?" Emma stuttered. *"On drugs?"* The moment the words were out of her mouth, she realized just how naïve she must have sounded. Of course, the woman meant drugs. What else could Coral have overdosed on? But it was just so shocking to learn that Luna's mother had taken *anything* to the point that she might have overdosed and *died*. Had Noah been using, too?

Oh, God, I don't want to know. Please don't tell me. She couldn't take any more shocking revelations right now.

"Heroin." The woman shook her head sadly. "It's gotten its claws into so many of the young people around here."

"Do you—" Emma swallowed hard, and then found herself asking the question she'd just sworn she wouldn't. Because what if he'd been under the influence when he was driving the car? What if he'd been keeping drugs in the house when Maya was there? "Do you know if Noah was using, too?"

"Oh, goodness." The woman gave a vigorous shake of her head. "I don't think so. He was always trying to get Coral to go into rehab and get clean. After that one time he had to Narcan her, and the paramedics came, I would always hear them fighting about it. She did try, God love her. For Luna's sake, I know she tried. But when I heard that she'd passed, I just assumed..." The woman shuddered.

Emma pressed her hands to her temples. *Paramedics? And Narcan?*

Wasn't Narcan a nasal spray meant to treat an opioid overdose? Emma remembered seeing a couple of billboards that said you could get it from the Health Department if you had a loved one who suffered from addiction. Was that where Noah had gotten it? And if he'd been carrying it around, had he been expecting Coral to overdose?

The other woman must have picked up on Emma's distress because she reached out a reassuring hand. "Oh, please don't look like that. Coral loved Luna more than anything. I promise you she did. That woman stopped using the minute she found out she was pregnant, and I really think she stayed off of it for months, maybe years, longer than she would have because of that girl. But addiction is a monster that some people just can't fight."

Suddenly exhausted, Emma slumped back against Coral Butler's door. She shook her head slowly, trying to clear it, but it was like a fog had settled in.

"Are you okay, honey?" The woman swung her door open wider. "Do you want to come in and sit down for a minute?"

Emma took a deep breath and blew it out slowly. What she wanted was to get out of here. Not just this apartment complex or this town; she wanted to get out of this entire strange reality she'd somehow stumbled into, and back to her real life.

But my real life is gone for good.

"Honey?" the woman repeated.

"No. Thank you. I'm fine." Emma forced a smile that she had a feeling came out looking more like a cringe. "Really."

"If you're sure."

Emma nodded. "Thanks for the information. I really appreciate it."

"Oh, it was no problem." The woman cocked her head. "Did you say Noah is in the hospital?"

Emma nodded.

"Well, I'll be praying for him. What a sweet man. He always made a point of saying hello and stopping to chat for a bit. My kids don't visit enough, so it was very kind of him. And whenever he saw that I had a package by the mailbox, he carried it up for me."

"Thank you," Emma said, with a weak smile. "That means a lot." And she meant it. For days, all the ways Noah had lied and betrayed her had been piling up. It was comforting to hear that he was at least kind to old ladies. That maybe somewhere underneath it all, the man she'd married wasn't a completely terrible person.

Emma said goodbye and headed back down the stairs to the parking lot. As she climbed into the car, she looked up to find the older woman waving at her. Maybe someone nice would move in next door once they cleared out Coral's things. Someone who would carry the woman's packages like Noah had.

Emma backed out of her parking spot and turned the car toward downtown Millersville. She'd only made it a couple of blocks before a wave of nausea crested over her, and she slammed on the breaks. A car behind her honked and swerved, and Emma jumped at the sound.

Oh my God, what am I doing?

Emma yanked the steering wheel to the right and pulled the car to the side of the road, out of the way of traffic. She clutched the dashboard with shaking hands and stared out the front windshield as the woman's words slowly began to register.

Coral Butler had been addicted to heroin. She'd been using with Luna around, and had overdosed at least once, and Noah had saved her life.

How did he even know how to use Narcan? It must have been the most terrifying experience of his life to have to bring someone back from the brink of death like that.

And then what about Luna? Was she there when her mother had almost died? Suddenly, Emma found herself oddly grateful that Noah had spent so much time there with Coral, because it meant he was looking out for Luna. What would have happened if Coral had died when she was all alone with the child? The thought of it had Emma's heart racing. Would the neighbor have heard Luna crying in that apartment?

Emma shuddered. She couldn't bear to think about what could have happened. So, instead, she pulled out her phone and focused on the present. A text had come in from Maya: a photo of Maya, Sam, and Fatima posing for a selfie with Luna at a local ice cream shop. Luna's mouth was smeared with chocolate, and it was comforting to see the joy on the little girl's face.

Five minutes later, Emma stood at the circulation desk of the Millersville Public Library in front of a thirty-something man wearing a pair of khakis and a button-up shirt, sorting through a pile of books. He looked up and gave her a smile. "Hi, how can I help you?"

"Um." Emma paused. Alicia had suggested she try the library, but what exactly was she looking for here? Old newspapers? *That could take days to sort through.* Birth and death records? She was more likely to find those in the town hall building, and that would be closed on a Saturday. "I'm looking for someone who used to live in town."

"Hmmm." The man's eyebrows knit together like he was considering this. "Are you looking for old phone books?"

"I'm not sure what I'm looking for. I know someone who lived in Millersville a long time ago, and I'm hoping to find some information about him. Like, maybe his family, where he lived, where he went to school..." And then it came to her. Noah hadn't shown up in the Lawrence Academy records. But what about the Millersville high school? "What about yearbooks? Do you have any old yearbooks?"

"We do." The man nodded. "We have a whole shelf of them." He waved a hand to the right. "They're back in row 6E. Would you like me to show you?"

"No, I'm sure I can find them." Millersville was such a small town, the library wasn't much more than one large room cut up into sections with rows of shelves. And then she remembered that Alicia's suggestion that the town was so small, some people might even remember something about Noah. "Actually, you didn't know a family named Havern, did you? Or a man named

Noah Havern? They lived in this town probably... thirty years ago?"

"No, ma'am. I'm sorry. But I only moved here a couple of years ago."

Emma nodded. He was probably too young anyway. "Well, thanks. I appreciate it." She headed toward the shelves and located the long line of yearbooks on shelf 6E. She grabbed the a small pile from the years Noah would have been in high school and carried them over to a quiet, unoccupied table in the back of the library.

Emma started with the one from Noah's graduation year. She'd seen his birth certificate, so at least she knew he hadn't lied about his age. With some trepidation, she slowly flipped the pages past the freshmen, sophomores, and juniors, finally stopping on the people with the last names beginning with G in the senior class.

She paused there and realized her hands were shaking. Part of her hoped to find Noah's photo there so she'd finally know some truth about him and his previous life. But if she did learn that Noah had gone to high school in Millersville, then she had hard, irrefutable proof that he'd lied to her. And part of her still wanted to cling to the hope that this was all some sort of colossal misunderstanding.

"Get it together," Emma muttered to herself. "The ship on *colossal misunderstanding* sailed a long time ago."

A woman a few tables over cleared her throat and gave Emma an odd look. Emma flashed her a rueful smile and focused her attention back on the yearbook.

Just do this.

Before Emma could change her mind, she grabbed the page and flipped it over to the *H* section.

And there he was.

Emma sucked in a breath. There was no mistaking Noah. She was looking at the handsome young man she'd met on the student union lawn all those years ago—same floppy brown hair, same warm smile. Underneath his photo were printed the words *Noah Havern, Valedictorian.*

Emma stared at that. Why hadn't he just told her the truth about where he was born? Did he really think she would have minded that he'd grown up in a small town and hadn't gone to private school? He had to have known she wouldn't have cared about any of that. So, why else would he have kept it from her? He was even valedictorian, for God's sake.

From somewhere outside the window, Emma heard a church bell ring, and she checked the time on her phone. If she wanted to get home in time, she had to leave now. It wouldn't be right to make Maya wait with Luna any longer. She snapped a photo of the page with Noah's class picture on it and then slapped the yearbook shut and quickly reshelved it with the others.

As Emma hurried toward the front door, she passed by the circulation desk and waved to the librarian who'd helped her.

"Did you find what you're looking for?" he asked.

"I did. Or at least some of what I'm looking for."

"Well, if you want to know more about people who lived in this town, head over to Polly's Diner out on Little Lake Road. Polly has been there for forty years, and I'm pretty sure she knows everything about everyone."

"I will. Thank you so much."

21

TEN YEARS AGO

"I know it's not the Jersey Shore, but it was a pretty good vacation, wasn't it?"

From her seat on the passenger's side of the car, Emma gave Noah a happy grin. "It was absolutely perfect."

"I mean, Snookie wasn't there." Noah gave Emma a wink. "But the Upper Peninsula isn't too bad a substitute."

Emma rolled her eyes with a laugh. "I didn't mean I wanted our family to go to *that* part of the Jersey Shore. But, yes, the UP was wonderful, and I think it was even better than I imagined."

Emma didn't care one bit that they hadn't made it to the Jersey Shore for their vacation. In fact, she was growing pretty partial to their new home in Michigan. It was an area of the country that she never would have considered if Noah hadn't gotten a job here. She'd grown up on the east coast, gone to college there, and had always assumed that's where she'd live forever. But Michigan was a beautiful place, and they'd slowly been exploring everything the state had to offer.

Emma had to admit that Noah had been right about moving their family there. Noah had kept his promise that he wasn't going to travel as much once he'd started his new job in Grand

Rapids. His job was flexible—he could work at home or in the office—and he was home every night for dinner. He'd even planned this entire vacation.

They'd rented a little cabin in northern Michigan for the week. It was right on the lake and came with a rowboat, fishing poles, and a fire pit for the cool summer evenings. They'd brought a bag of beach toys for Maya to dig in the narrow strip of sand right next to the dock, and plenty of books to read on the wide deck. Emma had loved every minute. Noah had completely checked out from work—the house didn't have Wi-Fi, and cell reception was spotty—so they'd spent the whole week doing activities as a family. They'd laughed their heads off while they'd dunked Maya in the lake, built giant castles, buried Noah in the sand, and roasted marshmallows every evening after dinner.

It had been absolutely perfect, and Emma was still glowing from the memories on the ride back to Grand Rapids.

They were about an hour from home, on Route 37, when the car began shaking.

"What was that? What's happening?" Emma glanced at Noah.

"I don't know. I'm going to pull over." He hit the turn signal and merged into the right lane. The car was still shaking, and slowing down now, despite Noah pushing his foot on and off the gas pedal. "Something definitely isn't right."

Just as he'd managed to maneuver the car to the side of the road, it stalled completely. "Damn it," Noah muttered under his breath.

"Mommy?" came a voice from the backseat. "Why are we pulling over? Does Daddy have to pee?"

They'd pulled the car over about a hundred miles back when Maya was about to have a bathroom emergency in a rural area with no rest stops around. Emma gazed at the trees on one side of the road and cornfields on the other. This area didn't look much more populated. But at least they were on a major road. "No, honey. Daddy doesn't have to go to the bathroom. We're just having a little trouble with the car."

"Where are we?" Maya asked nervously.

"Nowhere." Noah shook his head. "Absolutely nowhere." There was something about the edge in his voice that had Emma glancing sharply in his direction. He was staring at a green highway sign about a hundred yards ahead that read, *Exit 102, Millersville, ¾ mile.*

"Daddy is just joking," Emma told Maya in a buoyant voice so their daughter wouldn't be scared. "See? We're not nowhere at all. We're just a short distance to that town there. Millersville. I'm sure a tow truck can take us there, and they'll have a mechanic who can help us."

"No." Noah reached across her lap to open the glove compartment and pull out their insurance information and the number for roadside assistance. "We're not going to Millersville to look for a mechanic."

Emma squinted at him. "Why not? It's right there. I don't think there's anything else around here."

"We'll have the tow truck take us back to Grand Rapids." He pulled out his phone and began dialing the number on the roadside assistance card.

"Noah, that's crazy. It will cost hundreds of dollars to have the car towed all the way home. We can leave it at a mechanic here, and I can call Alicia to come and get us. When the car is ready, we'll drive back to pick it up."

Noah dropped the phone into his lap and turned in his seat to face Emma. *"We are not leaving the car in Millersville,"* he said, voice rising. "Who knows what kind of mechanic we're going to find there?"

At that moment, Maya started to cry. "Mommy, I'm scared. I want to go home."

Emma turned to glare at Noah, whose harsh tone had no

doubt triggered Maya's reaction. Why was he being so stubborn about this? "Fine, whatever," Emma snapped, as Maya's whining grew more insistent. "Tow the car all the way home and pay the extra hundreds of dollars. I don't care." She unbuckled her seatbelt and then hopped out of the car to help Maya from the backseat. "Come on, Maya, let's leave Daddy alone. We'll go sit under that tree over there to wait." And with that, she slammed the door shut.

As she and Maya sat in the shade eating snacks from Emma's purse, she began to calm down. They were just tired from packing and cleaning the house that morning, and then from the long drive. No doubt Noah just wanted to get home, and he thought this was the fastest way.

There was no sense in getting in a fight over it and ruining their vacation.

Besides, when I look back on this trip one day, Emma told herself, *all I'll think about is the wonderful times we had. I'll never even remember the car breaking down or the random little town off Route 37 called Millersville.*

22

"Don't forget Luna's teddy bear." Emma shoved the stuffed animal into Alicia's arms. "And here's her train."

Alicia had offered to watch Luna for a few hours, and this was the first time Emma was leaving the girl with someone other than Maya. Luna didn't go anywhere without her wooden train. Emma piled it on top of the bear. "And I brought these Legos, just in case."

"Okay," Alicia said, balancing the toys in her arms. She shuffled into the living room and dumped it on the couch.

Emma pulled a box of macaroni and cheese from her bag and held it out to her friend. "I brought this for you to make for her lunch."

"Got it." Alicia took the box and set it on the coffee table. "Mac and cheese for lunch."

"And see if you can get her to eat some grapes."

"Grapes. Check."

Emma turned to give Luna a hug. "I'll see you in a few hours, okay?"

"'K," Luna said.

"Luna and I are going to have a fabulous time." Alicia

crouched down to Luna's level. "First, we're going to play Legos, then we'll have mac and cheese and then, I have a surprise for you. We've got ice cream for dessert."

"Yay!" Luna said, clapping her hands.

Emma grabbed her bag and was about to head out the door when she remembered something else. "Oh, make sure if you feed her grapes, you cut them in half. They're a choking hazard, otherwise."

"Emma," Alicia said, with a laugh. "We'll be fine. I have kids, and I watched Maya dozens of times."

Emma gave Alicia a rueful smile. "I know. I'm sorry. It's just been a long time since I left a kid with a babysitter."

"Uh, huh." Alicia raised an eyebrow and looked at her sideways.

"What?" Emma demanded.

"You're getting attached to her."

"I—" Emma gazed at Luna, who was halfway down the hall, chasing after Alicia's cat and giggling in delight. Her heart gave a funny little flip. "Maybe a little," Emma admitted, and then shook her head. Who wouldn't grow attached to a sweet little girl like Luna? It still didn't mean that she was willing to take on the full responsibility of a toddler, if that was what Alicia was implying.

"I've got to go." Emma gave Luna another wave and headed out the door.

Twenty minutes later, Emma stepped into her husband's hospital room and found him sleeping as peacefully as ever. She approached the bed, her gaze searching his face for signs that he might be starting to move, to regain consciousness, to wake up. Somewhere in there, was his brain doing the healing that Dr. Woodward had talked about? Or was this it—forever?

"Noah?" She leaned over the bed, only inches from his face. *"Noah, are you in there?"*

Emma wanted to believe that his breathing changed slightly, that he'd given a little gasp or hitch of his lungs or *something* when he'd heard her voice. But, deep down, she knew his chest was rising and falling in the same maddening rhythm.

A better person would be grateful for that. Noah's condition wasn't declining, and there was still a good chance he'd wake up. But all Emma could feel in this moment was resentment. He got to lay there and sleep while she was out here sifting through the lies and betrayal and wreckage.

"I guess I should mention that I took a little trip to *Millersville*, Noah." She paused, searching his face for signs of movement. "You know Millersville well, don't you? After all, you grew up there, right?" Still nothing from Noah. "You grew up there, and you lied to me about it. You lied to me about *everything*."

Emma pushed away from the bed and paced to the opposite wall and back. "Who are you, Noah?" she demanded, stopping in front of him again. *"Who are you?"* She took another walk across the room and then whirled back around. "I can tell you who you're not. You're not the man I married. You're not the man I fell in love with. That man doesn't exist." Emma stepped up to the bed again and leaned in. "All I know for sure about you is that you're a liar and a fraud. That's who you are." She bent closer until she was only inches from Noah's face. "You're a liar and a fraud—" Her voice rose with each word. "—and I will *never* forgive you."

And with that, Noah's eyes fluttered.

Emma gasped and stood upright. "Oh my God. Noah?" She held her breath, staring at his eyes, closed and unmoving. "Noah? Do it again. Move your eyes again."

His face remained expressionless, and his eyes were still.

Had she imagined it? Conjured up movement that wasn't really there because she wanted it to so badly?

"Noah, please. I need you to wake up. Maya needs you." And then in a louder voice: "Luna needs you. That poor child has lost everything. I can't do this alone."

And then, so quickly that she would have missed it if she'd looked away for even a second, Noah's eyes fluttered again.

This time, Emma was sure of it. She whirled around and ran to the nurses' station. Brittany was on duty again today.

"My husband, Noah. In room 402." Emma gripped the counter and leaned in. "I saw his eyes move just a second ago. They fluttered twice."

Brittany's eyes widened. "I'll call the doctor."

"Does it mean anything? Could he be waking up?"

"I can't say for sure." Brittany picked up the phone, dialed a number, and reported what Emma had told her to the person on the other end. "That was Dr. Woodward. He said he'd be here soon."

Five minutes later, Dr. Woodward was leaning over Noah, pulling up one of his eyelids and shining a light inside.

"Do you see anything?" Emma asked from her perch at the foot of the bed.

"Not sure yet," Dr. Woodward murmured, pulling out a pen and pressing the metal tip into the side of Noah's hand. He waited a moment, first watching Noah's hand and then his eyes. Finally, Dr. Woodward cradled Noah's head in his palms and pressed on his eyebrows.

Emma shifted from one foot to the other, her gaze scanning her husband for signs of life, but as far as she could tell, he was as still as ever. "I know I didn't imagine it. He definitely fluttered his eyes."

"It's entirely possible he did." Dr. Woodward nodded. "What were you doing when it happened?"

"I was—" Emma looked down at her hands, tempted to stretch the truth, just a little bit. But if it would help Noah to wake up, she had to be transparent. "Well, to be honest, I was sort of yelling at him."

"Sometimes eye fluttering can be the first sign that someone is regaining consciousness," Dr. Woodward explained, seemingly unfazed by her admission. "If Noah was upset by what you were saying to him, his eyes fluttering might have been a reaction to that."

"So, you think he heard me?" Emma asked, hopefully.

"Possibly." Dr. Woodward shrugged. "But I can't say for sure. Sometimes these movements are involuntary. But it's a good sign that it happened when you were showing a lot of emotion, and it could mean he was reacting to that. It definitely raises his score on the Glasgow Coma Scale"

"So, what do I do now?"

Dr. Woodward poked his pen into Noah's hand one more time, shined a light into his eyes, and looked up to meet Emma's gaze. "I guess you keep yelling at him."

———

From the outside, Polly's Diner was exactly what Emma had imagined a small-town diner would look like. The restaurant was housed in a brick building with a red-and-white striped awning about a mile or so outside of Millersville. Driving down Little Lake Road, Emma spotted it immediately by the cursive lettering on its light-up plastic sign.

Emma parked next to the only two cars in the parking lot and headed through the heavy glass door into the diner. Blinking in the dim light, Emma surveyed the brown vinyl booths lining one wall and the Formica-topped wooden bar on the other. Less than half a dozen customers occupied the seats, drinking coffee and finishing off their sandwiches, and nobody even looked up when Emma walked in.

She'd intentionally come in mid-afternoon, between the lunch and dinner crowds, hoping that Polly would be more amenable to talking if she wasn't too busy. Emma spotted an older woman in an apron standing behind the counter and headed in her direction.

The woman placed a menu and a set of napkin-rolled silver-ware on the counter as Emma slid onto a bar stool. "Can I get you some coffee?"

"Yes, please."

A few moments later, the woman slid a heavy white mug onto the counter. "Do you know what you'll be having today?"

"Just the coffee, thanks."

"Okay, well, let me know if you need anything else."

Emma rubbed her sweaty hands on her pants. The whole thing made her nervous—questioning people, tracking down information like she was some kind of detective in a crime novel —and she hardly recognized her life anymore. For a moment, she considered throwing a ten on the counter and walking out of there, but her desperation to understand Noah's past outweighed her trepidation over talking to strangers, so she held out a hand to stop the woman from walking away.

"Actually... are you Polly?"

The woman pulled a rag from her apron pocket and began wiping the counter. "I sure am."

"A man at the library told me that you've been here for a long time and know everyone in town."

The woman cocked her head. "Did he, now?"

Emma wrapped her hands around her coffee mug, feeling the warmth seep through. "I'm looking for some information about a family that lived in town maybe twenty-five or thirty years ago."

"Are you a journalist? You writing a story or something?"

"No, nothing like that. Just trying to track down some information about someone I know."

"I don't generally give out information about folks in town to strangers."

Emma tried to give Polly a trustworthy smile. "I understand that. I'm not really a stranger—at least not to the person I'm asking about. It's my husband. His name is Noah Havern."

Judging by her raised eyebrow, Polly knew that name. "What is it you want to know?"

"He was in a car accident, and now he's in a coma." Emma looked down at the chipped Formica. Saying this part would never get easier. "The doctors aren't sure if he'll pull through."

Polly's face softened now. "I'm so sorry."

"I'm just trying to track down any family that might still live here. I want to let them know about Noah's condition."

"Noah Havern doesn't have any family in this town anymore."

At the firmness in her voice, Emma glanced up. "Are you sure?"

"Yep, I'm sure."

The front door jingled, and two men entered the diner and made their way to the counter.

Polly nodded in their direction. "Dylan, Pete."

"Hey-ya, Polly. How's business?" The man in a brown work shirt and boots slid onto the stool at the other end of the counter. His friend sat down next to him.

Emma waited patiently while Polly poured their coffee and sent their food orders to the cook in the back. Finally, the older woman made her way back to Emma's end of the counter. "I'm sorry, where were we?"

"I was asking if any of Noah's family members still live in town. Do you know anything about his parents?"

Polly cocked her head and gazed across the counter at Emma. "Didn't you say Noah is your husband?"

Emma nodded.

"How do you not know any of this?"

"I—" Emma felt a flush creep up her face, and she stared down into her coffee cup so she wouldn't have to meet the older woman's eyes. It was a great question. One she didn't have an answer for. "It turns out that I don't know as much about my husband as I thought I did." Emma's voice broke at the end. "That's why I'm here. To find out... what I'm missing."

Emma looked up in surprise when Polly reached out and patted her hand. "Well, I can tell you that I'm not surprised that Noah would want to keep his past a secret. From what I remember, it wasn't exactly a fairy tale. Noah had a pretty rough time of it."

"He—did?" Emma stared at the waitress, wide-eyed. She'd obviously figured out by now that Noah hadn't told the truth about growing up in Palo Alto, but she hadn't imagined that he'd made up the part about his childhood being a happy one. "Please," she whispered. "Please, can you tell me what you know?"

Polly glanced at Dylan and Pete at the other end of the counter. "Why don't we sit over here and talk so we can have a little privacy?" She waved at a table by the window. "We don't need the whole town knowing your business, do we?"

Grateful, Emma slid off her stool.

Polly yelled back to the kitchen that she was taking a break, and then she rounded the counter to join Emma at the table. "It's not that small of a town, but I knew Noah a little bit because he was a smart kid and he competed with my daughter for the top spot in the senior class. Lucky for him, he earned that spot and got himself out of this town. Went off to college and, judging from that nice car you've got parked outside, it looks like maybe he made something of himself. There was nothing and nobody worth it to come back for." Polly's eyebrows knit together. "Noah really didn't tell you any of this?"

Emma shook her head. "Can you tell me about his parents? Where are they now?"

Polly hesitated. "It was a long time ago, and I didn't know the family well. But if I remember correctly, Delia Havern—Noah's mother—she died of breast cancer." Polly bowed her head. "Terrible tragedy. She was so young."

Emma's breath caught. She didn't know what she'd been expecting, but it wasn't this.

Polly nodded. "That was a couple of years after I opened this place, so maybe close to thirty-five years ago. I didn't know Delia, but I remember people talking about it, with her being so young and all." She gazed out across the diner, shaking her head.

If Noah's mother had died over three decades ago, Noah would have been a little boy. Did Noah remember his mother passing? And what kind of trauma had that caused him?

But even if it was painful to talk about his mother, why not just tell Emma? There was nothing shameful about breast cancer. Why would he make up a story about her dying in a fire?

"What about Noah's father?" Emma asked. Noah had been the valedictorian of his class. After his mother's death, his father must have provided a stable environment, or Noah never would have had that kind of academic success. "Did he leave town, too?"

And if so, where is he now?

"Oh, he left town alright. A few years later, Gary Havern ended up in prison."

Emma slowly sank back into her chair. "Prison." Emma repeated, her voice measured. "Noah's dad went to prison." Of course he had. It wasn't even a question anymore. The only thing that would surprise her was if she found out Noah had told her the truth about something.

"Yeah, it was a real shame. Again, I didn't know him, but I heard he got caught up with the wrong crowd. People will do anything when they're desperate for money."

Emma tried to imagine it. Noah's mother dead, his father in prison. And Noah a child, maybe only a couple of years older than Luna. What had happened to him after that? "Did he have grandparents who took him in?"

Polly face twisted as she tried to recall. "You know, it was a long time ago and my memory isn't what it used to be. But I believe Noah didn't have any family members to take him. When his dad was convicted and sent away, Noah ended up in foster care."

23

It had been a week since the last rain, and dust and gravel kicked up behind the car tires, drifting across the farmers' corn-fields. Emma had turned off the two-lane highway about five miles back, onto a narrower road that wound past cow pastures and sprawling old barns with peeling paint and sagging door-frames. Keeping one hand on the wheel, Emma held up the directions Polly had scrawled on a napkin.

About 1500 feet past the rusted-out bus, make a right at the double wide.

Up ahead, Emma spotted the bus that must have been parked on the side of the road two decades ago. The tires were long gone, the door torn off, and a tree grew out from the wind-shield. Around the next bend appeared a pale blue trailer with a makeshift front porch set back off the road, next to a turn-off on the right. Though it was completely unnecessary—she'd only passed about two cars in the last ten minutes—Emma flipped on her turn signal as she steered the car onto a smaller, unpaved lane that disappeared into the woods.

Emma eyed the road ahead—it was really more of a fire lane than a road, actually, with two bare lines of tire tracks and weeds growing in between. For a moment, her foot lifted from the gas pedal. This was truly the middle of nowhere. Her cell phone reception had vanished when she'd turned off Little Lake Road, and nobody but Polly knew she was out here, looking for Noah's former foster home. She really should have texted Alicia before she left the diner, but where would she have said she was going? *Past the rusted-out bus and right at the double wide to find a man named John?*

Alicia would have absolutely told her to turn around. But Emma had come this far, and she needed to finish this. She pressed her foot back onto the gas, yanking the steering wheel to the left and then the right as she swerved to avoid potholes. The lane took a turn down a steep hill, and the trees formed a canopy overhead, dimming the sunlight to almost dusk.

Emma's nerves kicked in again, and she would have turned around if the road had been wider. Another half a mile ahead, her car finally broke through the trees and into a clearing.

Emma slammed on the breaks, eyes widening as she took in the crumbling wooden structure with a sagging front porch, overflowing garage full of cars in various states of repair and, finally, the algae-coated pond with an oil barrel floating in the middle.

There had to be a mistake. Emma scanned Polly's directions.

There's only one house. When you've found it, you've found John Picken.

Surely, Polly didn't mean *this* house, did she? Maybe Emma should have taken a left and not a right at the double wide. There was no way that Noah had grown up here. There was no way anyone even lived here anymore.

Emma was about to put the car into reverse and head back into town when she spotted movement by the garage. Her heart clattered as a man appeared from between a truck up on blocks and a Dodge Dart missing its hood. He wore a dirty pair of coveralls, heavy boots, and a trucker hat with the word *Valvoline* across the front. By the gray in his long beard and the stooped way he walked, Emma would have guessed he was at least seventy.

This had to be John Picken.

Cautiously, Emma opened her car door and stood up, keeping the keys in the ignition and one foot on the floormat in case she needed to dive back inside and peel off.

"I don't fix European cars." The man wiped his oil-stained hands on a rag that didn't look much cleaner.

"Excuse me?"

"Your car." He hitched his chin in her direction. "Can't fix it."

"Oh." Emma shook her head. "I'm not here for car repair."

"Well, then." The man turned to head back into the garage. "Get the hell off my property."

"Wait. Please." Emma called to him. "Are you John Picken?"

"Maybe." He swung back around. "Who's asking?"

"My name is Emma. Emma Havern." She emphasized her last name, hoping to see a spark of recognition.

But the man just stared blankly. "So?"

Maybe this wasn't John Picken after all. Polly had said Noah had been a foster child with the Pickens for years. Even if it was a long time ago, surely, John would remember him.

"I think my husband Noah—Havern—used to live here. He used to be your foster son."

The man crossed his arms across his barrel chest. "I didn't have any foster kids."

"Oh, I'm so sorry." Emma's insides flooded with relief. This definitely wasn't the place then. "I must have been mistaken."

The man shrugged. "My wife used to take in those fosters.

But they sure weren't mine. I didn't bother with them unless they got in my way." He waved his arm as if he were back-handing an imaginary person.

Emma's shoulders tensed. Oh, God. This *was* the place. Had this man swung at Noah like that? She studied the prop-erty again, noticing all sorts of things she'd missed the first time: decades of old garbage—bottles and cans and old car parts—piled up next to the garage; broken, boarded-up windows on the house; an old mobile home that didn't look much better than the bus down the road, parked in the dirt. And then there was the wet, swampy smell that permeated everything.

Surely it hadn't been like this when Noah lived here. Surely social services wouldn't have allowed this, even decades ago. But...

Emma turned her gaze to John Picken. Even if this place had been in better repair once, it seemed unlikely that John had been much improved in his younger days. Maybe Mrs. Picken was a nicer person, though. It sounded to Emma like she'd taken in more than just Noah. "I heard from the woman at the diner in town that your wife died a few years ago. I'm so sorry."

"What are you sorry for?" John sneered. "You didn't know her, did you?"

"I—no." Emma blinked. "But I'm sure it was difficult for you."

"It wasn't difficult. She was a miserable old witch."

Emma blinked at that. Even if Mrs. Picken had been a miserable old witch—and Emma was starting to believe she might have been—people usually didn't speak ill of the dead like that. "She must have had a good heart, though." Emma could hear the desperation in her voice. She needed to believe it more than she actually did. "She took in all those kids, after all."

John spit in the dirt. "The state paid three-, four hundred bucks a month, per kid. That's why she took them in. Her heart didn't have nothin' to do with it, lady."

Oh, God. Poor Noah. This was awful. A nightmare. And if she was horrified after being here for five minutes, what had it been like for Noah to end up here for years?

"What did you say your husband's name was?" John asked.

"Noah Havern." Emma could hear the wobble in her voice as she found herself hoping that John didn't remember him. That Noah had been able to stay off this guy's radar.

"Yeah, I remember him. The smart one." He cracked his knuckles. "Too smart for his own good."

Emma didn't want to know what that meant.

"He and those other two kids were always together. Like three musketeers or some shit. There was that other kid who ended up in prison, just like his father. I don't remember much about him. And then what was the blond girl's name—Cora or something?"

Emma gasped.

Cora or something.

Oh my God.

Her vision blurred and she started swaying.

No. I am not going to faint in John Picken's yard.

She reached to grip the car door and hold herself upright while she battled to pull more air in her lungs.

John had to be talking about Coral. He *had* to be.

Emma took another gasping breath. Noah had grown up in foster care with Coral Butler. They'd been inseparable, apparently. And, years later, he'd uprooted his family and moved them hundreds of miles away so he could live within an hour of her. He'd kept her hidden away and fathered a child with her.

But why?

Why marry Emma in the first place, why go through this whole charade, and spend decades lying about who he was? If he was in love with Coral that whole time, why not just be with Coral?

"So, what do you want with me?"

Emma blinked as John's voice dragged her back to the rundown clearing in the woods. "What?"

"Why. Are. You. Here?" John spoke slowly, deliberately. Threateningly.

"I—" She'd planned to let John know that Noah was in the hospital and to see if he wanted to come and visit. But it was clear that John would have no interest in that. And she had no interest in ever seeing John again. "No reason. I am here for no reason at all."

And before John could react, she got in her car, yanked the steering wheel to the right and did the fastest U-turn of her life out of there.

She drove as quickly as the potholes would allow back through the woods, made a left at the double wide, and gunned it onto the paved road leading back to town. Finally, when Emma was a couple of miles away, she pulled the car over and leaned her head against the steering wheel.

And then, as she sat there with her hands shaking and her mind whirling, it came to Emma. Why Noah had married her and not Coral. Why he'd gone to all this effort to fake his entire life, to marry someone he'd clearly never cared for, when he could have spent his life with the woman he loved.

Because there was one part of Emma that Noah did care for. He cared for it very much.

Her family's money.

24

EIGHT YEARS AGO

Emma hung up the phone in a daze and stared out the kitchen window, across the garden to her pottery studio. She was at a loss for what to think about the call she'd just had.

"Who were you talking to?" Noah's voice cut into her thoughts as he walked into the kitchen and pulled open the fridge. "Was that Alicia?"

"No..." Emma pressed her hands to her temples. "It was my father..."

Noah raised an eyebrow. He knew Emma didn't talk to her father much, especially since her mother had passed away. And usually when she did, it was a version of the same conversation —all about him and his business and latest golf game. He asked about Maya on occasion, but never about Emma. He never wanted to hear about her latest art show, or what she was working on; didn't care about the profile they'd written about her in the Sunday arts section of the *Chicago Times*.

Her father had never approved of her art, and he'd always been disappointed that she hadn't gone into the family business. He was going to leave his money to a distant cousin, he'd always told her. One who hadn't disappointed and embarrassed him.

"He's decided to write me back into his will."

Noah closed the refrigerator door and turned to look at her. "Well, that's good news."

Emma's brow furrowed. "Is it?"

"*Isn't* it?" Noah shrugged. "I mean, he can't take it with him. Who else is he going to leave it to?"

"I don't know. I don't care. He told me years ago he was going to leave it to a cousin." Emma waved a dismissive hand. "He could leave it to charity, I guess."

"So, what did you say?" Noah took a few tentative steps toward the kitchen counter and slid onto a stool across from her.

"I told him not to."

Noah opened his mouth and then closed it again, as if he wanted to say something, but worried maybe he shouldn't.

"What?" she demanded. "What were you going to say?"

"Just—" Noah paused, and then, "Emma, are you sure?"

Emma looked at Noah sideways. "I don't want him using his money to manipulate me. I wanted to study art and be a teacher. He cut me off. Why does he want to write me back into his will now?"

But Emma knew why. Her mother had passed, her father was getting older and thinking about what to do with his finances. A little over a decade ago, Emma was that poor art student who'd embarrassed him. Now she was married to a man her father respected, one who had even gotten a job at his friend's company. She lived in a nice house in a community similar to where she'd grown up. She might not have gone into the family business, but otherwise, her life had turned out an awful lot like her father had wanted it to.

"Maybe if, just once, he'd ask about me and my artwork. Maybe if, just once, he'd show some interest. But he doesn't care about me. All he cares is that he doesn't have to be ashamed to talk about me to his friends at the country club. That I'm acceptable to him again. No thanks. We're doing fine on our own."

Noah squinted across the counter at her, and she could have sworn there was a hint of disapproval in his expression. "What about Maya?" he finally asked.

"What about her?" Emma demanded.

"That money will go to Maya someday."

Emma gazed around their beautiful, comfortable kitchen. On the island sat a bowl of fruit and a plate of Maya's favorite banana muffins. They'd baked them together that morning and the whole house still smelled amazing. A breeze outside picked up, rustling the curtains Emma had sewn out of some pretty linen fabric she'd found in a thrift store. The dishes and cups in the cabinets were all her own designs: she'd made them in pale, soothing blues and mint-greens, two of her favorite colors. It wasn't like they were struggling. By any standards, they were more than comfortable. Noah had moved up in his company, and Emma earned a good living with her pottery. What more did they need than this?

"Maya doesn't need to be rich." Emma argued. "We're saving enough for her to go to college, so she won't have to worry about student debt. Anything else, she can get a job and work for, like we did."

"But what if she wants to buy a house? What if—I don't know... she wants to travel, or start a foundation, or—" Noah shrugged. "Having a nest egg will give her the security to follow her dreams."

Emma shot him an incredulous look. "Plenty of people follow their dreams without a nest egg. *We* did. And we're better off for it."

Noah sighed and shifted in his seat. "Well, it's your family. I'll leave it to you to navigate."

But Emma could tell he disapproved. It was clear he thought she should take the money and, for some reason she couldn't quite articulate, it bothered her. "If it makes you feel any better, I told my dad I don't want his money, but he said he's leaving it to me anyway."

She peeked across the kitchen to gauge Noah's reaction.

He *did* look like he felt a little bit better about that.

25

"Maya, don't slam the door," Emma whisper-yelled as she came into the living room. "I finally got Luna to sleep." It had taken about six books to even get the girl to calm down, and then another three until she grew sleepy enough to agree to lay in the crib.

When Alicia had promised Luna ice cream, Emma should have told her not to give it to her after 5 p.m.

"Is it true?" Maya demanded, still standing in the entry way in her coat.

Emma stopped short at the quiver in her daughter's voice. "Is what true?"

"Is it true about Dad?"

Emma's heart stuttered. "What—what have you heard?"

"A bunch of kids at school are saying that Dad had an affair with the woman who was in the car with him, and that Luna is his love child. Is it true?"

Emma's mouth dropped open. "Where would they even come up with that?" She tried to keep her voice even, but she could hear it shaking.

"I don't know. But a girl started the rumor and now everyone is talking about it."

Oh my God, who told her?

"Maya, why don't you come in and sit down, and then we can talk more." Emma knew she was stalling, but she needed a minute to think.

"I don't want to sit. Next, you'll be telling me to calm down."

Emma held up a hand. "I'm not telling you to calm down. I just want to have a conversation about it." Oh, God, she was blowing this, wasn't she? Damn whoever started this rumor. *And how did they find out?*

Emma knew that she couldn't keep Noah's secrets forever. If Luna really was Maya's sister, she deserved to know. But Emma had thought there would be time to make a plan, to figure out the gentlest way to break it to her. And definitely only after they got the tests back and had the DNA confirmed.

"It's true, isn't it?"

"I—" Emma sighed. "I don't know for sure."

"*For sure?*" Maya's tears spilled over. "Oh my God. So, you suspected? And you didn't say anything?"

Emma nodded.

"How could you keep this from me?" Maya screamed at the top of her lungs.

"*Maya*," Emma scolded. But it was too late. A wail came from the direction of Luna's room. Emma closed her eyes. She was so tired she could sleep for a decade.

"This is so messed up. I hate you! And I hate Dad, too." Maya turned and ran up the stairs. A moment later, her bedroom door went crashing into its frame. Luna cried louder. Emma sighed and headed in the little girl's direction.

Half an hour and five books later, Emma finally left a sleeping Luna in her crib and limped out of her room. She eyed her bedroom door at the end of the hall, picturing her bed waiting there for her. All she wanted to do was just lay down for a minute. Just one minute. And then she could go deal with this latest crisis.

But she couldn't. Because while Maya's reaction had been a little extra-dramatic, she wasn't wrong. This situation *was* messed up. And Maya had gotten caught in the middle of it. So, instead of heading for her own bedroom, Emma shuffled over to Maya's and gently knocked on the door.

"Maya, can I come in?"

"Go away," came the tearful reply.

"Please? I really think we should talk about this." Emma pressed her ear to the door, and for a moment, there was silence. Then in the next moment, the lock clicked, and the door was flung open.

"Fine." Maya turned her back to Emma and walked to her bed. "Talk." She dove face-first onto the mattress and then grabbed her pillow, pulling it over her head.

Emma made her way into the room, stepping over the land-mines of discarded clothes and books scattered across Maya's floor. When she got to the bed, she perched on the edge next to where Maya still lay buried. "Maya." Emma tugged at the pillow. "Honey, sit up so we can talk for real."

Maya sighed, rolling onto her back, and when she tossed the pillow aside, Emma's heart squeezed. Her daughter's face was red and puffy, and her cheeks still wet from crying. Maya looked so much like she had when she was a little girl and would come home sobbing after she fell and scraped her knee. But Maya wasn't a little girl, and these weren't just cuts Emma could cover with a Band-Aid. These were real, adult problems, and Maya wasn't that many years away from adulthood. She deserved to know the truth.

"The thing is, I didn't tell you about Luna because I don't know."

"But you suspect."

"Yes. I do."

"Did you know Dad was having an affair with Luna's mom?"

"No." Emma hesitated. "I still don't know for sure. I don't know anything for sure."

"So how do we find out?"

"Well, the nurses in the hospital gave both Dad and Luna DNA tests. The results take about a week to ten days. So, we should hear something soon." Emma reached over to smooth Maya's hair off her forehead. "Maya, I promise you that I would have told you Luna is your sister the minute I knew for sure. But there wasn't anything to tell yet. I don't even know who could have started this rumor."

"Jessica Bigby. She posted it online."

Emma's eyebrows shot up. "Connie Bigby's daughter?" *Damn it.* The neighborhood gossip who'd asked all those questions when they ran into her the other night. Emma had seen the gleam in her eye. Of course she'd started a rumor about Noah and Luna. She'd probably reveled in calling all her friends the minute Emma had walked away.

"Yeah."

"Ugh, I hate that horrible woman," Emma said, and then glanced at Maya. She realized she wasn't being a very good example. "Uh, sorry. I shouldn't say that."

"It's okay. Her daughter is just as horrible. They're a horrible family," Maya said with a watery laugh. And then her face turned serious. "So, if Dad really is Luna's father, does that mean she'll live with us forever?"

Emma looked down at her hands. She wished more than anything she had the answers. But conversations like these made her feel more lost than ever. "I don't know. There's a lot we still need to work out. Luna's mother named Dad as Luna's guardian in her will. But Dad is still in a coma."

"Would you *want* Luna to live with us forever?"

"I—" Emma hesitated. These were the sort of adult decisions a sixteen-year-old who still saw the world in black and white couldn't completely grasp. Even if Emma wanted Luna to live with them, it didn't mean it was the right decision for Luna, or for her.

"Well, I would want her to." Maya crossed her arms over her chest, and Emma envied her daughter's ability to feel certain about anything. "She might be my sister. And if Dad doesn't make it, then Luna would be like a little piece of himself that Dad left behind."

Emma's throat burned with emotion. Maybe, a moment ago, she'd been wrong to think her daughter was too young to understand the nuance of this situation. Maya was articulating the most painful truth with a maturity and grace far beyond her years. Emma gave Maya a sad smile. "That's a lovely way to think about it."

"But—" Maya sat up abruptly. "What if Luna *isn't* Dad's kid?"

"It's a possibility." Anything was a possibility these days. And Emma didn't want Maya to get her hopes up that Luna would be staying with them forever.

"So, if Luna isn't Dad's kid, and Dad doesn't wake up, will they take her away from us?"

Emma was surprised by the hollow feeling that thought left in her stomach. She reached out to put a gentle hand on Maya's arm. "Well, there could be some other family who might come forward and want to take custody. Luna's real dad, or maybe a grandmother or something."

"But her mom left Luna to us."

"She left her to Dad." Emma paused, shaking her head. "No, in fact, she didn't leave her to anyone. Luna is a child. Coral's will is a statement of her wishes for Luna's guardianship, but a judge ultimately decides what's best for her. And that could be another family member."

"But what if there's no family member?" Maya's voice was rising again. "What if she's not Dad's kid, and nobody else wants her? Do we just ship her off to foster care?"

Emma closed her eyes and was hit with a wave of memories from earlier that day. The oppressive stench of the rotting pond, the piles of garbage, the broken windows. And John Picken curling his dirty hand into a fist and cracking his knuckles. That was Noah's experience of foster care.

Times would be better now. They must be. Kate was an amazing social worker and she'd make sure Luna ended up someplace safe, wouldn't she?

But even Kate had admitted that the system was over-crowded, and how could Emma stand by and risk any child ending up in a place like where Noah had grown up? Let alone sweet Luna? Emma pictured the little girl sleeping in the bed down the hall, her little body curled around her elephant, her favorite train clutched in her hand. Luna's eyelashes looked so long fanned out against her pink cheeks, still flushed from the endless energy she'd expended all day. She was so innocent, so trusting, so *good*. How long would it take for someone like John Picken and his miserable witch of a wife to steal that away from her?

Emma shook her head. She could never, ever let that happen. But did that mean she was willing to take on the responsibility of raising a toddler all over again? She gazed across the bedsheets at her daughter. Surprisingly, caring for Luna hadn't been that difficult, in part because of Maya. The teenager had really stepped up and helped out in a way that Emma never would have predicted. Emma's heart expanded as she reflected on the fact that her daughter was turning into a compassionate and responsible young woman. It had been so lovely to see her and little Luna together these past days. Maya had been so sweet with Luna, so protective, even when so much of her own world was falling apart.

"Maya, let's see what the tests say, okay? And focus on getting Dad to wake up. That's the best thing we can do for Luna right now." Emma managed a strained smile. "Are you going back to the hospital to see him tomorrow? The doctor said your singing boosted the nurses' morale."

Maya grinned at that. She'd always loved an appreciative audience. "I'll tell Sam and Fatima. We've been working on a three-part harmony of 'Seasons of Love', from *Rent*."

"And what are we going to do about this Jessica girl? The one spreading rumors? Do you want me to call the principal? Surely, they have rules about social media and bullying."

"God, no." Maya reared back in horror. "Please don't call the principal. That would make things so, so much worse." She hesitated, pulling her pillow to her chest. "Besides, it might be true what Jessica is saying. Luna might really be my sister." Her mouth curved into a hopeful smile.

"Let's take it one day at a time, okay?" Emma reached over to pull her daughter into a hug, and for once, Maya gave her a squeeze in return. Emma stood up and headed back to the door. "I'll let you get to your homework."

"Mom?" Maya's voice called, just as Emma was about to pull the door shut behind her.

She popped her head back in the room. "Yes?"

"Is this why you kicked Dad out? Because you thought he was having an affair?"

Emma shook her head. "No. I didn't know anything about Coral at the time." She hesitated, and finally settled on, "Marriage is complicated. Someday, you'll understand that."

"If he did have an affair with Coral, do you think you can forgive him and let him come home?"

Again, Emma envied her daughter's ability to see the world in such simple terms. *Noah had made a mistake, and he could be forgiven.* Maya couldn't imagine all the layers beneath that one transgression. The lies, the betrayal, the way

Noah had used Emma so callously. "One day at a time, okay?"

Back downstairs, Emma's phone was ringing with Alicia's name lit up on the screen. When she'd picked up Luna from Alicia's house, Emma had given her friend a brief rundown of what she'd learned that day in Millersville, but it had been approaching Luna's bedtime, so they'd agreed to talk later that night.

"So, I called a friend of mine who works in law enforcement," Alicia began, without even saying hello. "And asked him to look into Noah's father, Gary."

Emma's eyes widened. "Wow, you work fast."

"Well, Noah always told everyone his parents were dead, right? And Polly at the diner said Noah's mother died of cancer."

"Polly at the diner shared more about Noah's life in twenty minutes than Noah shared in twenty years," Emma said bitterly.

"Oh, honey." Alicia's voice softened. "This has been so awful for you."

"No, no." Emma shrugged her off. "I can't wallow in it anymore. I need to do something. Tell me what your friend said."

"Okay." Alicia cleared her throat. "Polly told you Noah's father went to prison. So, I got to thinking... he could still be alive."

Emma sank down on the couch. "I hadn't thought of that."

"My friend was able to look into old prison records for the federal penitentiary, and it turns out that Noah's father was incarcerated for seventeen years."

Emma pressed against the back of the couch. *Seventeen years. For what?*

"Driver's license records show that he's been living in a trailer park on Little Lake Road, just outside of Millersville, since he got out about two decades ago."

Little Lake Road. Emma was becoming more familiar with Millersville than she ever would have imagined. "I was probably right near there today, on my drive to John Picken's."

"I think you should go back."

Should I? The questions about Noah piled up. Noah had probably been about six or seven when Gary had gone to prison. Had they talked since then? Had Noah ever seen his father again? And if Emma tracked the man down, what would be the point of it? What could she hope to learn?

The truth.

Emma could finally learn the whole truth about Noah's past. Where he came from, what had really happened to him, and how he'd turned into a person who was capable of lying to her at every turn. Forgiving him was too much to ask of anyone. But maybe, at least, Emma could understand him.

Emma sat up and grabbed a pen and note pad from the coffee table drawer. "What's the address? I've started this, and I'm going to finish it."

26

Two days later, Luna was back with Alicia, who'd been given strict instructions not to feed the child ice cream after 5 p.m. And Emma was back on Little Lake Road, headed out of downtown Millersville. She was using GPS this time, so there was no *turn at the rusty farm equipment* type of directions to follow.

The trailer park was a short turn off the two-lane road, so it was easy to spot. Emma had probably passed by there the other day, on her way out to John Picken's house, but at the time, there hadn't been any reason to even glance over this way. Now, though, Emma parked in a small lot next to a bank of mailboxes and stepped out of her car to study the neat rows of single-wides laid out on a grid of gravel roads that made up the Pine Hollow Trailer Park.

"Can I help you?" An older woman approached pushing two babies—probably her grandchildren—in a stroller. "Are you looking for someone?" Her voice held a note of wariness that made Emma suspect that people in the trailer park kept an eye out for strangers sniffing around.

"Yes, I'm looking for Gary Havern."

The woman studied her for a moment, her eyes sweeping

from Emma's dark gray flats up to her cashmere cardigan. Then her eyes shifted to Emma's late-model Audi. "What business do you have with Gary Havern?"

"I—" Emma was a little surprised to be asked so directly. People in her world usually talked around things without ever coming right out and saying what they meant. She thought about Connie Bigby's sneaky, subtle interrogation about Luna's parentage. Maybe this woman's directness wasn't such a bad thing. "Gary is my father-in-law."

The woman's eyebrows shot northward. "Huh. Wasn't aware that Gary had any kids."

"Yes. He does." *Grandkids, too,* Emma thought, and then realized she'd automatically included Luna. "Do you know where he lives?"

"You'll find him one block over and two doors down. His is on the right." The woman gestured down one of the gravel roads. "Beige trailer with dark brown shutters. He's usually on the porch this time of day."

"Thanks. I appreciate it." Emma nodded and headed in the direction the woman had indicated. The trailers varied in color and the types of foliage planted around them, but all of them were well-kept, with wooden porches added on to the fronts.

It seemed that Gary wasn't the only resident who liked to sit out this time of day, because Emma lifted a hand to wave at a number of people as she walked. Nobody else questioned her purpose there, but she could feel their eyes following her as she continued on her way.

A few more doors down, Emma came to a beige trailer with brown shutters and a porch painted to match. Several feet above her, a man sat in a plastic chair with a cup of coffee in one hand and a newspaper held up in front of him.

"Hello?" Emma called.

The man flipped the top half of the newspaper down so he could peer down at her through thick glasses.

"Yes?"

She didn't know what she'd been expecting—maybe an older version of Noah. But it was hard to tell if this man and her husband were related or not. The man had Noah's height and slim build, but his hair was completely gray and mostly receded, and his face was covered in a thick beard.

"Um. Hi. I'm looking for Gary Havern."

"Well, you found him."

Suddenly nervous, Emma shoved her hands in her pockets to have something do with them. "Hi," she murmured breathlessly.

"And you are—?" The man lowered his newspaper to his lap.

"I'm Emma." She hesitated, and then, "Emma... Havern."

Gary's eyebrows rose and, almost in slow motion, he lowered his cup of coffee to the table in front of him. "You're Noah's wife."

Emma hadn't been expecting that. "How did you know?"

"Well." He cocked an eyebrow. "Kids these days have something called *the Google*." He gave her a wry smile. "You can find out anything about anyone."

Not anything! Emma wanted to assert, thinking about all the things she hadn't known about Noah. Like this man in front of her, for example. But instead, she asked, "So, you checked up on Noah?"

"Every now and again, yep." He shook his head. "Never thought I'd see him or any of his family, though. What could possibly bring you here?"

"Well." Emma looked down at her shoes and kicked at a piece of gravel. "I wanted to let you know that Noah—he was in a car accident last week. And now he's in a coma. The doctors aren't sure if he'll recover."

Gary's eyes widened, and he flopped backwards, shrinking

into the chair. "I—well. I had no idea." He gave his head a shake as if he were trying to knock this news out of it. "I... My goodness... that's... well, that's—" Gary dropped his head in his hands.

Emma gave him a moment to process this, not sure what else to do.

Finally, Gary lifted his head and she saw tears there. "I guess what I'm trying to say is that it's really awful," Gary finally managed. He swiped at one eye with the back of his hand.

"Are you alright?" Emma hesitated for a moment, and then decided to climb up on the porch and perch on the edge of the chair across from him. She reached out a comforting hand and then yanked it back, folding it in her lap instead.

Gary gave a humorless laugh and shook his head. "Folks would argue that I don't have the right to care about Noah, and they'd be right. But I do. I always did. And I always will." He shrugged and then used the hem of his flannel shirt to wipe his eyes.

Emma wasn't quite sure what to say to that. She didn't know anything about his past, or how he'd ended up here. How *Noah* had ended up here. "Mr. Havern—"

"Call me Gary."

"Gary." Emma cleared her throat. "The truth is that Noah had always been very private about his childhood. To be honest... I don't know a whole lot about how you ended up in prison, or how Noah ended up in foster care."

Gary gave a slow, sad shake of his head. "I can't say I blame Noah for not wanting to talk about it."

"But... he's in a coma. And he has a daughter who could lose her father without knowing anything about his past." Emma didn't mention that Noah might have two daughters. That was a conversation for another day. "She's your grandchild. I was hoping..." Emma trailed off.

Gary gave her a long look. "What is it that you want to know?"

"Well..." Emma said. "I guess I want to know what happened? How did you end up going to prison and leaving Noah alone?"

Gary took a heavy breath, held it for a minute, and then blew it out slowly. "I haven't talked about this in decades."

"Please?" Emma could hear a hint of desperation in her voice. She'd come this far, and the truth was so close. There was a time in her life when she wouldn't have dreamed of asking a near-stranger such personal questions. But these past few weeks had changed her, and she was no longer willing to tiptoe around.

And, at the end of the day, Gary wasn't a stranger. He was Noah's father.

Gary hesitated for another moment, and then he nodded. "Things were fine until my wife got sick."

"I heard about that. I'm so sorry," Emma murmured.

Gary nodded his thanks. "We weren't rich by any means, but we got by, and we were happy. I worked as a day laborer for a construction company, and they didn't offer health insurance or anything like that. And after my wife died, the bills started piling up."

Emma remembered back to when Polly told her about Noah's father going to prison. *People will do anything when they're desperate for money,* she'd said.

"My boss at the construction company knew what kind of a mess I was in, and he offered me some jobs on the side. Transporting packages from point A to point B, that sort of thing. I didn't know what was in the packages, and I didn't ask." Gary met Emma's eyes. "I knew my boss was in with some rough people, but I figured none of it would touch me. And the money really helped us to stay above water."

"But you were wrong about it not touching you?"

Gary flinched, and his face seemed to age ten years. "One night I was hired to drop off a car in the Upper Peninsula. I was just supposed to leave it in a deserted parking lot and take the bus home." He hesitated, picking up his coffee cup and then setting it down without taking a sip. "But it turned out the Feds had been tracking my boss and his associates for a while, and I got stuck in the middle of it."

"You got caught."

"Yeah." Gary looked away. "I got caught alright. When I got to the parking lot, they were waiting for me. They searched the car and found about fifty kilos of cocaine. I went to prison for twenty years for drug trafficking. Got out in seventeen for good behavior."

Emma was momentarily speechless. "Why... why didn't you turn your boss in? You were just the delivery guy. Surely, they would have wanted your testimony about who was really behind the business."

Gary nodded. "Sure, they did. But my boss had connections, and they threatened my family. So, I kept quiet."

"And Noah went to foster care."

Gary turned in his chair to face Emma. "Not a day goes by that I don't regret what I did. That I don't wish I could go back and change things. But I told myself that at least I could take solace in the fact that Noah made it. That he got out of this town and made a life for himself. Went to college. Met a pretty girl and got married." He gave Emma a sad smile. "At least I could take solace in the fact that he turned out to be such a better man than me."

Emma released a shaky breath. How could she possibly tell this poor man the truth? That his son had turned out to be a liar and a fraud? Maybe Gary had made bad choices, but at least he'd had good intentions. "Did you ever reach out to Noah? After you got out of prison?"

"Once."

Emma sat up in her chair. "You did? When?"

"I came to the church on your wedding day."

"On our..." Emma gazed out at the mobile home across the road. Noah's father was at their wedding? How was it possible? There were three hundred people there, but surely someone would have noticed a complete stranger—

And then it came to her.

"You were across the street!"

Gary nodded slowly.

"You were the man Noah went over and talked to." She could still picture it. Noah's hunched shoulders and straight back. His arm waving, as if to tell that man to go away. "You argued."

"I didn't expect anyone to see me. I'd read your wedding announcement in the *Times*, and I—" Gary hung his head. "I just wanted to see him. Just one time. So, I took the bus all the way to Boston, and I stood there on the sidewalk. Just for a glimpse. I didn't think Noah would notice me, or recognize me if he did." He turned to Emma with a wistful expression. "You sure looked beautiful that day. And Noah—well, Noah looked like he thought you hung the moon and the stars. You two reminded me of me and Delia on our wedding day."

"You even wore a suit." Emma could still picture it. The lapels were worn, and his shoes were scuffed, but he'd dressed up for their wedding. More than anything, Emma wished she'd jumped out of the limo and followed Noah across the street. What if she'd met Gary all those years ago? Would Noah's secrets have come out then? Would she have been able to forgive him and move past it?

Emma gave a slight shake of her head. Not if it turned out that Noah never loved her. That he was using her for her parents' money. She also remembered the other conversation on their wedding day. The one where Noah wanted to network with her dad's friends to get a good job. No, if all of this had come to light years ago, she never would have stayed with Noah, and then they wouldn't have had Maya.

There was no use in rehashing the past.

"Noah told you to go away, didn't he? He didn't want to see you—?"

"He sure didn't, and who could blame him? By then, almost two decades had gone by, and I very nearly ruined his life. Why would he want me back in it?" His pain was so real, Emma could feel it coming off him in waves. Gary's eyes welled up again, and he swiped at them, shaking his head. "God, look at me. You're the one who should be crying, not me. You're the one whose husband is in a coma."

"Well, I've had a little more time to process it."

"I really appreciate you coming to let me know. What made you do it? Lord knows you didn't have to."

"You're Noah's father. And you're Maya's grandfather." Again, her thoughts drifted to Luna. The DNA tests would reveal whether Gary was Luna's grandfather soon enough.

Gary cocked his head, a sad smile tugging at his lips. "Maya. That's your daughter's name?"

Emma nodded.

"It's beautiful. I bet she's a lovely girl, and I bet you and Noah are wonderful parents."

Emma thought of Maya holding Luna's hand as the toddler took an unsteady step off the curb. "She is a lovely girl. I'm really proud of her."

Gary grabbed the arms of the chair and pulled himself to his feet. "Would you mind waiting here a minute while I run inside?"

"Sure." Maybe he needed to visit the bathroom. Or it could be that he just needed a moment to get ahold of himself. Her appearance had to have been a shock to him after all these years.

While she waited for Gary to return, Emma gazed off down

the road and spotted the older woman with the stroller headed in her direction. Emma raised her hand in a wave.

"I see you found him," the woman said, stopping in front of Gary's porch. She pushed the stroller back and forth in a rhythmic motion so the babies wouldn't wake up.

"I did." Emma held up a hand against the glare of the sun. "Thanks again for your help."

"Gary is a real nice guy." In contrast to the woman's words, Emma detected a hard edge to her voice. "He's always helping out people in the community. Doing repairs or driving the elderly people to doctor's appointments."

"That's really nice of him," Emma murmured, wondering where the woman was going with this.

The woman pushed the stroller forward and then pulled it backward again. "We all know he's been to prison, and we don't care about any of that. So, if that's why you and your family have been staying away, I just thought you should know the whole community thinks he's a good person."

Emma gave a slow nod. She didn't know this woman at all, but it *was* reassuring to hear that Gary was well-regarded and people around here cared about him. It meant something that this woman had gone out of her way to stick up for him. "Thanks for letting me know."

The woman gave a wave and then continued down the road with her stroller.

A moment later, Gary appeared in the doorway of the trailer clutching a white envelope. "Sorry about that." He made his way back to his chair and sat down.

"No problem." Emma gazed at the object in his hand.

Gary cleared his throat and fumbled with the flap on the envelope. "I know it's a lot to ask, but I wondered if maybe I could give you this." With shaking hands, he pulled out an old photograph and held it out to Emma. "It's for Maya. I thought she might like to have it."

Eyes wide, Emma took the photograph and turned it over in her hands. "Oh."

She stared down at a yellowing photograph of a young woman that looked like it had been taken in the 1970s. The woman had long, pin-straight hair and wore a short black skirt and maroon turtleneck. She gazed into the camera with a smile that looked familiar to Emma.

Emma looked from the photograph to Gary and then back again. "This is Delia, isn't it? This is Noah's mother?"

Gary nodded. "That was taken before we married." His eyes softened as he stared at the picture in Emma's hands. "I thought she was the most beautiful woman on Earth." He tilted his head. "Still do."

"I can see the resemblance to Noah." Emma traced a finger across the woman's face. And maybe Maya, too." *And Luna.* Luna had those same dark eyes.

"I wonder if you'd keep that. Noah might despise me, but he sure loved his mama. And Lord, did she love him back." Gary wiped his eyes again.

Emma felt her own eyes well up. "I know Maya will love to see her grandmother." She carefully tucked the photo back into the envelope Gary had given her and slid it into her purse. What an absolute tragedy this whole situation had turned out to be.

"Thanks." Gary gave a nod.

"Listen, Gary," she said on impulse. "Would you like to come to the hospital to see Noah?"

Gary's head whipped in her direction, and Emma's heart nearly broke at the look of hope on his face. "I—" And then in the next moment, he deflated. "I couldn't." He stared down at his hands, shaking his head.

"Why not?"

"I'm the last person he wants to see. I couldn't do that to him, not in his state."

Emma reached out a hand and gave Gary's arm a gentle squeeze. "Gary, come to the hospital. Please. He's your son." If Noah wasn't going to pull through, shouldn't his father have the chance to see him once before he died? And if Noah did wake up... Well. Wasn't it about time to start healing from the past? Poor Gary had seen his share of suffering.

"What if, somehow, he knew I was there? What if I made things worse?"

"Nothing could make things worse, trust me." Emma stood up, brushing off her jeans. "And you know what? If Noah has a problem with you being there, he can wake up and tell us himself."

27

Emma met Gary in the hospital lobby, and they rode the elevator up to Noah's floor together. Emma entered the room first, and then held the curtain aside for Gary. He walked slowly, with a slight limp, and Emma wondered if it was an injury he'd gotten in prison, or just the effects of old age and a hard life.

As soon as Gary saw Noah lying on the hospital bed, his face drained of color. "Oh, dear Lord Jesus." He bowed his head and made the sign of the cross. When he looked up, Emma gestured at a chair, but Gary shook his head. "No, thanks. I can stand. I won't be staying too long."

"You can talk to him," Emma urged. "The doctor said it's helpful for him to hear our voices."

"Are you sure?" Gary's face twisted with uncertainty.

Emma gave him an encouraging smile. "I'm sure." She backed up to give him a minute.

"Okay." Gary took a couple of tentative steps toward the bed and cleared his throat. "Noah, it's... it's your dad. Gary." He shuffled a little closer and reached out to steady himself on the bed rail. From all the way across the room, Emma could see his hand was shaking. "I didn't think you'd want me here, but your wife—Emma—she said it might be good for you. Lord knows I've never done anything that's good for you in your whole life, so you're probably thinking, 'Why start now?' And you wouldn't be wrong." Gary's shoulders slumped. "I have no right to be here now. But... well, I guess I'm selfish, Noah. I'm a selfish man because I wanted the chance to see you and to say some things to you, and I thought this might be my only shot." He paused, his shoulders rising and falling from the effort of his breath. "I've got two things to say to you. One is that I'm sorry. And the other is..." Gary's voice broke, and he scrubbed a hand across his eyes. Finally, looking at his son, he took another breath and murmured, "The other is that I love you."

And then, Noah's eyelid twitched.

Emma gasped, and Gary swung around, wide-eyed. "Did you see that? Is that normal?"

"No. He's only done that a few times. It might mean something. He hears you." She hurried to the bed to stand next to Gary. "Noah, wake up. I know you're in there. *Wake up.*"

Gary leaned forward. "Listen, son. You've got a beautiful wife here, and I understand you have a daughter, too. They're here waiting for you. Don't throw it away like I did."

Noah flinched, and his arm gave a little spasm.

"Noah, come on. Please?" Emma scanned him for signs of more activity, but he was as still as ever. She tried all the tricks she'd seen the doctor do—pressing below his eyebrows, poking his hand with a pen from her purse—but Noah seemed to be done with whatever movements he was going to make. She sighed and slumped in a chair.

"I'm sorry." Gary sat down next to her. "I really hoped he'd wake up, if only to tell me to piss off."

Emma dropped her head into her hands. "For a moment, I really thought..." She sighed. "Anyway, I appreciate you coming. I know this wasn't easy."

"I should probably head out and leave you to it." Gary grabbed onto the arms of the chair and pulled himself to his feet. He shuffled toward the door, and then stopped and turned around. "Thank you for this. Truly. I'll never forget it."

Emma gave him a sad smile. Gary turned back toward the door just as Alicia walked in with Luna.

"Look who I brought," Alicia announced, swinging Luna's hand. She stopped when she noticed Gary there. "Oh, hello."

"Gary, this is my good friend, Alicia..." Emma began to explain, but her voice trailed off when she saw the older man's face.

Gary's eyes had frozen on Luna as if a ghost had walked into the room. "That child—" He began to sway, reaching out a shaking hand and fumbling for something to grab onto.

"Gary! Are you okay?" Emma rushed over and took his arm to steady him. She helped him back to the chair, and he slowly lowered himself into it, gaze still riveted on Luna.

Alicia slid Luna's hand into Emma's. "Should I get the doctor?"

"No, no. I'm fine." Gary waved her off. "It's just—I wasn't expecting that. You only mentioned having a teenage daughter." Gary looked from Luna to Emma and back. "So, who is this?"

"This is Luna. She's..." She hesitated. Judging from the way Gary had nearly passed out on the floor when he saw the child, she had a feeling Luna looked an awful lot like Noah did as a child. And that might tell her everything she needed to know about whether Luna was Gary's granddaughter. "She looks like Noah, doesn't she?"

Gary squinted at Luna. "Maybe a bit."

Emma and Alicia exchanged confused looks.

"Wait," Emma said. "If she doesn't look like Noah, why did you react like that when you saw her?"

Gary gave a wave in Luna's direction. "Because that child is the spitting image of Joshua when he was that age."

What? Who?

Gary shook his head, sadly. "It just brings back all the regret."

"Joshua?" Alicia demanded, thankfully saying what Emma was too stunned to verbalize. "Who the hell is Joshua?"

Now it was Gary's turn to look confused. His gaze swung back and forth between Emma and Alicia. "What do you mean, who is Joshua?" He held up his hands, palms up. "Joshua is Noah's younger brother."

28

"Noah has a younger brother," Emma murmured, bent over in her chair, her head in her hands. "Noah has a younger brother."

Emma really had fainted this time, her vision going white and knees buckling. Luckily, Alicia had managed to reach out and yank her up by the shoulders, shoving her into a chair before her head hit the floor. They'd called in the doctor, who'd shined a light in Emma's eyes, checked her reflexes, and prescribed her plenty of water, a good night sleep, and a visit to her primary care physician.

Now, both Gary and Alicia stood in front of her with matching concerned expressions. Luckily, Luna had no idea what had happened and was happily using the stethoscope she'd pilfered from the doctor to listen to her elephant's heart.

"I'm so sorry, I thought you knew," Gary repeated in time to Emma's murmurings. "I thought you knew. Why would Noah keep his own brother a secret?"

Emma shook her head. Other than the fact that Noah kept everything from her, she had no idea. But Gary didn't know about any of the lies or secrets. "Are there other siblings I don't know about?"

"No." Gary shook his head. "Just Joshua."

Where is Joshua now?

And then it came to her.

Oh, God.

"Joshua is in prison, isn't he?"

It was something that John Picken had said to her. He was talking about Coral and Noah, and he'd called them the *three* musketeers. There had been a third child living in that foster home, and she'd bet her life it was Joshua. "Noah's foster father told me that there was a kid in the house who went to prison. *Just like his father.* It was Joshua, right?"

Gary nodded slowly, and she'd never seen anyone's eyes look so sad. "Joshua was in and out of prison on drug-related charges for years."

"Did you have more of a relationship with Joshua than you did with Noah? How do you know he was in and out of prison?"

"I know because..." Gary ran a hand over his eyes as if he could wipe away the whole terrible ordeal. "Because it was the worst day of my life to see my own son walk into my cell block."

"Oh." Emma stared at Gary as the tragedy unfolded yet wider, and in every direction. "Oh, no."

"It was the drugs that got him." Gary shook his head. "Those doctors, they'll prescribe oxy to everyone with a crick in their back. Nowadays, kids in small towns can buy it on the street corner like it's a pack of gum. And when the pills get too expensive, they'll move on to heroin, fentanyl. It numbs more than just physical pain." He glanced up at Emma, his eyes haunted. "You know what I mean?"

She pictured little Noah, Joshua, and Coral living in John Picken's place. The fear and horror they must have experienced every single day. What had Coral's neighbor said? *Addiction is a monster that some people just can't fight.* Or maybe it was better to escape into drugs than it was to live with a real, live monster.

"Is Joshua still in prison?" If she'd found Gary, maybe they could locate Joshua, too.

"Joshua—" Gary hung his head. "Joshua died of a drug overdose a couple of years back."

———

Gary headed home soon after that, and Emma and Alicia sat in the matching vinyl chairs and stared at Noah.

"What else is he hiding from me?" Emma asked, pressing her palms to her eyes in an attempt to stop her head from spinning.

"What else is there *to* hide?"

"I keep asking myself that, and then something else comes along." Emma would have given anything to go back to those days of blissful ignorance, when she'd had no idea who Noah really was. When her battered, bleeding heart was still intact. "Do you think he ever had any feelings for me at all? I mean, we have a daughter together, for God's sake. Was this all a game to him?"

Emma closed her eyes as the images filtered past. Noah's smile lit up by the afternoon sun as he looked down at her lying on a picnic blanket. The warmth in his eyes, the little catch in his throat when he told her he loved her. The wonder on his face as he held a tiny, blanket-wrapped Maya in his arms, minutes after her birth.

Was Noah a psychopath? The best actor in the world?

"Was there a tiny part of him that really did love me?"

"Oh, honey." Alicia shifted her knees in Emma's direction. "Don't let this ruin all your good memories. You and Noah were happy together for a lot of years, and of course he loved you." She reached out a comforting hand. "But after what he lived through, maybe he didn't know how to do anything but lie and sneak around. It's how he learned to survive."

Emma took a shaky breath. And then there was Coral, whose presence hung in the room. Coral, who Noah had been through everything with since childhood, who he'd stood by all these years. Had he been able to be truly honest with Coral? Emma hoped so. There was a comfort in knowing that at least her husband hadn't spent his life hiding from everyone who was close to him.

Luna toddled over with her new stethoscope in one hand and her wooden train in the other. "Snack?"

It was getting late. Maya would be home from play rehearsal soon and everyone would need dinner. Her body felt like it was slogging through quicksand. She was so tired she almost envied Noah's ability to just lay there and sleep uninterrupted. Emma grabbed the arms of the chair to pull herself to her feet, but she simply couldn't force her body to make the effort.

As if she sensed Emma's feelings, Alicia stood up. "You know what? Let me take Luna home. I'll get a pizza, visit with Maya a little, and then get Luna to bed. I can relax at your place as long as you need. You stay here and don't rush home, okay?" She gave Emma a lopsided smile. "I know hanging out with Noah isn't much of a break, but it's all I can offer you at the moment."

Emma sank back in her chair. "Thank you. I just need a little silence to process everything." She hitched her chin in Noah's direction. "And at least I don't have to worry about him interrupting me."

Alicia leaned over to give Emma a hug, and then she took Luna's hand, and they headed out.

Emma leaned her head against the back of the chair as exhaustion overtook her, and a minute later, she was asleep.

She dreamed of her wedding day. She and Noah were in a

beautiful old chapel with stained glass windows and towering vaulted ceilings. But suddenly, everything shifted, and in the next moment, they stood in the center of John Picken's rundown shack. Broken glass was scattered at their feet, and the fetid stench of stagnant pond water mingled with the sweet smell of the wedding bouquet in her hands. Just as she and Noah were about to promise to love each other for better or worse, the walls of the shack began to creak and pitch. A board dropped from the ceiling, and then another, and she dove out of the way before she was buried beneath them.

Noah. Where is Noah?

Emma spun in circles as the ground vibrated beneath her feet.

There, by the door, Noah stood with his hand outstretched. All she had to do was grab it. But an arm clenched around her shoulders and yanked her backwards. *John Picken.* She tried to fight her way free, to get to Noah, but the walls were closing in on her. And just as the ceiling collapsed, she realized that Noah wasn't reaching for her at all.

He was reaching for Coral Butler.

Emma jerked awake with her heart racing and her back soaked in sweat.

It was only a nightmare, she told herself. *Only a nightmare.* But as Emma gazed across the narrow space between her and her husband lying there, unmoving, she realized that this was a nightmare, too. One she didn't seem to be able to wake up from.

Slowly, she got out of her chair and stepped up to the bed. Noah's chest rose and fell. Rose and fell. Just like her feelings for him. She hated him, and she loved him, all in the same breath. But somewhere along the way, her anger had evaporated, and in its place was nothing but soul-crushing sadness.

Anger and sadness, two sides of the same coin.

"Please, Noah," she whispered. "Please wake up." Emma didn't think she could cry anymore, but here she was, her throat burning and her eyes filling. "Whatever you've lied about, whatever you've done, it doesn't matter anymore. What matters is Maya, and Luna. Don't make them grow up fatherless like you did."

And then, just like earlier that day, Noah flinched.

"Noah, wake up," Emma pleaded. "Please *wake up*." She grabbed his hand and pulled it to her chest. "You can do it, Noah." A hot tear streaked down her cheek and splashed on his palm.

The arm she was holding twitched, and then the other one, its cast clanking against the bed rail.

"Noah." Emma demanded. "*Wake up*."

His head jerked, then—Emma's breath caught—Noah let out a low groan.

"Come on, Noah." She leaned over him, speaking even louder. "I know you're in there."

Noah's head jerked again, and then his eyes fluttered once, then twice. And slowly... they opened.

"Oh my God," Emma murmured, her shoulders shaking with sobs now. *Please, let this be it. Please let him be awake.* "Noah?"

But he just stared at her face, blankly. As though he didn't know her at all.

29

Dr. Woodward and Brittany rushed around, checking Noah's pupils and reflexes, and asking him if he knew his name and what year it was. Noah was confused, disoriented, and he drifted in and out of consciousness. Emma stood back and let them work, her heart swinging wildly between hope that Noah would recover, and fear that he'd stay in this half-asleep state forever.

The next time Noah opened his eyes, he managed to mumble a few answers to the doctor's questions and demonstrate that he could move his arms and legs on his own. A wave of relief flooded through Emma when Noah stated his name, and Maya's, and when he turned his head to look at Emma after the nurse had asked him if he was married.

"His Glasgow and FOUR scores are through the roof," Dr. Woodward said when he pulled Emma aside. "His brain was injured and needed some time to heal. But I'm very hopeful he's on the road to recovery."

Still, every time Noah's eyes closed, Emma's heart slammed into her ribcage, and she waited in agony until he opened them again. As he lay there—only sleeping, she hoped—Emma thought about texting Alicia to let her know what was happening, but she decided to hold off on sharing the news.

Just in case.

When Noah drifted awake again, a couple of hours later, his eyes looked clearer, and he was able to communicate with the nurse in a few short sentences. The doctor immediately started another battery of tests to determine if Noah could move his limbs and tilt his head on command. Apparently, he passed them all with flying colors, because Dr. Woodward shot Emma an enthusiastic thumbs up.

"What happened?" Noah croaked, his muscles shaking with the effort of lifting the cast on his arm off the bed.

"You were in a car accident, out on Route 37," Dr. Woodward explained. "Do you remember any part of it?"

Noah shook his head weakly.

Dr. Woodward patted Noah on the shoulder. "Don't worry about that. It's normal for patients to forget the moments leading up to an accident. Especially if a head injury is involved. It may come back to you, or it may not."

Noah nodded and drifted off. He dozed for two more hours, and Emma was reassured by the fact that he rolled over on his own, snoring slightly and occasionally mumbling in his sleep, just like he used to when he slept in their bed. It all felt so normal, so familiar, and she began to allow herself to believe he might really be out of the woods.

Around midnight, Emma headed for the hospital cafeteria to grab a cup of coffee.

When she returned, Noah was awake, seemingly alert. Someone had even raised the back of his bed so he could sit up. He looked exhausted, but he smiled when Emma walked in, and something about that tugged at her heart. She was so tempted to crawl into the bed next to him, lay her head on his chest, and pretend everything was okay, just for a little while.

"Hey," he whispered, hoarsely.

"How are you feeling?" she asked, setting her coffee on the side table and moving closer the bed.

"Weird. Tired."

She picked up a cup of ice water that one of the nurses had left and offered him the straw. He shook his head.

"Can you tell me what happened?" he rasped.

"You still don't remember anything?"

Noah closed his eyes. "I remember getting into the car," he murmured. "I remember..." And then his eyes flew open, and his stricken gaze flew to Emma.

He remembered Coral and Luna.

She nodded.

"Emma." His heart monitor began to beep louder.

Emma pressed a hand on his chest. "Don't overdo it, Noah. We can talk tomorrow."

Noah's eyes pleaded with her. "Please tell me."

It didn't seem like a great idea to upset him. But he was already upset. And as much as it broke her heart to witness just how much he clearly loved Coral and Luna—his other family—she couldn't keep something like this from him. If it were Maya who'd been in that car, Emma would be beyond desperate.

"Emma," Noah choked. "Coral... and Luna... please, are they...?"

Emma took a shaky breath. "Coral and Luna were in the car, too, Noah," she said, gently. "Luna is fine."

"Oh, thank God," Noah murmured, his shoulders relaxing.

"She's been staying with us."

The fine lines around Noah's eyes deepened in an expression that vacillated between surprised and grateful. "You took her in?" he asked breathlessly.

"I did. She and Maya have grown close."

"What about Coral?" he whispered weakly.

"Noah." Emma reached out to put a hand gently on his arm. "Coral died in the accident."

Noah sank back against the pillow and closed his eyes, turning his head away from her. He stayed that way for so long that she began to worry that he'd drifted back into unconsciousness.

"Noah?"

When he swung his head back to face her, his cheeks were streaked with tears.

It shattered her heart into a million pieces. "I'm so sorry," she whispered. And she was sorry, as irrational as it was that she should be sorry to see him devastated over the woman he'd kept a secret from her, but she was. He'd loved Coral, maybe he'd always loved her. They'd been inseparable through their childhood; they'd survived unspeakable trauma together. And now, Coral was gone. "I know how much she meant to you... I know you loved her."

Noah lifted a hand and swiped at his tears. "Emma, there's so much I need to explain to you." He said it so weakly, she had to lean in to hear it. "I've kept so much from you."

"I know."

"Do you?" His eyes shifted to hers. "What do you know?"

Emma pushed away from the bed. "We should talk about this another time. You're exhausted, and you need to rest."

"Emma, please."

She hesitated for a moment as the last week and a half came back to her. The shock of secret after secret coming to light. Her own pain and sorrow that she'd had to bury to put on a good face for Maya and Luna. And the number of times she'd sat in this room, willing Noah to wake up so she could tell him how angry she was.

"Okay. You really want to talk about this?" She held up a hand, counting on her fingers. "I know about your parents, that they didn't die in a fire. I know you grew up in Millersville, you had a brother named Joshua, and your father went to prison. I know about the foster home at the Pickens' place." She cast her angry expression in his direction. "And, obviously, I know about Coral and Luna. Is there anything I'm missing?"

Dazed, Noah slowly shook his head.

Emma turned away from him to stare out the window at the streetlights shining in the distant neighborhoods across the city. Finally, she turned back to face him. "I just want to know why, Noah." She kept her voice calm, measured. "Was it about my parents' money? You and Coral, and maybe Joshua too—*the three musketeers*—did you plan it all out?"

Noah closed his eyes and shook his head. "No."

"You were the smart one with the good grades and all the potential. You'd go off to college and pretend to be someone you weren't. Join Theta Chi Delta and meet a rich girl and use her daddy's connections to get a good job. And then maybe someday, he'd leave all his money to you."

"It wasn't like that, Emma," Noah said, sharply. "It was *never* like that." His hands shook, and his face was as pale as the sheets on the bed.

Emma took a step backward, pressing her hands to her temples. "We should talk about this another time. This isn't good for you—to get so upset."

"No, I need to explain this to you." He reached out weakly to stop her. "Please. I need to."

Emma sighed, her shoulders drooping. "Go ahead. Explain."

"You're right. I pretended to be someone I'm not, but that's because I was a *nobody*." Noah's face contorted. "I was a nobody with a father in prison and a foster father who smacked me around every chance he got. The only thing I had going for me was that I was smart."

Noah gazed across the room as if it hurt so much, he couldn't look at her. "I worked so hard to get scholarships to a good college because it was my only chance to get out. I didn't intend to lie to people." He shifted his eyes to Emma. "I swear I didn't. But when I got to Cartwright, everyone had parents dropping them off and helping them set up their dorm rooms, and all I had was a receipt from my bus ticket and a suitcase full of second-hand clothes..."

Emma remembered it—freshman drop-off day. At least for the girls, it was almost a competition to see who had the cutest dorm set-up and best wardrobe to wear to parties. What would it have been like to walk in there with a past like Noah's?

"I couldn't tell them who I really was, so I said my parents died in a fire and all our things were destroyed. And then I... turned myself into the person I'd always wanted to be." His face flashed with longing. "The person I'd imagined when I was growing up. Someone with loving parents who went to a good school where nobody bullied me because I lived in a trash heap outside of town and had to walk three miles each way just to catch the school bus." He grimaced at the memory. "I told the fantasy I'd been living in my head since I was six years old. Since the day my dad left the house one day and never came back."

Despite herself, Emma's heart squeezed. "Oh, Noah." She'd spent five minutes in that trash heap with John Picken, and she'd never forget it. The fear, the smell, the hopelessness of it all. Who wouldn't want to leave that place and forget it ever existed?

"I just wanted to have every opportunity that the other kids at Cartwright had. I wanted the connections and the job opportunities a fraternity like Theta Chi Delta could offer me. And I knew if I told the truth, they never would have wanted me."

He was right. A 200-year-old Ivy-League university where 30 percent of the students were legacies wasn't exactly a haven of openness and acceptance. Noah would have been an outcast. This explained why he'd lied to everyone at Cartwright. But it didn't excuse his lies to one person in particular.

"What about me? You didn't have to lie to me."

Noah was silent for a long time, his head bowed. Finally, he looked up. "By the time I'd met you, I was so deep into the lie, I almost believed it myself." Pain slashed across Noah's face. "I kept promising myself that I'd tell you the truth, but I kept putting it off. And then I met your parents and saw where you grew up, and I just—I couldn't."

"You know none of that mattered to me.' Emma could feel her anger rising. "The fancy house, the country club. I didn't care about those things."

"I know you didn't, Emma. *But I did*." He looked away as if he was ashamed to admit it. "It's so hard to explain how it eats away at you when you grew up like I did... How people tell you you're trash for so long that you can't help believing it." His shoulders drooped. "I *did* want your dad's connections. I wanted every little bit of help I could get to get the best job and make the most money, because it wasn't just myself I was responsible for."

"Joshua and Coral."

Noah nodded. "They didn't have the opportunities I had. Neither of them was very good in school, and they both struggled with addiction." He scrubbed a hand across his eyes. "Joshua started using when we were in high school. He got in with the wrong crowd, and ended up in prison before his eighteenth birthday, and... it was all my fault." Noah's voice cracked. "It was my job to protect him. I was his big brother, and I failed. The only way I could help him was to hire a lawyer, get him a spot in rehab. And nobody is handing those out for free on the street corner. Especially not to people like us."

Emma remembered the woman at Coral's apartment talking about Coral's addiction, how she'd tried to stop using so many times. And then Gary saying Joshua had used drugs to escape from his pain. There were thousands, probably millions of stories like Joshua's and Coral's. It was heartbreaking.

"Emma." Noah fumbled for her hand, but she backed away. "I never expected to fall for you. But I did, and it changed my whole life. It was you who gave me everything I'd been imagining since I was a kid. The family, the house full of love, and Maya. I should have told you the truth. But I was terrified to lose you. If you don't believe anything else I ever tell you again, I need you to believe that I love you."

Emma wanted to believe him. She was so close to believing him. But there was one piece of the puzzle that didn't fit.

Luna. And Coral.

All those times Emma thought Noah was traveling for work, and he was really going to see Coral and Luna. The neighbor had talked about how close they were. A family.

There were still so many unanswered questions, but at that moment, Brittany bustled into the room and approached Noah's bed. "I'm sorry to interrupt, but it's time for our patient to get some rest." She pushed a couple of buttons on the machines monitoring Noah's vitals and then reached for the control to lower the bed. "You've got a lot of healing to do, and you're going to need all your energy."

"I've been resting for days," Noah argued. "I need to talk to my wife."

Brittany shook her head. "Your wife is welcome to come back first thing in the morning."

Noah reached out a hand toward Emma, his face straining from the effort. "Please, Emma. Come back tomorrow, and we'll talk more."

Maybe it was for the best that they cut it off here. Emma didn't know if she could take much more shock and emotional upheaval today. Her mind whirled with Noah's revelations while her body ached with exhaustion. It felt like a hundred years ago that she'd sat on Gary's porch and told him his son might be dying. And now Noah was awake, and claiming he'd always loved her, telling her the most heartbreaking story she'd ever heard. Emma had no idea what to do with that.

She looked at Noah for a long moment, and then she nodded. "Okay. Tomorrow." Maybe a little rest would help her healing, too.

"Thank you." He rolled his head on the pillow to look at her, his face tightly drawn and his eyes sad, and oh God, how she wanted to believe he was sincere. But she didn't know if she'd ever be able to him trust again.

With one more long look in Noah's direction, Emma turned and walked out the door.

She was almost to the elevators when the alarm sounded. Emma came to a stop as the noise rang out through the hall, low then high, low then high, like an ambulance siren. Was it a fire? Someone in trouble? She looked toward the nurses' station for a signal, but one nurse was barking instructions into the phone and the other had grabbed a metal rolling cart and was hurrying down the hall. A robotic voice came over the intercom repeating, "*Code blue, code blue,*" over and over.

Didn't that mean someone was having a heart attack?

Emma backed up against the wall as a doctor in a white coat blew past her, followed by a nurse in scrubs. Whatever it was, it had to be an emergency. Her gaze followed the medical personnel down the hall to see where they were going. She'd grown familiar with the families of the other patients over the past week and a half. They hadn't exchanged names, but they'd smiled in the elevator or said hello at the coffee machine. Wished each other well. They'd all been through so much. She hoped whichever patient was in crisis, they'd be okay.

The doctor and nurse darted into a room, followed by another nurse.

And then, Emma realized whose room it was.

She took off down the hall and skidded to a stop inside the room just in time to see Brittany performing compressions on Noah's chest while Dr. Woodward unraveled the cord of a defibrillator.

"Noah! Oh my God. *Noah.*" Emma ran toward the bed, but another nurse grabbed her arm and held her back.

"You can't be in here, ma'am. You need to leave."

Frantic, Emma wrenched her arm from the nurse's grasp. "That's my husband."

The nurse jumped in front of Noah to wedge himself between Emma and the hospital bed. "You need to get out of the way and let us work."

"*Move aside*," Dr. Woodward barked, shoving past her to drag the crash cart to Noah's side.

Oh my God, this isn't happening. "He was awake a minute ago," she told the nurse. "He'd just woken up."

The nurse gave her a hard shove into the corner. "Stand there and don't move."

Emma backed up against the wall, her eyes frozen on Noah's pale face and motionless body. Had he gone back into the coma? How had his heart stopped?

Please, Emma prayed as they tore open Noah's hospital gown and pressed the pads of the defibrillator to his chest. *Please don't let him die.*

"*Clear!*" the doctor yelled as someone activated the defibrillator.

Noah's body jerked, his chest rising up and head rocking back against the mattress. Emma's gaze flew to the heart monitor above his head. The line that she'd been watching zigzag for the past week and a half now crept from one side of the screen to the other, flat and lifeless. That reassuring beep-beep-beep was now one long tone without end.

"*Clear.*"

Noah's body jerked again. The line jumped and then leveled out.

Please don't let him die.

How could this be happening? He'd been awake and talking, just five minutes ago. People didn't wake up from comas and then just...

"Clear!"

Was it her fault? She shouldn't have upset him with all her interrogations. Or maybe his heart was broken over Coral.

"Clear!"

Please God, don't let him die. We need him. Maya and I need him. And Luna needs him, too.

"Clear!"

Noah's body jerked one last time, and Dr. Woodward slowly lowered the defibrillator paddles to the bed. Then he turned around, looked at Emma, and said, "I'm sorry. We did everything we could."

30

It was long past midnight, and the house was silent when Emma slipped through the front door. She'd sobbed the entire way home, so hard that twice she'd had to pull the car over to clear her eyes of blinding tears and catch her breath. But now she was all cried out and blessed numbness had taken over.

Noah was gone. She'd been bracing herself for that possibility for days, but there was really no way to prepare herself for the death of the man she'd loved for two decades. Even with the lies, the secrets. No matter what his transgressions were, she'd loved him with her whole heart. And now he was gone.

A traumatic aneurysm, the doctor had said. It was unusual but not unheard of that they could be late in presentation, not showing up on brain scans until days or weeks after a brain injury. The aneurysm had burst, triggering cardiac arrest. There was nothing anyone could have done, and no way to predict it. These things just happened.

Emma gently closed the door behind her. Maya and Luna would be asleep. Alicia had texted hours ago to let her know not to rush home, and Emma hadn't had a chance to text back. Nobody even knew Noah had woken up from the coma.

Emma was glad she hadn't shared the news and given them false hope. She glanced up the staircase where her daughter lay sleeping in her bedroom, still believing that her father was alive and might come home.

Emma turned away and walked into the living room. She'd let Maya sleep for one more night before her whole world crashed around her. Let her daughter hold on to one more "before" moment, before her life moved into "after" forever.

She stopped in the doorway and gazed at Alicia sleeping on the couch. Emma didn't know what she would have done these past weeks without her best friend. Alicia had loved Noah like a brother, and this was going to be devastating for her, too.

Maybe I'll let her sleep a little bit longer before she has to hear the news, too.

Emma tiptoed into the kitchen and poured herself a glass of water. Someone had grabbed the mail from the box and left it in a neat stack on the counter. Out of habit, Emma sorted absently thought it, looking for bills. The house, the bills, they were going to be completely her responsibility from now on.

It was too overwhelming to think about, so she gave the mail a shove. It slid across the counter, revealing a nondescript white envelope with Emma's name and address typed across the front. Curious, her gaze slid to the top left-hand corner, where the name of the sender was located.

SecureDNA Inc.

Noah and Luna's paternity test results.

Emma grabbed the envelope and tore into it, yanking out the letter and smoothing it on the counter. Her gaze roamed the page, scanning a table of numbers that meant absolutely nothing to her. "What is this? What does this *mean*?" She finally got to the bottom of the page where a paragraph was typed. A narrative report of the findings.

Emma held her breath and started reading.

Interpretation: *Based on the analyses of the DNA loci listed above, Noah Havern does <u>not</u> show the genetic markers which have to be present for the biological father of the child Luna Butler. The probability of paternity is 0%.*

Emma gripped the counter with shaking hands. Noah *wasn't* Luna's father. Did this mean he hadn't had an affair with Coral after all? So, why had he been sending the other woman money and visiting every week? Could it have all been as innocent as friendship, and their shared childhood history? Emma kept reading, searching for answers.

Conclusion: *Based on our analysis, it is practically proven that Noah Havern is not the biological father of the child Luna Butler. However, our lab recommends further testing, as the genetic markers are present to indicate that Mr. Havern may be a third-degree relative of Luna Butler, such as an uncle/aunt or niece/nephew.*

Emma gasped.

Noah *wasn't* Luna's father, but someone was... someone who had been closely related to Noah.

Joshua.

Noah's brother must have been the father. Which meant that Noah was... Luna's uncle. The pieces began to slot into place. All the time he'd been driving back and forth to Millersville, the weekly visits with Coral and Luna, the money he'd been sending for the past two and half years... they were for his brother's girlfriend. His brother's child.

Emma remembered the shock on Gary's face in the hospital, like he'd seen a ghost of his deceased younger son. Gary had said that Joshua died a couple of years ago, probably right around the time Luna was born. And that was when Noah had started traveling so much for work again. The three of them—

Coral, Joshua, and Noah—they'd been the three musketeers. But Coral and Joshua had been struggling with addiction, and Noah was the oldest, the person who felt responsible for them.

Even before Luna was born, Noah had moved their family to Grand Rapids, only an hour from where Coral and Joshua lived. Had he been trying to help them get clean, even back then? She could still picture the anguish on Noah's face when he told her that it was his job to protect Joshua and he'd failed. Noah hadn't been able to save his younger brother, but he could save his younger brother's child. Noah knew about Coral's addiction. The neighbor said he was always trying to get her to stop using. Had Noah encouraged Coral to draw up a will, naming him the guardian, just in case Coral overdosed?

Emma slid onto a barstool next to Luna's highchair. Alicia had cleaned up the dinner dishes, but she'd forgotten to put Luna's sippy cup in the dishwasher. It was the red one with the picture of a truck on it. As soon as Luna had seen that cup in the store, she'd reached for it, fussing until Emma had agreed to buy it. Emma's lips tugged into an affectionate smile, her body relaxing. A couple of minutes ago, Emma would have sworn she'd never be able to smile again. But Luna could do that to her. This past week and a half, that little girl had slowly wormed her way into her heart. And, she suspected, into Maya and Alicia's too.

Luna was Maya's cousin and Noah's niece.

And she's mine too.

Luna was her niece, but she'd grown to be more than that. Emma had been the one to care for her, to hold her, to rush in at midnight and dry her tears when she cried. She thought of that fierce maternal instinct she had to protect Maya. She felt it just the same for Luna. She'd grown to love Luna like her own daughter. She could never send her to foster care, into a system that had allowed Noah, Joshua, and Coral to end up with a family like the Pickens.

Emma hoped with all her heart that at least Noah had felt safe, had felt loved, when he'd been here in this home and this marriage to her. Noah certainly hadn't been perfect. He'd had demons she never could have imagined. But he'd been a caring man, and a loving father.

Emma dropped the DNA test results on the counter. She'd fight for Luna, to keep the girl here with her and Maya. She'd honor Noah, and Coral and Joshua too, by raising Luna the best she could. She'd give her a loving home where she didn't have to live in fear, to live with secrets. Where she'd never feel anything but love.

EPILOGUE

One year later

Emma clutched the bouquet in her hands, breathing in the scent of early spring blooms. Bunches of tulips, daffodils, and a branch of forsythia, all picked from her garden earlier that morning and bundled together with a piece of twine. And, of course, she'd added a few peony stems. Her favorite flower, the kind she'd carried at her wedding, and that Noah had worn on his lapel. The kind he always used to pick up for her on a whim.

For months after Noah had died, Emma couldn't walk past the bunches of peonies in the grocery store flower section without breaking down. But then that spring, Maya had discovered the pink-tipped flowers blooming in the backyard—the ones Emma had planted that first year they lived in the house—and had begged to bring a bouquet inside.

The peonies reminded Maya of her father, too.

How could Emma say no? Once the flowers sat in a vase on the dining table, Emma realized that the joy on her daughter's face soothed the pain of missing Noah more than just about anything else could.

Maya walked on the cobblestone cemetery path next to Emma now, in a knee-length black dress that made her look so much more grown up than her seventeen years. She was carrying a similar flower arrangement. And clutching Maya's finger with one chubby hand, a bouquet in the other, was Luna, wearing a rainbow tutu with a flower tucked behind her ear. At three years old, she was still a little unsteady on her feet as she veered off to chase a butterfly between the gravestones.

It was a beautiful old cemetery, full of mature trees and statues memorializing generations of local families. Luna quickly disappeared in a grouping of bushes.

"Luna!" Emma called, her breath hitching in her chest. "Be careful! Don't get lost!" Parents always said they were more laid back with their second child, but Emma found herself worrying over everything when it came to Luna. The little girl had been a bright light in an otherwise terrible year. Emma couldn't imagine what she'd do if something happened to her.

"I'll get her," Maya volunteered, taking off between the gravestones to chase after the child. The two girls giggled as Luna ran faster, and Maya pretended she couldn't quite catch up. Emma watched them go, her heart constricting at the sound of Maya's laughter.

When Emma had broken the news that her father had died, Maya had been inconsolable. She'd climbed into bed and stayed there for days, crying until she wore herself out enough to fall into fitful sleep. In vain, Emma had tried everything she could think of to coax her daughter to eat, to come downstairs, to allow her friends to stop by.

After about a week of the same, Emma had put Luna down for her nap and called Maya's doctor, leaving a message with the answering service. While she'd waited for a call-back, she took a quick shower, and when Emma had turned off the water, she'd been shocked to hear laughter coming from the direction of Luna's room. Emma had wrapped herself in a towel and hurried down the hall.

She'd flung the door of the room open to find Maya and Luna sitting on the bed, reading *The Book with No Pictures* and giggling uncontrollably.

"Maya!" Emma had said, her heart pounding. "I'm so happy to see you in here."

"Luna woke up and was crying," Maya had explained. "I couldn't just leave her." She'd gazed across the pillow at Luna. "She lost her parent recently, too, and—" Maya's chin wobbled. "I think she needs me."

Luna had looked over and noticed Maya watching her. "I love you, Maya," she'd said in her little girl voice, and with that, both Emma and Maya had started crying.

"I love you, too, Luna."

Maya had come downstairs to eat dinner that night and had gone to school the next day. It hadn't been easy, this past year, but the three of them had gotten through it together.

"Sorry I'm late!" a voice called, dragging Emma back to the cemetery. She looked up to find Alicia running down the path.

"You're not late," Emma said, leaning in to give her best friend a hug. "I'm so glad you could come."

"Of course I came." Alicia hugged her back. "I'm so happy for your family, Emma. You all deserve this."

"What do you mean, *my* family? You're part of this family, too," Emma reminded her. "Thank you for all the times you took care of Luna so I could work this past year." *It really does take a village,* Emma realized with a smile, as she spotted the last member of their little party making his way down the path.

"Grandpa!" Luna's little girl voice called from behind a gravestone where she'd been hiding from Maya. She took off across the grass, her little legs churning as she ran toward a man in a gray suit. He crouched down, holding out his arms, and Luna ran into them.

The man stood up a little unsteadily, and then took Luna's hand as they made their way toward the group.

"Gary!" Emma said with a smile. "Don't you look nice."

Gary straightened his tie as his cheeks turned pink. "Well, it's an important occasion. I thought I'd dress up a little."

Emma was grateful she'd insisted Gary stop by the hospital to see Noah before he'd died, and that he'd had a chance to say goodbye to his son. The woman in the trailer park had been right. Gary was a good man. When he'd heard about Noah's death, he'd started stopping by once a week to drop dinner off on Emma's doorstep. For the first few months, he'd absolutely refused to come inside when Emma invited him, saying he didn't want to be a bother. Finally, one fall afternoon, she'd managed to convince him to stay and sit on the porch for a while. It turned out that Gary loved show tunes as much as Maya did, and he knew a few card tricks to impress Luna. Now, he came for dinner once a week and both Maya and Luna adored him.

"You look just like Dad in that suit," Maya said, brushing away a tear. "I wish he could be here."

Gary nodded, quickly swiping at his own eye.

Emma's gaze swept across their little group. Noah would have been so happy today, knowing that in a few short hours they would all be heading over to the courthouse where Emma would officially adopt Luna. He'd sacrificed so much to protect that little girl, and now Luna would be theirs forever.

"I can feel his presence today, can't you?" Emma gestured to the gravestones arranged together under a sprawling maple tree. "All three of the musketeers are here in spirit." She leaned over and carefully placed her flowers on one of the graves—*Noah Havern, loving husband, and father*.

Then Maya stepped up and set her flowers on the grave

next to it. *Joshua Havern.* Her uncle, Luna's father, and the man Noah had done so much to protect.

"Go ahead, Luna. You can put your flowers down." Emma took the little girl's hand and led her over to the final grave. *Coral Butler, loving mother.*

Luna set down the last bouquet of flowers in front of the gravestone. "This is where my other mommy is," she told Emma.

"That's right, honey," Emma said with a smile. "She loved you very much. Just like we do." And then with one last look at her husband's grave, she turned and headed with her little family to the courthouse.

A LETTER FROM MELISSA

Dear reader,

I want to say a huge thank you for choosing *His Secret Daughter,* and I hope you enjoyed it. If you'd like to keep up to date with all my latest releases, just sign up at the following link. Your email address will never be shared, and you can unsubscribe at any time.

www.bookouture.com/melissa-wiesner

This story was a bit of a departure for me because it's the first book I've written where I didn't know how it would end when I started writing. I unraveled Noah's past life right along with Emma, secret by secret and chapter by chapter. And I admit that I surprised myself with the ending! (I will forever treasure my editor Ellen's note at the end of the book which read: "I ACTUALLY CANNOT BELIEVE you've done this, Melissa." Shocking an editor I've worked with on three books feels like a huge accomplishment!)

The only thing better than hearing reactions from my editor is hearing reactions from readers. Were you as surprised by Noah's secret life? Did you root for a happy ending for Emma, Maya, and especially little Luna? If you enjoyed the story, I would love it if you could leave a short review. Getting feedback from readers is wonderful, and it also helps to persuade other readers to pick up one of my books for the first time.

Please be in touch! You can reach me on my website or on social media.

Best,

Melissa Wiesner

www.melissawiesner.com

facebook.com/MelissaWiesnerAuthor

twitter.com/Melissa-Wiesner

instagram.com/melissawiesnerauthor

ACKNOWLEDGMENTS

His Secret Daughter is my fourth novel with Bookouture, and working with this wonderful publisher has been an absolute dream. Every time I open my laptop and see a supportive and encouraging discussion in the Bookouture author chat, read another round of brilliant and insightful comments from my amazing editor, or hear about the marketing and publicity teams' innovative ideas to get books in front of readers, I feel so grateful to be a part of the Bookouture family.

A special thanks to:

My editor Ellen Gleeson who somehow always seems to know exactly what my books need to make them better.

My copyeditor Belinda Jones who patiently endures typos, timeline inconsistencies, and characters whose names mysteriously change halfway through my books.

Sarah Hardy from the publicity team, who has always done an amazing job generating buzz for all of my titles.

As always, thank you to my family for your encouragement and patience with my deadlines.

Finally, my most sincere gratitude to my readers (with a very special shout-out to the Seabright Book Club for being my most dedicated fans and a whole lot of fun to talk books with!).